DEATH BY
MEDITATION

BRIAN
STAFF

DEATH BY MEDITATION
BY BRIAN STAFF

A WordisWorth Book
First Published in Print in 2013
Printed by CreateSpace

Death by Meditation is also available as an ebook

Library of Congress Control Number: 2012952350

ISBN: 978-0-9802474-3-5

Editor and Designer: Alison J. Macmillan

DECIDING

Closing my eyes to meditate sent an invitation to every thought I'd ever had to start stomping around my mind like a herd of rampaging bull elephants. Thoughts that I'd success-fully repressed for years made glittering guest appearances, and thoughts that I'd never thought before kicked and yelled to attract attention. I was so bad at it that I can't really claim my two weeks of sitting on a cushion achieved anything in themselves. But the other experiences I had at Ravenswood lodged their indelible stamp on my personality, just as much as the cushion left its imprint on my backside, and, like the cushion, they were experiences that were misleadingly soft at first, but excruciatingly painful later.

Whatever induced me? Well, Fiona recommended it. We had shacked up on an impulse some years ago, and we lived together for one month and one day. They say failed relationships don't often turn into good friendships, and I would agree, but we didn't have a good relationship and we don't have a good friendship. We were as bad as lovers as we are as friends. Where she once forgot to call me to say she would be home late - very late, two days late, in fact - she now forgets to send me birthday cards. Similar failings applied and apply to me, but more so, as she reminds me each time we get-together over a bottle or two or three of wine.

After a month of co-habiting, she plucked up the courage to tell me she thought it wasn't working, which was remarkably good timing from my point of view, because I was just about to tell her exactly the same thing. We then had an embarrassing, ingratiating conversation in which we both tried to convince each other we still liked each other a lot but that a live-in relationship was rather premature. Really we should have said we drove each other up the wall, and neither of us could wait to get away from the other. Given that I'm normally quite forthright, I don't know why I didn't just say what we both felt, but I didn't, and instead we spent the next day being unnaturally nice to each other and agreeing vigorously with whatever the other one said until we could effect the physical split.

We carried on seeing each other, and after about a year I noticed the normally muddle-headed Fiona acquiring an impressive degree of calm and assurance. I assumed she had done something to herself or somebody had done something to her, either physically or mentally, that I would like to know about. Actually, her new persona was so impressive that I got quite to fancy her again.

"It's wonderful, Peter. It's a way of putting everything in perspective - your thoughts, your emotions, your view of yourself and other people. You would get a lot out of it."

"Why me in particular?"

"Anyone with a brain would benefit from it."

Well, I would seem to qualify on those terms, although my ex-wife might disagree. Both she and my daughter – I assume she prefers to be described as "ex-daughter" – seem to want to have nothing to do with me, and categorise me as the original sad clown.

It is an irony that a man who draws cartoons for a living to make others laugh does his best to avoid crying his eyes out most of the time. Well, to be perfectly honest, I don't think I've cried in the past 10 years, but I suspect that I would, if I could. Emotional constipation drove me to adopt my perch on the meditator's cushion, as much as anything else.

"It helps you make sense of your life, and … and well, you begin to understand that there's another life that's larger than us," said Fiona.

I didn't have a clue what she meant, but this other-worldliness she portrayed was so alluring I thought I could do with some of it. Full of enthusiasm, I booked myself into Ravenswood, a "retreat and meditation facility."

When trepidation set in I tried to think positively. I live in a flat in Kensington, in a once exclusive, then genteel, but now anonymous area, like any other swathe of flatland in London that hasn't managed to acquire some sort of label - be it complimentary or derogatory. But Ravenswood was in Wales. I supposed the dampness of Wales wouldn't be much worse than the fog of London. In Wales you have smelly, matted sheep for neighbors. Here I have grotty individuals surrounding me who get more uncouth every time there is a change of tenants. My neighbors have metamorphosed from old ladies, to middle-aged couples, to young couples with children, to young couples without children, to yuppies, to punks (employed), and now to punks (unemployed) who, despite being unemployed, seem to have more disposable income than anyone else I know. Wales' exiled hippies would be mellowed by dope, unlike my punks spiked up with Red Bull and 'E'.

Be realistic I told myself. Even the name Ravenswood stinks of countryside, dirt tracks leading nowhere, and if they did lead by any chance to a pub, it would be so far away I probably wouldn't be able to breathe by the time I got there, having overdosed on fresh but alien country air.

But what did I have to lose? I was pretty desperate. Age 44, no assets, neither financial nor those that draw women, unless you count an ancient Porsche that spends most of its time being repaired or sitting in the street waiting to be re-paired; the amount of time it spends being driven rather than vandalizing my cringing bank account is insignificant. And I was so influenced by the effect Ravenswood had wrought on dizzy Fiona that I thought it was probably worth a try. As I had no holiday plans, or any other sort of plans come to that - for then or for the rest of my life – the portents seemed to conspire to hurtle me into the unknown.

Christ, I thought, it's going to be hard enough to go to the damn meditation place, but what if someone asks me where I'm going? Frankly, I was a little ashamed of what I was thinking of doing. I have credentials as a disparager to pre-serve, and if I start sending out mixed messages my reputa-tion might veer off into the uncharted territory of the loony liberal area, which wouldn't do at all. I've struggled hard over the years to establish myself as the negative, curmudgeonly sod I am, and it would be like wearing a three-piece suit after spending years in a snug and soothing pair of old Levis. If my friends find out I've taken to dabbling in something that sounds even the slightest bit wishy-washy, I could expect the phone to go quiet and stay quiet. This wouldn't be a problem if I was good at making friends, but I'm not. It takes ages for me to get comfortable with other people so, when I do, I don't want to let them get away that easily.

§

"I'm going to Wales for a few days for a rest", I told Carstairs, a Fleet Street editor who uses a lot of my stuff, and that makes him a treasured friend.

"You're in need of a rest?" he'd said, loudly enough for the rest of the office to hear. "What the fuck have you ever done that you need a rest from? Your life is one long bloody rest. Why the hell do you need to go to Wales to do it? The last time anyone saw you break sweat was when that bar-maid at The Wanker split her skirt when she was bending for a fresh bottle of Teachers."

For clarification, let me say "The Wanker" is not the real name of a pub I frequent - it was given that name after a discussion about its proper name (The Prince of Wales). "Wanker" is, however, an eminently suitable name for Roger Carstairs. Despite publishing my stuff for over 20 years, he delights in telling me that both my work and myself are "absolutely fucking pathetic", or worse. You could say he's a "down to earth figure who keeps me grounded in reality". But he isn't; he's just an obnoxious prick, and I can't afford to let go of one of the few friends I have by consorting with

Hare Krishnas in a namby-pamby Welsh meditation centre. I shouldn't go.

§

"I'm not going to go to Ravenswood," I told Fiona. "Getting there's too much of a hassle."

"You've got a car haven't you?"

"Well, yes, but it's playing up. Here in London, I can get out, kick it, curse it and get a cab home when it breaks down. Who wants to be stuck up the M4? It's more hostile than you with PMT."

"Get it fixed."

"Yeah, and I'm really going to fit in arriving in a Porsche. What message is that going to give to that lot of abstemious dropouts? They'll probably ostracize me even before I get my legs crossed when they see what I drive."

The reason I bought a Porsche in the first place was, almost exclusively, to impress people, primarily women, who once smitten by the P-word are never quite as disappointed by the creaking, leaking and reeking reality as they should be - I speak of both the car and its owner with this description.

"Suit yourself. Could you leave now, please, I want to go to bed," she said.

"I could join you."

She handed me my jacket.

§

My best bet would be to take public transport; for one thing it's cheap. I don't earn much. I had a couple of good income years a long time ago and I've spent every year since trying to convince the tax man that my (almost completely honest) tax return is neither a joke nor a lie. In fact, I sometimes exaggerate my income just to make myself feel better, even if it does mean paying a few more quid in tax and ex-daughter support. Secondly, taking public transport would bestow upon me the advantage of being in keeping with what I expected to be the austere, slow and depressing nature of Ravenswood. I doubted whether Wales had advanced beyond the pony and trap, but the chap I spoke to on the phone when I booked told me they could collect me from the local train station. I had attained enlightenment even before getting there. Rail lines in Wales had survived government butchering of the network in the '60s.

"Oh, you've got a car then?"

"No," he said, and there was a long pause that made me think either he was being funny, or he was being cynical, or he was mad; until he went on to say "we've got a van." Another pause, and if I hadn't heard him chuckle I think I would have probably cancelled my reservation on the spot.

"Do you need a deposit or something?" I asked.

"Oh, well, no, well, yeah, I suppose ... hang on a minute."

I heard him calling out to someone else. "Do we want a deposit?" I heard a "yeah" in the background, then a "yeah" from him, to me.

"How much?"

"Er," to me, and "how much?" to the other voice, and "10 quid" from the other voice, then "five quid" from him.

"Is that all?"

"Yeah, well ... yeah. It's vegetarian here, you know?"

I assumed that was a non-sequitor to discussion of the deposit. If it wasn't, I was clearly missing some important and valuable attribute of the vegetarian lifestyle.

"That's okay," I said, lying.

"Good, because some people find that a bit, you know, difficult."

"Not me. Not that I am one, but I can handle it." It felt as though we were discussing some mildly shameful form of sexual deviancy. "So you'll pick me up at Aberfenny station?"

"No."

"I thought you said ..."

"Oh, sorry, yeah, well, not me, I don't drive, but someone will."

After that phone call I changed my mind again and decided not to go. They didn't even take credit cards - in fact, I don't think the bloke even knew what a credit card was.

But I got to thinking about my mid-life crisis. I had reached the desperation phase, and I thought I'd be better doing something like mediation rather than going off to India on an impulse to help the starving millions, or embarking on some other life-changing but inevitably disastrous exercise like parenting abandoned elephants in Kenya. The India thing was particularly hard to shake off, but every time the thought lurched into my head, I realized how completely ludicrous it was – some days I can barely manage to feed myself adequately, so how the hell did I think I could help even one other person to eat, let alone an emaciated tide of humanity?

I decided I would go, if only to fail and prove that any attempt to sort myself out was pointless, and I could just go on being confused without feeling I had to do something about putting it right. This line of thinking, perverse as it may sound, actually brought me considerable comfort, as if knowing my confusion was irremediable would allow me to stop thinking I could fix it and relax peacefully into a state of decline I was powerless to correct or influence. Is that Karma, Dharma or Bullshit?

By the way, as you develop a mental picture of me you should know that I'm a physical and moral coward. My ex-wife fell for me partly because she thought I was "so strong" - a statement based on two provocative cartoons I'd drawn (when completely drunk, I should add). I was amazed when she said it, and equally amazed that it took her a year or so to find out that it was so wrong. My cartoons are a facade, not a weapon but a shield. Through them I can say what I wouldn't dare say myself, be the person I might wish to be, not the one I am.

§§§

ARRIVING

The first part of my journey passed in a blur. I'd got up pre-dawn to give me plenty of time to catch the train from Paddington, but I still ended up bundling myself onto the Inter City just seconds before it pulled away. I slept until mid-morning, and by then I was hungry enough to try a British Rail sandwich and a cup of coffee. As I ate, oblivious to the landscape slurring and blurring past the rain-lashed window, I tried to work out why I was enjoying it so much, and I realized I had eaten hardly anything for almost 24 hours, my only calorie intake since yesterday lunch time having been in the form of a variety of second-rate red wines and a few tapas.

I had got drunk with a woman I'd been trying to get into bed for about a year. When we got back to my flat I was hoping to achieve my goal without too much difficulty, but after a bit of frantic fumbling on the sofa, she suddenly catapulted from my arms and sprinted to the bathroom in order to throw up most of the drink and all of the tapas I'd been plying her with for the past four hours. I managed to dump her limp and rancid body into a taxi about an hour later, and repaired grumpily to my lonely bed. This episode seemed both ominous and apposite - ominous in that it bode badly for the fortnight of frustration that loomed ahead of me, and apposite in that it clearly demonstrated the unfulfilled and unsatisfactory state of my life that had caused me to sign up for this nonsense in the first place.

I got another coffee and settled down to gaze out of the window as the view became more and more rural, by which I mean, more and more hostile. I just don't understand the countryside. When I was a student, living in a hovel in Pimlico, I used to listen to "The Archers" on Sunday mornings, and I convinced myself I could take up the life of a rural gentleman with consummate ease, so I found myself a job on a farm during the summer vacation. But as soon as the first cow dung splattered onto my pristine Wellington boots, I realised this was, most assuredly, not the place for me.

I find all those fields, enormous sky and strange smells fundamentally unsettling. If I can't see tarmac or touch concrete or smell car exhaust, I get a distinct feeling of uneasiness, and for some reason the rural equivalents in the shape of corrugated iron, barbed wire and tractor fumes don't comfort me in anything like the same way. Oh well, perhaps I would be able to rid myself of my idiotic phobia, which I'm sure must have some deeply rooted subconscious significance that I could do with unearthing and tossing out.

Gazing out the window was very relaxing once the first rush of rural aversion had subsided, and when an elderly lady sat down opposite me and attempted conversation, I wasn't too keen to communicate, but I was at least civil, an act of chivalry for which I was to be rewarded, sort of.

"My daughter's getting on at the next stop. I hope she manages to find me alright."

"Well, she's only got to walk through the train. It's not as if she doesn't know what you look like."

And, sure enough, the daughter was spotted on the platform as we pulled up at the next station, waved to frantically from the window, and a few minutes later she was sitting opposite me. The daughter was, without doubt, one of the top 10 most desirable women I have ever seen, and although I'm aware that most women are starting to fit into this category as I grow older, I still believe she was an outstanding example of womanhood. I couldn't take my eyes off her, and the fact her mother was kind enough to classify me as her "new friend", meant I qualified for a lot more smiles than I normally get from beautiful women.

But how the hell do you pick up a woman when she's sitting next to her mother? The difficulty of this feat reminded me of a friend who claimed he'd once screwed his girlfriend on the sofa whilst her father snored in an armchair in front of the television, not six feet away. A story I didn't believe, but which has supplied me with some graphic sexual fantasies over the past 20-odd years. After a while it was obvious the old lady and I had more in common than the daughter and I - probably even more in common than the mother and daughter - and I ended up wishing the beautiful woman had possessed the older woman's character, outlook and liking for me.

I alighted at Swansea and spent an hour and a half waiting for the connection to Aberfenny. I tried to use this time to get into the right frame of mind, but as I had bugger all idea what the right frame of mind is when you're about to intrude upon a retreat centre it was utterly impossible, so I drank insipid tea from Styrofoam cups and wandered around reading timetables, information posters, advertisements, graffiti and anything else I could find written in English rather than Welsh on the walls.

It was a pleasant sort of day by my extremely limited experience of Welsh weather, by which I mean it was mild, grey and almost dry, and I was just starting to feel a little excited about my trip - which I was almost willing to promote to calling an adventure - when I came close to experiencing a panic attack.

An announcement that a train was just about to leave for London bellowed over the intercom. It crossed my mind I could sprint across the station and jump on it and, by early evening, I would be sitting in The Wanker, heaving a huge sigh of relief and contemplating a pint of Guinness. In fact, it didn't just cross my mind, it actually stuck there for about a minute, and I took three or four faltering steps in the direction of the London-bound platform. Then I stopped, forced myself to stand still, but felt a compelling nausea well up inside of me and a cold sweat well up outside of me. I was going to make myself go to Ravenswood.

I watched the London train ease away from the station, and there was a slight, juddering pause in its movement, as though it was asking me if I was sure I didn't want to leap on board. But as it picked up speed all I could do was picture myself sitting in a seat by the window downing a Johnny Walker miniature and watching the unfriendly Welsh scenery and unwelcome aspirations of self-improvement slip away from me, a contented smile spreading across my face as my crackpot idea disappeared in the wake of my rescuer. I carried the impression of squandered salvation with me all the way to Aberfenny station, and Roger.

§

Roger was not in the business of caring what impression he left on people, which was just as well, because the impression he left was distinctly off-putting. He was tall and skinny, with close-cropped hair and one earring. He was clad in denim from head to toe, even denim sneakers. Not totally abnormal so far, you might say, and you'd be right; even most of his features were quite ordinary. What made Roger remarkable were his piercing grey eyes and his mouth, or rather, what came out of his mouth. Roger lived by two, self-imposed rules.

Rule One was he never said anything he didn't feel, no matter how harmless; and Rule Two was he always said things he did feel, no matter how hurtful. Rule One meant that words and phrases of social lubrication like "nice to meet you", "thanks", "please", "how are you?" and so forth, were wholly absent from his vocabulary. In fact, all pleasantries were extinct from his vocabulary, and I got the impression if anything even slightly sociable escaped his lips, he would immediately go off and commit suicide for the shame of having broken Rule One. Rule Two, on the other hand, meant that comments like "that was a stupid thing to say", "you're ugly", "this food tastes like dog shit", etc., had to be expressed, no matter how painful they might be to the recipient or a third party's sensibilities.

I'm not saying there's anything wrong with honesty. In

fact, I've been known to practice it myself on divergent occasions, but the older and wiser I get, the more I become convinced honesty has a very limited role to play in the world of smooth social intercourse, and blunt individuals like Roger have no place in the warm, two-faced environment most of us inhabit. I wondered if Roger's persona was born out of the directness and honesty his ardent pursuit of truth and enlightenment demanded, but I preferred to believe he was really just a fucking obnoxious git.

Conversation on the way to the Centre was sparse, mainly because Roger didn't respond to idle chatter and only responded in the most perfunctory way to direct questions. When he had an opinion to express, he expressed it without further explanation, such as by saying "You smell" to me, just after we'd got in the van.

"Eh?"

No answer.

"What do you mean?" I said.

"You eat meat."

"Yes, sometimes." I'd had a ham sandwich on the train, although it had a texture that could have been pink cheese.

"Meat eaters smell."

"Of what?"

No answer, but an electric, withering look. I suppose I was to infer that meat eaters smell of meat and the smell isn't a good one, particularly if the one doing the smelling is a militant vegetarian.

"I'm surprised you can smell me, the stench in this van is overpowering enough to mask anything."

No answer. I looked in the back and saw remnants of straw on the floor, plausibly the spills of animal transportation or some earthy agricultural product, and very recent, to judge by the odor.

"Humans weren't designed to eat meat, that's why it makes them smell."

"Humans weren't designed to tell other humans they smell," I said. But if I thought I could improve Roger's sociability with a smart rejoinder, I was expecting miracles, and miracles are not things of which I have experience, so I doubt their existence.

Another of Roger's characteristics was he had no sense of humor or irony. I mean absolutely no sense of humor. It was as if it had been cut out of him and destroyed. This was probably a consequence of his completely factual view of life, because humor, as a cartoonist knows only too well, largely consists of taking reality and distorting it slightly - not violating it too much, which becomes absurd or childish - but just enough. For Roger, no such distortion was permitted, so humor was as meaningless to him as nonsense is to the rest of us. When I came to understand this, I actually started to feel sorry for him as I would feel sorry for anyone lacking a vital organ or faculty, but in those first few minutes of our acquaintance, I assumed his weirdness was being directed at me personally, and I didn't like it. I resolved then and there that if the rest of them were like this, or even if half of them were like Roger, I wouldn't be stopping more than the time it took to order a taxi to take me back to Aberfenny, Swansea and eventually - and I got rather emotional when I thought of it - London.

The rest of our journey proceeded in silence, which gave me ample opportunity to study the surroundings, which were predominantly green and getting greener by the minute. A main road led to a byroad, which led to a minor road, which led to a very minor road, which led to a lane, which led to a minor lane, which led to a track, which we bounced along for about 10 minutes before coming to a gate, which prompted Roger to say "Open the gate", which I did, and then closed it behind the van and re-boarded. We carried on bumpily for another five minutes before reaching a collection of buildings that turned out to be the Ravenswood Retreat Centre.

"Why's it called Ravenswood?"

"Don't know," said Roger, but the fact there seemed to be no sneer in his voice made me feel positively warm to him. It's amazing how you can adjust to people and their bizarre characteristics. Roger said nothing more, and it was clear he had no intention of saying anything more, so I followed him into the largest building, which looked as though it had once been the main farmhouse. The other buildings clustered around it had probably been barns and other outhouses, but now appeared to have been converted into accommodation of some sort. It was neater than I'd expected. I'd been worried it might be a ramshackle, drafty and leaky affair, or even that I'd be expected to live in a wigwam or a teepee or some other sort of New Age construction.

Still following Roger, although not knowing if I was meant to, I ended up in the kitchen, and I assumed I hadn't been meant to, and I felt as stupid as if I'd followed a desultory waiter into the storeroom of a restaurant, believing he was taking me to a table. But then he announced "New arrival" to the back of a woman who was busy at the sink. She turned round and a smile stretched across her face from ear to ear. She looked younger from the back than she did from the front. She wore no make-up and her voluminous black hair had a lot of grey in it, but after the taciturn Roger the sight of a smiling face was a huge relief.

"Oh, you must be, er ...?"

"Peter Wickham."

"Yes, from London. I'm Monica. Welcome to Raven-swood. Did you have a good journey, Peter?" She asked this question as though the answer was important and not just out of politeness. I'm not used to promoting small talk to the status of being important or interesting, so I struggled to think of something to say that was worthy of the attention she was willing to invest in my every utterance. Needless to say, I didn't succeed.

"Well, yes, I suppose so, a bit long, a bit boring, but no problems."

"Trains go so fast, don't they?" she said with an intensity and an earnestness that made me wince.

"Yes, I suppose they do, but they're meant to, aren't they?"

"Yes, but I find I get giddy just looking out of the window." I was getting the impression she was the type who would get giddy scrubbing a potato, which appeared to be what she was doing. Roger had poured himself a cup of tea and was sitting at a huge butcher block table - in the middle of what was a sparse but homely room - watching us as though we were two strange and mildly disgusting animals in a zoo that had no reason to be communicating with each other.

"Do you want some tea?" he said. I took this offer as an indication that Roger and I were becoming firm friends, by his standards.

"Yes, please."

"Cups are over there, teapot's there, milk is in the fridge and sugar's over there," he said, staring into his tea and indicating locations with careless inclinations of his head, but at least he was speaking to me, or at me.

"Sit down Peter, if you'd like to," said Monica "and tell me what you do in London, if you want to."

I sat opposite her. Her piercing gaze seemed to be drilling deep into my brain, or soul. In any other setting I would have assumed that a woman who sits staring at me intently and smiling is asking to be flirted with, but I didn't think this about Monica. Not that she was unattractive. With a bit of attention she may have been pretty, but I somehow got the message she always behaved like this.

"I draw cartoons."

"Oh, cartoons. You mean for children, like The Beano or The Dandy or something?"

"No, for adults, for newspapers, political mainly."

"Oh, like Hogarth?"

"Well, I wouldn't quite put myself in that league."

"Bateman?"

"Er, no, not in that league either."

"Giles? Schulz?"

"No, you'll have to go lower."

"Well, how about, oh what's his name, Scoff or something like that?"

"No, not even in that league, I'm afraid. I guess you could say I'm a minor cartoonist, but I make a living out of it, and have done for nearly 20 years."

"Strips?" said Roger.

"Who does?" I said. Not meaning it to be a joke, and he not taking it as one.

"Do you draw cartoon strips?" he said, slowly, deliberately and condescendingly.

"No," was all I could think of by way of a pithy response.

"What do you call yourself?"

"Wickham."

"No, I mean in your cartoons. What do you sign them? What's your *nom de plume*?"

"Wickham."

"Oh."

It always turns out like this. I suppose about one in 10 people who question me about my work say they think they've heard of me, one in a hundred can recall seeing a cartoon of mine, and one in a thousand say they like them and sound as though they might mean it. I don't know if others who are half in the public eye find it the same, but when strangers hear I do something in the media, they start to interrogate me quite fiercely, as though I'm making it up and they want to get at the truth.

A friend once told me it's because they want to find out if they've really heard of me and they're not just imagining it, but to me it sounds more like they don't believe it and they're trying to expose me as a fraud. I don't care that much anymore, and when people claim they know and like my work I tend to interrogate them in return to make sure they're being honest, to themselves and to me.

I'm a little paranoid about it, but you wouldn't meet a plumber and demand to know "Who do you work for? Are you a better plumber than such-and-such? Is your work admired by your customers? Do you know lots of other plumbers? Do you unblock the toilets of many famous people?" and so on, would you?

"I've never heard of you," said Roger, helpfully.

"I'm devastated," I said, flatly.

"But we don't often get newspapers here," said Monica, conciliatorily.

"I'm not offended; I do it for money, not for fame."

"You'd make more money if you were famous," said Roger.

"Who's the richest man in the world?" I said.

"Don't know," said Roger.

"So if he doesn't need to be famous, nor do I." I felt smug when I said this, but it didn't seem to register as a joke, a put-down or even a clever analogy with either of them. In fact, it didn't seem to register at all. Monica was still staring at me, smiling but silent. Roger was looking vacantly into space as he slurped his tea. I was overcome by feeling that I couldn't say anything that would surprise, upset, amuse, impress or even bore them. Everything would be heard, processed and, perhaps, replied to. Everything would be taken literally and responded to in a similar vein. This sort of precision and logic may be comforting to some, but to me it's disconcerting enough to be frightening.

I live in a world where the literal is to be avoided. Publicly, I would say the literal world is boring, mundane, unfunny and flat, but in private I would say I've never matured enough to be able to live in the rarefied atmosphere that exists in the real world, and I prefer to stay in comic-book land where we all breath laughing gas, everyone is a caricature, and where we can hide behind farcical images personalities that are too frightening to contemplate without humor. I need a veneer of ridicule to make the world acceptable to me, me acceptable to the world, and me acceptable to myself. Fortunately, for the sake of my career and sanity, a lot of people seem to share my knee-trembling weakness. Some of those on whom I base my cartoons terrify me, particularly the political ones, but as soon as you equip them with a long nose, fat lips, droopy ears, a big beer-belly and outrageously sized bums, tits and genitals (depending on what you can get away with in the commissioning publication), they become less threatening - the more bizarre they look, the more human they seem, to me at any rate.

"And you live in London." Monica had come back to life.

"Yes, Kensington-ish. A bit too much Earls Court and not enough Sloane Square."

"Don't you find London a very difficult place to live? All that noise and traffic? All those people?"

On the contrary, I thought. I find London to be just about the only place I can live. I know all the nasty things about the place, and most of them have happened to me or close acquaintances, but it's not a matter of liking or disliking it. My organism needs a city to survive. I'm like a germ that feeds on filth, physically and professionally. I can't even begin to conceive how I could live anywhere else. As soon as I leave London I start to lose my paranoia, my furtiveness, my cynicism and my distrust. How can a cartoonist operate without these essential stimuli? As I consider this, I start to worry that after my trip to Wales I may not be able to produce any sellable work for a month - I shall be polluted by niceness. I'd better stick close to Roger if I want to maintain a healthy dose of abrasiveness.

"London's a shit hole," he said, as if reading my mind.

"Yes," I replied "it is, and that's exactly what I like about it."
"Dennis will be here soon," said Monica, changing the subject to something she probably felt more comfortable with than shit holes, "and he'll tell you about Ravenswood and

what we do here. I think it's always best to get that from Dennis before anyone else. He's so lucid. How did you find out about us?"

"A friend recommended it."

"Who was that?"

"Fiona Lowry, she was here about two months ago."

"Remember her," said Roger. He said it in such a way as to imply he remembered something specific about her, and if it had been anyone other than Roger I would have expected him to expand on this statement by adding some characteristic of Fiona - great legs, for example - or allusion to something she'd done - perhaps that she kept falling asleep during meditation, which she'd admitted to me she'd done a couple of times, and she possibly snored if she did, because I learnt during our brief cohabitation that Fiona snored in her sleep, nicely but noticeably, and would often awaken herself with a shout which, the first time she did it, scared me half to death.

"Oh, I remember Fiona," said Monica, nodding and smiling, but otherwise remaining inscrutable. I had already learnt that nods and smiles were her baseline appearance, and they implied nothing about the subject in hand. I don't know why - and I never know why I feel this, although I frequently do - but I wanted to say "And what did you think of Fiona?" I have this pressing need to get a fix on people, to triangulate an opinion so that I can validate, reject or reconsider my own impressions. If someone had said - Roger, I suppose - "She was a twat", it would have served to either shore up my own view or prove, by my reacting against his statement, that she is not a twat, but until somebody says something, my own feelings about her swim around in a soupy, unformed mush.

My friends probably think I'm a shameful gossip, and I am, but I don't do it because I like badmouthing people, I do it because it's my way of making concrete my opinions, which otherwise might never coagulate. Not that I don't have opinions. Ask me what I think about Margaret Thatcher or Lester Piggot or Helen Mirren or Michael Jackson and I'll give you chapter and verse, but ask me what I think about my wife or my daughter or Fiona or any number of other acquaintances, past or present, or even myself - in fact, especially myself - and I'll flounder helplessly unless you have an opinion I can use as a point of purchase. As my wife would say, I lack a centre of gravity, but whether she means gravity as in powerful force, or gravity as in taking things seriously, I've never got her to clarify.

§§§

MEETING

Monica showed me to my room. I'd insisted on a single room when I'd made the booking. Fiona told me that some people shared rooms, but I was buggered if I was going to put up with that. Partners aside, I'd not shared a room with anyone since my second year at college. Of course, if I'd been offered a voluptuous 18 year old nymphomaniac as my roommate, I would have been prepared to alter the habit of my adult lifetime, but I didn't expect this particular option to be tabled, and I assumed I was more likely to get a smelly, tedious, garrulous, male grunter.

The room was in the main house. It was small and simply furnished; just a bed, desk and 3-legged stool, with an agreeable view across the valley on one side of which Ravenswood perched. To a nature lover the panorama would probably have been unexciting. To a city dweller it was pleasant without being too intimidating - wide open spaces with lots of sky and distant mountains would probably have made me nauseous. There was a vase of flowers on the dressing table. They had been chaotically arranged, or probably not arranged at all, just stuffed in the vase, but that made them look all the more natural.

"Nice flowers."

"Yes," said Monica "Roger put them there for you."

"Roger?"

"Yes, you know Roger."

"No, I don't think ... What? You mean Roger in the kitchen?"

"Yes, didn't he tell you his name?"

"Yes but, yes, oh yes, of course."

She left me to unpack, which I did while stealing furtive glances at the vase of flowers, and seeing an image of Roger's insouciant features staring out from between the stems whenever I did.

§

As I wandered around the grounds, I ruminated whilst absorbing the atmosphere of the place, which was primarily damp and lonely. The door of one of the larger outbuildings opened and a man emerged. He was striding across the yard towards the main house when he spotted me and stopped in his tracks. He swung through ninety degrees and made for me like a guided missile, extending a hand as he did and saying "You must be Peter. Is that right?"

"Yes, and you could be Dennis."

"Correct."

He was about my age, with plenty of white hair – the word "flowing" springs to mind. He was slender, tanned and stooped a little from his 6 foot plus height, He wore what looked like a hand-knitted sweater, khaki slacks and healthy slip-on shoes that looked something like clogs and were probably made by a serious-minded Scandinavian. He was smiling broadly and genuinely.

After Roger's ferocity - the pre-flowers Roger, that is, I hadn't made my mind up about the post-flowers version yet - and Monica's smile-at-everybody-and-everything counte-nance, this was a refreshing change. If he runs the place, I thought, it might just be tolerable after all. That was a quick reaction to a 10 second acquaintanceship, but I always trust first appearances. No matter how many times I've been told not to do it, by myself and others, I always find the long-term impression I have of someone is the same impression I got at first sight or sound. My mid-term opinion may alter, but the first and enduring ones are nearly always identical.

"Would you like to have a chat?" he said, gripping my arm and steering me towards the main house and a room off the hallway set up as an office. Dennis was obviously happy with the idea of being Dennis, which was admirable, but also a little intimidating to someone like me who can see advan-tages in being almost anyone other than himself, but is too cantankerous to change his ways.

"I won't ask you to tell me about yourself. We'll do that later in the evening so you can tell everybody at the same time and spare yourself a lot of effort." He smiled and then sipped something from a mug that looked as though it hadn't been washed recently, and was silent for a few seconds. I had already learnt that smiles, tea and silence were major components of life here. "I'd just like to tell you something about Ravenswood and what we do, and then you can ask me any questions that may occur to you. Okay?"

"Sure."

Silence while Dennis thought.

"The first thing I should tell you is nobody will ask you to do anything you don't want to do. Or rather, they may ask, but if you don't want to do it, you don't have to. We ask you to honor the unwritten rules of living in a community, like respecting the space of other people, doing your share of domestic chores, and generally not rocking the boat, but beyond that it's important you feel completely at ease. Ravenswood gives people the chance to look into themselves, and we offer help in doing that, but people need to feel secure if they are attempting that degree of introspection, and if you feel threatened it could be unpleasant and even damaging, so you must feel comfortable."

More silence. I was tempted to mention that having stony-faced Roger collect new guests from the station didn't exactly achieve the goal of putting people at ease.

"Of course, there may be times when you'll want to take a risk, and if you do, we'll be there to support you, and when I say we, I mean all the residents, not just the staff - we expect the residents to support each other in their quest for ... for whatever they're looking for." He laughed.

"You notice I don't specify what anyone is pursuing. People come here for so many reasons I try not to guess at what they're seeking to achieve. It can be anything from divine enlightenment, to help with a particular problem, or even just a refreshing break. We don't ask, we wait for people to tell us, if they want to."

More silence. Silence is powerful stuff if used correctly, and Dennis organized his silences very effectively.

"The basis of life here is meditation. Do you meditate?"

"No."

"That's no problem. The principles of meditation are simple, it's the practice that's difficult, and for most of us only time can improve the practice. By coming here, you've awarded yourself a space in your life to work on something you feel the need to work on. Meditation gives you the freedom in your mind to see to the heart of the problems, confusions, contradictions or whatever else it is you want to address, and if you don't want to address anything specific, meditation gives you the ability to relax into a degree of inner peace that's simply not attainable in the hustle and bustle of everyday life."

He spoke like a textbook, or like a tape on the art of meditation. Every word was measured and precisely delivered, but somehow he made it sound very natural. Fiona had described him as "charismatic", and although charismatic occupies a leading place in my list of words most to be avoided, it was a struggle not to think of it as he spoke. Although it was comfortable to sit and listen to him, it was also slightly spooky. I could imagine a bloke like Dennis engendering slavish obedience in his followers. He had the magnetism I would expect to find in a cult leader. He had power, and power unsettles me, which probably explains why I spend so much time trying to ridicule powerful people through my work.

He went on to outline the daily schedule, which started at 7 a.m. and ended at around 9 p.m. and sounded like a lot of hard work, even if meditation did come up a lot.

"But don't worry," he said, "you can skip any session you like, except the work details," a smile "and we encourage everyone to take part in the reporting-in meetings at which we share experiences with each other. It probably sounds a bit confusing to you, but you'll get the hang of it quickly, and the daily program is posted in the hallway outside. If you have any difficulties, we'll help, and I try to make myself available whenever I can." A long pause. "Do you have any questions?"

As he said this, I realized I really didn't have a clue what I was doing there. My goal of sorting myself out seemed as stupid as a child's wish to be an astronaut or a pop star. It was a puerile aspiration I would probably have grown out of if Fiona hadn't worked on me as insistently and effectively as she did.

"I really don't have a clue what I'm doing here."

I expected a quizzical look, maybe even a disappointed look. He laughed.

"Then you're exactly the sort of person we like here. The Zen Buddhists call it "beginner's mind". You have no preconceptions. You are in exactly the right mental state to make terrific discoveries."

But I'd already made exactly one terrific discovery - tomorrow I was going to get exactly the first train back to terrific London.

We left his office and went into a large room next to the kitchen. Food was laid out on a table at one end and people were already seated at different tables, eating. It was quiet.

"Help yourself," said Dennis "sit where you like, talk to whom you like, say what you like, or say nothing."

The food was some sort of nut roast. There was a huge bowl of very organic-looking salad - by which I mean that most of the ingredients looked vaguely ominous and completely inedible - and a large dish of roast potatoes. I took a bit of each and joined two people who were sitting alone at a table but not talking. One of them was a young girl and the other an older man. They both smiled when I sat down, but the girl looked unhappy and the man didn't look like he would be a bundle of fun at the best of times. We introduced ourselves. She was Amanda, quite pretty, very feminine and young, which made her painfully attractive to a middle-aged man who is watching his youth and youthful attributes spin ever faster down the plug hole of missed opportunities. The man was Ruben, but he didn't give any impression of wanting to say much.

Amanda seemed to cheer up as we chatted. Her eyes sparkled when she looked at me, and although it was probably coming from some inner sense of transcendental peace, I chose to interpret it as being mildly flirtatious, and I felt a wholly inappropriate reaction stirring in me - inappropriate for a retreat center, that is, but completely appropriate for a randy, ageing male when confronted with a lithe, young girl. Within seconds my mind had transported me and Amanda to my bedroom, where I was peeling off her natural fibre clothing and neatly filled wholemeal underwear, and getting ready to rid of her of the sexual frustration that, I hypothesized, she might be suffering amidst the likes of Ruben and Roger.

"Why have you come here?" she asked.

"I don't really know. My life seems to have got a bit bogged down in the day to day stuff. I thought a bit of peace and concentration might sort me out."

"Sort you out," muttered Ruben. I turned to look at him, but he was just staring into space.

"Yes," I said, expecting him to ask me something or make some sort of comment, instead of which he continued to gaze into the distance. I turned back to Amanda and felt another jolt of sexual chemistry do a lap of my body. I knew I shouldn't be feeling this way. She was far too young to give me a second thought, and I was translating her friendliness into a physical interest that almost certainly wasn't there. But I was hanging my hat on the "almost" rather than the "certainly", and hormones don't take much account of logic, well mine don't. Maybe, just maybe, we were on the same wavelength.

"How about you?" I asked her.

"Oh, I come here quite often. I have a lot of gaps in my life, and coming here seems to fill them, and cheaply. I'm an actress, so I don't make much money and spend far too much time resting."

"Gaps," said Ruben, still staring blankly ahead of him and showing no signs of wanting to converse.

"What do you act in?" Stupid question. A bit like asking me what cartoons I draw.

"Anything."

"What do you like to act in?"

"Anything that has an interesting script and a good director. What do you do?"

I wanted to tell her I'm a famous cartoonist with a Porsche, and shouldn't we slip down the pub and have a good time then sneak back here and have an even better time. But instead I told her I'm an undistinguished, hack cartoonist she's probably never heard of, and I didn't even mention motor cars, let alone Porches, or fornication.

"Oh, how wonderful!" People sometimes say that, but they don't know the half of it. My work is 1% inspiration and 99% the drudgery of sketching up the idea and touting it around the bilious sods I have to deal with. "I'd love to see some of your work." And I'd love to show it to you, as we chat over a bottle of wine in some romantic spot, or even as we frantically explore each other's bodies in some dark outhouse, vacant cow shed or silent byre.

"Work," said Ruben. Ruben didn't look stupid, or even temporarily half-witted. He actually looked intelligent and quite handsome in a rugged, hairy, Friends of the Earth kind of way, so I assumed he was just a little spaced out that day, overdosed on meditation, or perhaps he was a Professor of Etymology, some sort of Henry Higgins who was treating us as research material in a study of the use of language in bizarre social situations.

A big, blowsy woman burst into the room. If you asked me, I couldn't tell you what the dictionary definition of "blowsy" is, but the sound of it summed up this woman perfectly. She was big. Her clothes were voluminous. She was full of extravagant gestures. Her voice swooped all over the place, from high to low, from left to right, from cultured to common, it was as though she, despite her bulk, was being carried around on a strong breeze - her ideas, her words, her arms, her dress, all were billowing and flapping in a gale of uncontainable energy. I had the impression of wind blowing around the room, disturbing the peace.

She sat at our table, and talked endlessly about herself and gave us the minutiae of everything that had happened to her that day. When she fired questions at us about ourselves, she took whatever we said as an opportunity to turn the spotlight back on herself. I told her I'm from London, and she spent 10 minutes giving me her cock-eyed, incontestable opinions of the place. Amanda told her she'd had a good meditation earlier, and the big woman told us about her meditation in excruciating detail. Ruben muttered "deep" to nobody in particular, and she told us about an experience she once had whilst travelling in Norfolk with a friend who is destined to be the next Virginia Woolf, although she didn't clarify in what acts or accomplishments - literary, sexual or suicidal - her friend planned to emulate the doyen of the Bloomsbury Set. The big woman's name was Zara. She made me long for Roger's company.

Whilst she talked and we ate, it occurred to me the food was actually quite good. The nut roast was not at all like compacted sawdust in texture and was less bland than I'd expected; the salad failed to intimidate me - despite the annoying tendency for various green bits to stick haphazardly out of my mouth whenever Amanda looked in my direction, probably giving her more the impression of a straw-sucking yokel than an urbane sophisticate; and the roast potatoes were sensational. When I added up the pros and cons of the place - Amanda, potatoes and Dennis on one side, Roger, Ruben and Zara on the other - I was still favoring an early departure next morning, but if Amanda went on to show any inclination, or even an intimation of an inclination, I could have been persuaded to change my mind.

"I paint myself," said Zara, interrupting my musing.

"What color?"

"Pardon?"

"What color do you paint yourself?"

Ruben snorted – it could have been a laugh or just a regular snort.

"No, I mean that I paint works of art," she explained, no hint of a smile on her face, no hint of modesty in her claim to produce "works of art", which is a brag that no artist I've ever known has made. "Landscapes, portraits, still lives, collages. I also throw pots."

"Amazing," I said.

"Amazing," echoed Ruben. I glanced at him out of the corner of my eye, expecting he was still floating in his surreal hyperspace, picking up words at random and bouncing them back at us, but I detected a grin hovering around his mouth, and his eyes darted fleetingly and conspiratorially in my direction. I started to like him, just a little.

"Do you exhibit?" asked Zara.

"Only to passing females."

"Say again?" she said, reminding me I've always harbored ambivalent feelings about people who say "say again".

"No, I don't do any art other than cartoons, and I'm not good enough or well known enough to attract interest." I hoped this show of modesty on my part would affect Zara and get her to tone down her self-directed effusions, but it didn't. She was perfectly literal when it came to the self-deprecation of others.

"I've exhibited." she said, and went on to tell me where her pictures had been hung, her pots displayed and her collages laughed at - collages are usually laughed at by serious artists, aren't they? - but I didn't listen. She left eventually, probably disconcerted by the lack of interest we'd shown in her. But no, a person like that is never disconcerted - she would have ascribed our silence to imbecility, and would have interpreted my humble statement about my artistic ability as nothing but a pathetic fact. At times, I'd like to be brazen like her, sweeping through life on an unstoppable wave of incontrovertible opinions like a raucous and unrepentant fart.

I glanced at Amanda and Ruben. They were wearing identical expressions, smiles that spoke volumes regarding their feelings towards Zara, and I felt warmer towards Ruben and hotter towards Amanda as a consequence. People had started to drift out of the dining room, which with Zara's departure was quieter than ever.

"What happens next?" I asked.

"There's an evening meditation at seven. We're silent after that."

"Silent?"

"Yes, nobody speaks until breakfast tomorrow."

"Why not?"

She giggled, girlishly, which set various parts of me trembling.

"Quiet and stillness are an important part of being here. If you stay silent for a time in a social situation, when you're amidst other people, strangers, like here, where you'd normally be talking, you start to realize how meaningless words often are, but how powerful they can be when used properly. I did a silent retreat once. For seven days nobody said anything and then, when we gradually started talking on the eighth day, we used very few words but used them to tremendous effect. It's very illuminating."

"Illuminating," said Ruben, and I smiled at him, and he grinned back. I was starting to understand the man. I bet he'd been on lots of silent retreats. In fact, I bet his whole life was one long, almost-silent retreat. I couldn't conceive of going seven days without speaking, even though most of what I say - and hear others say - would benefit from never being exposed to the ears of others.

Dennis joined us and started to tell me what would happen next as he nibbled at an incredibly small portion of food. As he did so, Amanda got up and left, followed by Ruben. She smiled at me as she did so, which caused me to miss the first few seconds of what Dennis said.

"… and the evening meditation is my favorite. It's very peaceful."

"You'd better tell me how to meditate."

"Don't worry. I intend using your arrival as an opportunity to give everyone a quick refresher. Some of the people here have been meditating for most of their lives, some of them longer than me, but it doesn't hurt to be reminded of what we're supposed to be doing. Meditation can be very self-indulgent, but it should really be highly focused without being goal-orientated."

"Sounds like a contradiction."

"Not at all. I once learnt to play the violin, and my teacher told me one day that the biggest problem his students faced was understanding how easy it is to play the violin. What he meant, I think, was that you should never feel intimidated by what you're trying to do, and if you set objectives you will be, and your progress will be dictated by your conscious mind and not by something deeper."

"Oh."

"Don't worry, you'll soon see what I mean. By the way, how do you feel about introducing yourself to everyone?"

"Fine."

"Good, then I'll ask you to do that. They're a very sympathetic audience." Yes, I could imagine most of them would be, but I doubted if Roger would appear to be sympathetic, and I had no hope of Zara being able to keep her mouth shut, and I was damn sure I wouldn't be able to take my eyes off Amanda, or my brain off the erotic mental images of her, of which I had begun to construct an extensive portfolio.

§§§

DISCLOSING

At 7:30 we assembled in the building I'd first spotted Dennis coming out of. It had once been a barn, and still looked very much like a barn, in that it was just one large space with nothing between the floor and the rafters. There were colorful pictures on the walls of what looked - to my wholly untutored eye - like Indian Gods, and at one end of the room a big stone Buddha, surrounded by fresh lilies, gazed placidly from a raised platform. There was a sweet, burning smell in the air and people were perched on cushions around the periphery of the room. In other words, it was exactly as I had expected, and feared, it would be. Why couldn't we just sit in an ordinary room, in comfortable chairs, with Spencer and Matisse reproductions on the walls, with no funny smells and no intimidating statues?

Dennis told me to collect a few cushions from a pile by the door, and perhaps a blanket or two, and to pick a spot and arrange things so that I could sit on the cushions with my legs crossed loosely in front of me. He told me to find a comfortable position with my back as straight and as vertical as possible, but not to worry too much about a specific posture for now, he'd talk about that later. He walked to the end of the room, prostrated himself dramatically before the Buddha, which deepened my sense of ill-ease, and then settled himself in front of the statue, facing the rest of us, with the Enlightened One peeping over his left shoulder.

I then spent what felt like an age getting myself into a vaguely comfortable position. I couldn't remember when I had last sat on the floor with my legs crossed, and I wasn't even sure I'd ever done it, although I probably sat in a similar posture as a child at the insistence of some bullying or cajoling teacher who thought children were capable of doing things like that.

It has long been a mystery to me as to why women have a propensity to sit on the floor now and again, but they do, and I have not infrequently joined them there so as to launch some sort of romantic attack. Floor sitting and an ability to hold a conversation on the subject of curtains are two of the salient characteristics that will always convince me of the radical dissimilarity between the sexes, a dissimilarity in which I take great comfort. My contortions went on so long and seemed to make so little progress that I started to sense the gaze of the others on me, and I began to feel embarrassed, angry and stupid in that order, but then I noticed Amanda giggling to herself as she watched my efforts, and my self-consciousness disappeared immediately, to be replaced by a hollow, tingling feeling in the pit of my stomach.

I looked at my fellow retreatants. Roger was there, his eyes shut and his legs entwined in a tangle of limbs that looked like the most uncomfortable position known to man or spider. He was rocking gently and seemed to be murmuring something. Amanda, when she wasn't chuckling at my pathetic antics, was getting herself arranged amidst a convoluted mass of cushions and blankets. Monica was there, sitting as still as a rock, her eyes shut and a beatific smile on her face. Ruben had his legs stuck out straight in front of him - he was gazing around the room and may have been humming to himself. Zara stormed in, collected cushions and blankets, marched to a vacant spot and settled herself down extravagantly and with more limb movements than a hyperactive crane fly.

The others, still strangers to me, were a mixed bunch, their only common feature being that few of them looked normal, by which I mean that if you saw them in the street you would never think them to be married people with well-adjusted children, who drive new Fords to humdrum office jobs every day, go to the Mediterranean to souse themselves in booze for their holidays, and spend Christmas eating turkey and getting sick on a surfeit of Drambuie and Southern Comfort.

They looked like artists, or dropouts, or students, anarchists even. I doubt if the Tory party would get a single vote out of the whole roomful, and the Inland Revenue probably didn't get very fat out of them either. They were anti-war, pro-abortion, anti-nicotine-smoking, pro-weed-smoking, peacefully anti-government, pro-free healthcare, anti-private medicine and anti-fascist, avowed vegetarians to the last man and Ms. The males either had very short cropped hair or very long unruly hair, the females likewise. Half the men wore earrings - one each - but only Amanda of the women wore any, and she sported an extremely large pair I thought must hurt her ears, but which I would love to pull and nibble at playfully. The clothes were baggy, colorful, handmade, probably self-made in many cases. The expressions were intelligent and peaceful. They were definitely not a run-of-the-mill audience.

The room fell completely silent, and then proceeded to do the seemingly impossible by getting silenter and silenter. It got so silent it was spooky. Rural noises from outside became increasingly noticeable. I had the distinct impression that if someone broke wind in Swansea, I would hear it clearly, and if I broke wind here - which the nut roast was starting to make a painful inevitability - it would shatter eardrums and precipitate breakdowns. My senses, deprived of the normal chatter and clatter that assails them, seemed to be reaching out beyond the room for contact with something human or mechanical I could relate to and be comforted by. I imagined that after a concentrated immersion in this oppressive aural vacuum, a silence-phobia would emerge to displace my countryside-phobia. There were over 20 people in the room. How could they be so bloody quiet? After what seemed like an age, Dennis spoke, quietly, but in the hushed room he was as audible and attention-grabbing as Hitler at Nuremberg.

"Tonight we have a new arrival, Peter. Peter has kindly agreed to tell us something about himself." He smiled and nodded towards me. I saw heads turn in my direction, some smiling, some blank. Some faces remained staring straight ahead, some with their eyes closed. I noticed Zara look up to the roof and stay looking at the roof, as though she already knew about me - second-rate cartoonist and lousy artist - and could plunge into her own, self-admiring reverie as I spoke, confident she wouldn't miss anything worth hearing.

Silence closed in on me, and when I started to talk my voice echoed around the room, vandalizing the peace. I felt as if I was telling a dirty joke at a funeral.

"Hello. Yes, I'm Peter. As you can see, I'm a middle-aged man. I live in London, beyond my means. I draw cartoons for a living, political cartoons. I'm freelance. I get some stuff in the nationals, magazines and so on, but I have more luck with the provincial press and fringe magazines, sub-Private Eye kind of things. I drink too much at times, well, most of the time really. I ..." and then I couldn't think of anything else to say. I was silent for a while, which I knew would be acceptable, and then I started off again, and I quite surprised myself.

"I'm not sure why I'm here. Well, that's not strictly true. I do know why I came, but I don't know what I'm going to do here. A friend recommended the place, and she thought it might help me put my life in order. I'm just confused, basically. Male menopause stuff I suppose. I could have bought a Harley Davidson, but I thought it would be cheaper to come here instead. I'm half way through my life, half still to go, the less exciting half, so what do I do with it? My talent, what little I had, is leaving me, my looks, what little I had, are leaving me. Just about everything is leaving me, including my wife - well, she's left me already, actually. So I want to know what I can usefully do now. I ...," and again words escaped me. I seemed to be getting insidiously drawn into saying more than I'd intended, saying things that were expected of me rather than things I felt. Words were being sucked out of my mouth by the listeners' ears, meeting their requirements, not mine, not that I clearly knew what was required of me in company like this.

"I've never done anything like this before." I went on,

ignoring the screamed advice of my brain to shut the fuck up. "It's not my kind of thing really. To be honest, I'd made my mind up to go back to London in the morning, but I may have changed my mind." Why the hell did I say that? Why did I tell them I was tempted to flee? Had I changed my mind about leaving? There were a few grins and at least one chuckle. Just as I didn't mix with people like them, I suppose they didn't mix with people like me, but whereas they were amused by the strange new animal, I was disconcerted by the incumbent menagerie.

"Er, that's about it really." Silence, then some "thank you, Peter" comments, some smiles, some nods, and one final "thank you, Peter" from Dennis. It felt weird, as though they'd actually been listening to me, even though I'd had so little of substance to say. I can spend hours in a pub, spouting off half-assed witticisms and cracker barrel philosophy to a few inebriated, sympathetic cronies and feel, by the end of the evening, they haven't listened to a word of it, not even the good bits. But a few disjointed statements to a bunch of complete strangers and I feel as though they were actually interested, except Zara, who was still staring at the ceiling as if it was infinitely more interesting than I could ever be.

Dennis then reminded everyone about the importance of posture. What it came down to was that if you kept your spine straight and were in a comfortable enough position to be able to endure an hour without moving and without your legs going numb, or even going black and falling off, you were okay, and that advanced yoga positions like the full lotus weren't necessary. Roger glanced disparagingly in his direction at this point, from which I gathered that Roger had mastered the full lotus and was exhibiting his mastery at this very moment. This was my first exposure to the unstated and - in the context of the allegedly uncompetitive environment of a retreat centre – inappropriate and cutthroat contest for the best and most difficult meditation posture, as if the entanglement of your legs and spirit are inversely proportional.

Meditation sounded straightforward, in theory. You simply observed your breath and tried to exclude all other thoughts from your mind. Thoughts were to be gently brushed aside, and concentration always returned to the breath. There should be no objectives. The mind should be left completely open to whatever feelings and sensations came to it, but always refocused on the breathing. Without doubt, said Dennis, the best mind to have going into tonight's meditation was Peter's - as Peter had no idea what was going to happen next, so he was completely "open-minded" in the truest sense of the term. Of course, this was patent hogwash, as I knew bloody well that as soon as I shut my eyes my mind would throw up a provocative image of Amanda, and I would spend the rest of the session either thinking about her or the erection that would be forming embarrassingly above my crossed legs, waiting to pop out of my jeans and point accusingly at my chin, standing at attention like a grubby schoolboy in a classroom of well-scrubbed virgins. But it was nice of him to single me out for special attention.

Dennis went on to tell us we should observe silence until breakfast tomorrow, and then only break it if we felt inclined to do so.

"Silence," he said "is a wonderful tool for gaining self-awareness. Words are frequently a distortion of what we really feel, and can lead us into all sorts of ambiguities and trivialities that are a major enemy of constructive introspection and mindfulness." There was a lot of nodding at this, so I assumed that chatty individuals, like my friend Fiona, either found the going pretty tough or were dismissed as spiritual lightweights by the other attendees. But if Fiona was a light-weight, God knows what they would make of me. At least she had the inclination to fit in, I didn't even have that.

Dennis then tapped a dinky, little gong three times and we settled down to meditate. Well, the others settled down to meditate, whilst I proceeded to close my eyes and watch a million random images float across my mind's eye for the next hour. As part of his homily Dennis had said the rudi-ments of meditation are simple, but the correct practice was the hardest thing in the world. I had thought it a foolish thing to say, particularly to one who was finding just about everything in life impossibly convoluted and intractable, but within a few minutes I thought that he had, if anything, dramatically understated the complexity of the task ahead of me. It seemed that just about every experience I'd ever been through made an appearance eventually, some that I'd completely forgotten I'd ever had. My legs started to ache like hell and I spent the last 15 minutes - which felt like a long, painful and otherwise uneventful lifetime - trying to get into a bearable position without making too much noise. I did manage to focus on my breathing now and again, but after a couple of breaths my mind threw up a new scene demand-ing my immediate attention, and it would be minutes before I realized I'd wandered off and had to try to get back to what I was supposed to be doing. The crazy rush of endless im-ages was like drowning is supposed to be, but in this case there was no easeful death to put me out of my misery.

I felt as if I was taking a train journey through my life, and instead of concentrating on the book I was trying to read, I was staring aimlessly out of the window to watch things zip past. But while a train journey, even on British Rail, has some sort of sequence to it, the journey my mind took me on during that first meditation was completely, mischievously, random. It wasn't as if my thoughts were lofty, profound, or anything to be proud of. I must have spent at least 10 minutes trying to work out how I could submit a plausible tax return this year without either giving all my money away or ending up in prison. Another five minutes were consumed by trying to work out if I'd brought enough pairs of socks with me, and about the same amount of time went on trying to remember if I'd been optimistic enough to pack any condoms. If things turned promising with Amanda, I had no idea where I could buy condoms. I didn't even know if they sold condoms in Wales.

When the gong went at the end of the session, marking what was, without any doubt, the longest hour of my life - with the possible exception of those hours when my ex-wife frog-marched me to a Wagnerian opera - I felt a huge sense of relief, but also a nagging feeling of disappointment. If anyone had asked me how it had gone - which, fortunately, they were unable to do because of the compulsory silence - I would have felt very shamefaced to admit I'd just squandered an opportunity to gain spiritual enlightenment by worrying about whether the gurgling of my stomach could be heard, how I would get back to the station to return to London, and how I could spike Zara's tea to put her out and shut her up. But, strangely enough, I also had a vaguely perceptible feeling of tranquility, and even the tiniest trace of fascination, because although I've spent more of my life worrying about my life than I have living it - if that's mathematically possible - I've seldom reflected on it as I did for the few minutes when my mind wasn't occupied by all the trivia. Several minutes out of an hour wasn't a big return on a painful investment, but it was something, and infinitely more than I'd expected an hour beforehand.

People gradually pulled themselves together, unhooked

their legs and drifted out of the room, although one or two, including Roger, seemed intent on staying. I maliciously hoped Roger wouldn't be able to disentangle himself, and, when he finally did, that one of his legs would come off in his hand, but I felt tranquil enough to find my spite quite endearing. It was dark outside, but lights illuminated the path back to the farmhouse. I noticed people entering some of the other buildings which, as lights went on inside of them, I could see provided more living accommodation. I tried to spot Amanda in the puerile hope she would beckon me into an outhouse.

Monica was just ahead of me as we entered the house, and she indicated by improvised sign language and a lot of silent and gross distensions of her mouth that hot drinks and biscuits were available in the dining room - in fact, her sign language was so ambiguous it could have been booze and a particularly energetic variety of oral sex that were being dispensed.

I helped myself to a cup of decaffeinated coffee and headed for my room, not having anywhere else to go or anything else to do, given that everyone else appeared to be doing the same. Once there, the silence hit me like an explosion. I was both invigorated and intimidated by it. I've probably been through whole days when I've not spoken much, but somehow the thought of not having a television or a radio or a conversation, and also feeling restrained about the last recourse of talking to myself, made me feel peculiar, rather tingly. I had visions of waking up in the night and screaming out something at the top of my voice, just to break the spell the silence was weaving over me.

But it didn't work out like that. As I sat in my room, sipping coffee and browsing through a book on Japanese Zen art I'd found on a shelf, I started to wonder if this place might do me some good after all. I was far from convinced, but for an inveterate cynic even a hint of weakening was surprising, and troubling. Of course, just by coming here I'd illustrated I was willing to find some value in the place, even though I didn't really know what it was all about. But no matter how skeptical I was, what intrigued me was the fact that such an uncomplicated, undramatic and unsuspicious thing as silence had stimulated me. My head started to nod as I gazed vacantly at the sparse, stylized images in the book, and something about them was peaceful and relaxing. By 9:30 I was in bed and dead to the world, which is the first time in years I've managed that particular feat without artificial assistance.

§

I awoke with a start. Some lunatic was stalking around the farmhouse ringing a hand bell, and from the volume they were achieving it felt as though they'd given it a few lusty shakes in my ear. It was 6:30, and this was either the wake-up call for the 7 o'clock meditation or the notification that Armageddon was about to happen. My head felt as though someone had removed my brain and replaced it with cotton wool. I'd slept like a dead man for nine hours, and thinking was going to take a considerable degree of effort.

I wanted a pee, I wanted a shave, I wanted a shower, but I only had time for the first of these. As I dressed, I heard the demented bell-ringer doing a tour of the grounds, obviously relishing his or her task of tipping us rudely from the gentle world of slumber into the cold light of day.

I staggered downstairs, intent on getting at least a few gulps of fresh air into my lungs before meditating, otherwise I knew I'd be asleep again within minutes of closing my eyes. Seldom had I felt so clearly that an organism can exist in three possible states, awake, asleep or dead, and at that moment I was very definitely being coerced into the wrong one - I would have readily settled for death if sleep wasn't available. A few people were milling about with cups of steaming liquid in their hands. I went into the dining room and found hot water in an urn and the other necessary components of the strong cup of coffee that would hold my eyelids up for a while longer. It was cheap instant coffee, and it tasted more of beef tea than anything, but the intimation of nausea it induced might at least keep me awake, either that or I would fall narcoleptically into a pool of frothy, brown vomit.

Outside the air was certainly fresh, cold in fact, but I inhaled deeply to try and get a shock into my system and some sense into my head. To put it mildly, the thought of spending another hour struggling with my numb legs and my chaotic mind, and probably having to put up a major fight against sleep, snoring and disgrace, was not enticing. What the hell, I asked myself, was I doing here? When did I last get up at 6:30? When did I last go a whole day, and night, without a drink? Why did I obediently heave myself out of bed this morning and not just say "screw it" and roll over for another few hours of warm and delicious sleep?

I thought about going back to bed, if only to show I couldn't be kick-started into action like a raw army recruit. Something was telling me to make a fuss, play awkward, be anarchic. It wasn't my conscious mind that was objecting, but something deep within me that was yelling for attention. It was like schizophrenia - the habits of a lifetime rallying them- selves against the whim of the moment on the battleground inside my head. But there I was, standing in a farmyard with a lot of other sheep, waiting to be herded into the meditation barn for another hour of physical torture and mental turmoil.

We filed in, sat down and waited for everyone to get settled. Dennis tapped his little gong and off we went. After bitching to myself for a few minutes I started to follow my breathing, and immediately an image of a little devil sprang into my mind.

He was a miniature man, completely naked and red from head to toe. He was wiry and constantly in motion. He didn't look evil as much as bothersome, and his facial expression was that of somebody who is extremely pissed off and is not going to stop being pissed off, no matter what anyone does to placate him. I've no idea where he came from, but there he was, an image as solid and detailed in my mind as if he'd walked into the room and stood in front of me. He jumped up and down, stamped his feet, and waved his arms about in frustrated, angry gestures. He was the eternal complainer, the grump, the grouch, the archetypal bloody nuisance, the sort of person you'd hate to be a neighbor, and there was no way he could settle down, relax or be anything other than severely disgruntled. Needless to say, it was obvious the devil was me, or at least part of me, the part that's always nit-picking and criticizing, but it was astonishing he'd just sprung into my mind like that. I'd never seen him before, even though I'd always known this bitching part of my character existed, and that it frequently dominated my personality.

I spent a long time looking at the little devil, observing his petulant, nonstop antics. He mouthed gibberish, but it was the angry gibberish of a man whose temper is permanently lost. I remember thinking my mind was doing this, but it was a part of my mind I wasn't controlling. When I tried to get focused on my breathing he would burst into view again and sneer at me. He wanted to be back in bed, somewhere else, doing something else, with someone else, and when he was doing that, he would want to be somewhere else again, with someone else, doing something else, and on, and on. As I studied his form, I wasn't at all surprised to see that he had a half-erect penis, big enough to be troublesome, but too flaccid to be useful - that, if I needed any further convincing, proved conclusively his perfect allegorical significance to me and my life, or lack of it.

He spent a few minutes running round my body, poking at it and drawing attention to my stiff legs, my itchy scalp, my sweaty feet, my malodorous, unshowered body and my slightly aching, sleep-addled head. I realized he was always with me and always had been, looking for something to complain about, giving me reason to feel sorry for myself, providing me with excuses not to do what I ought to do. Coming here to try and sort myself out was, of course, an enormous threat to him. Chaos and complaint were his lifeblood, and if I did anything to reduce them, his power would be sapped and his very existence put in doubt. But just as I saw he was damaging to me, I also saw that I liked him; I had a genuine affection for this silly little devil with the bothersome, undecided penis.

This was no big deal. I didn't think "Wow, this meditation is really powerful stuff!" As soon as I spotted my miniature devil it was obvious what he was. I knew all the time it was going on that I was consciously conspiring to keep him there so I could take a closer look at him, fill in the detail and be entertained by him. My subconscious mind may have thrown him into view in the first place, but now he was just another entertaining thought I dwelt on, mainly to avoid getting back to proper meditation.

I would probably have gone on thinking about him or my aching legs until the end of the session if I hadn't been diverted by the unmistakable sound of somebody snoring. To begin with I thought it might be me, my body having dropped off to sleep without bothering to inform my mind. But then I opened my eyes and traced the noise, without any difficulty, to a man who was sitting on the opposite side of the room. He was stocky and balding - an obvious snoring suspect to judge by his looks. I'd noticed him yesterday evening and considered him to be one of the more normal looking residents. He was my age or a bit older, and he could have passed for a bank manager if he hadn't been sporting a tattoo of a naked woman cosseted by a snake on his forearm. Of course, that didn't mean he still couldn't be a bank manager, but it lengthened the odds quite dramatically. Ruben, who was sitting next to him, lifted his arm and, while staring dead ahead unwilling to disturb his trance, patted his neighbor on the shoulder. Nothing happened, he patted again, and again, and eventually the sleeper awoke with a mumbled "Wa, wa, wassa matter?" before realizing what was happening. He looked embarrassed and smiled guiltily around the room before dropping his head and taking a few deep breaths. After a while he lifted his head slightly and shot a furtive glance in the direction of the Buddha and/or Dennis, hoping, I presume to gauge the reaction of one or both of them, but when I turned to look at them, they were both wearing inscrutable expressions, the only discernible difference being that Dennis had his eyes shut and the Buddha had a shorter haircut.

At long last the gong chimed. If this was all there was to it, just sitting on the floor between gong strikes, it was going to be a hard slog, and I doubted I would be able to last a day, let alone a couple of weeks. But I told myself it hadn't been a total disaster so far, and I should at least give it one full day to see what the program consisted of. In that way I would be able to claim my early departure was done on a slightly informed basis.

The episode with the little devil had been interesting, and if anything more profound came to light, well, who knows where it would lead? But then I caught myself. Can you sort out your life selectively and leave intact the nasty bits about yourself with which you are happy? If cynicism was the little devil's creation, did I really want to ostracize him when he's key to the way I make my living? I was starting to feel uneasy. If meditation is about deconstructing your persona, what the hell gets erected in its place? It was clear this argument was the red devil's making, but he had a right to his say. He'd been a welcome tenant in my body for the past 40-odd years, and it would be unfair to evict him now because he didn't match the Aquarian wallpaper I was about to hang. His irritable view of life had doubtless generated some of my best work, so he'd more than paid what he owed me for renting the space in which he angrily stomped around in my otherwise wishy-washy mind.

After worrying over this, I was one of the last to leave the meditation room, and as I put my shoes on at the door I found myself alongside the snorer.

"That was embarrassing," he said to me, from which I inferred either that it was now okay to talk again, or that he was putting his foot in it for a second time.

"I bet you're not the first person to fall asleep during meditation," I said, thinking of Fiona.

"No, but, you know, I get the impression they think I'm a dilettante, a lightweight, a bit of a joke, you know, and, well, I take it very seriously really, and, well. I don't know. I'm Bob," he said, and we shook hands, which was the first time any of the retreatants had given me a conventional greeting since I'd arrived. He looked like a Bob. A normal chap you'd meet in a pub and have a few beers with and feel quite alright about. Warm, friendly, non-threatening, just plain ordinary. In this environment he stuck out like a sore thumb, and he probably thought the same about me, hence our conversation about something as mundane as snoring. "You're Peter, the cartoonist. Interesting job, isn't it?"

"You'd think so, wouldn't you? But I guess it's just like any job, it has its bad bits, quite a lot of them, actually."

"Really? Sounds like fun to me."

"I should have given it up years ago, moved into a more lucrative side of art, or even given art up altogether and got a proper job. Too late now, so I just stumble on. What do you do?"

"I'm an astrologer." I did the astronomer/astrologer thing in my head, the same as when I try to remember the difference between a stalagmite and a stalactite, not that knowing the difference has had any major impact on my life, as far as I'm aware. It was a few seconds before I resolved which was which, and that he was on the horoscope side of the universe, hanging upside down from the ceiling of fantasy, rather than growing up soundly from the floor of reality.

I'd never met an astrologer before, at least, not to talk to, and he didn't fit my image of one at all. I mean, aren't they flowery individuals, effeminate if male, somewhat, well ... ? I don't know, but Bob just didn't look like one. Then I couldn't think of anything to say, anything sensible I mean, and I didn't want to subject the man to the sort of inane but well-meaning questions I get asked, like "Have you horoscoped anybody famous?" and that kind of thing.

"Do you do personal horoscopes or general ones?" This sounded sensible, but it was hard to show interest in something I couldn't take seriously.

"I've done columns in magazines from time to time, but not anymore. You only get broad generalizations when you treat people en masse. That sort of stuff may attract people to the science, but they only get anything really insightful out of it when you do them individually."

"Science? Not art?" I said, aware he could have asked "Art? Not graffiti?" about my profession.

"For me it's a science."

"And it's all about the movements of heavenly bodies?" I said, the image of Amanda spontaneously pushing its way back into my caricature of a mind.

"I call it the gravitational influence of stars and planets. I'm not one of the twaddle merchants. I know as an observed fact that people have different personalities depending on when they were born, and that they're also affected by gravitational alignments according to their birth date. I just translate the facts into how they'll be feeling in the future, and given we usually respond to our feelings by action, I can tell them how they'll probably be acting too."

It was as though I was talking to a mechanic about differential axles, or to a dentist about cavities, or to a brewer about hop varieties. He treated it like a matter of fact, no mystery, just the appliance of science.

"So it's all down to gravity, in a manner of speaking," I said.

"Yes, but what's gravity?" he asked. I don't normally get asked questions like that, not in my line of business and never on a stomach so empty my blood wasn't giving my brain the confidence to do anything more than find my way to breakfast. I only have the pretension to tackle weighty subjects after a substantial intake of alcohol, and even then I know more sense would be contained in the methane blown out of a cow's arse.

"We know about all the other forces," he went on, "electro-magnetic, nuclear and so on, and we all experience gravity, but nobody can point to it. All bodies possess it. The apple pulls the earth just as surely as the earth pulls the apple, it's just that the earth is bigger so it's observable effect is greater. But what actually is it?"

Again, I didn't feel I had a suitable answer. In fact, I didn't think I had anything suitable to say at all, but I could hardly change the subject, given the intensity with which we - that is, he - had embarked upon it.

"Gravity is mysterious, and nobody seeks to question it. We all just swallow the concept and assume we understand it. Believe me, if people knew as little about electricity as we know about the essential nature of gravity, they'd be a lot less willing to plug their kettle into it every morning. But you can't turn off gravity, so we just live with it and take it for granted, good or bad."

"Do many astrologers think like you?"

"Hardly any. There are a few who want to ground the subject in fact rather than wrap it up in hocus-pocus, but most astrologers like the mystery, and they don't even understand the science anyway. The mathematics is way beyond your average tea leaf reader. A lot of the people who look at the facts are trying to ridicule the subject, and if you come to it with that intention, you'll probably achieve the result you're after."

The next trap I had to avoid was asking him to do my horoscope, to see if he came up with anything startling. But again, I know what it's like to be asked to draw cartoons of people when they find out what I do for a living. It wouldn't be so bad if they didn't frequently seem to be so damn disappointed, or even insulted, when I oblige and do a sketch of them. I mean, I'm a cartoonist for Christ's sake! I'm supposed to make people look absurd. By the same token, if he'd told me about something nasty in my future I might have blamed him for it, as people sometimes blame me for their big noses and other cartoon-exaggerated features.

"What about astronomers. They, well, they scoff at it, don't they?"

"They think we're mad, and I can't blame them, most astrologers are mad. Actually, I'm as much astronomer as astrologer, I'm a something else, an astronomologer perhaps, but there's no category for that in Yellow Pages, so I'm stuck alongside the nutters."

I never knew you could find astrologers in the Yellow Pages, not that I've ever looked.

"How do you calculate it all?"

"I work on the same principles as the others, even the little old ladies with crystal balls who think it's magic, we all use the same basic methods, just depends how deep you go and how you interpret the charts. I keep it straightforward and factual, bang, bang, bang," he chops the air with his hand as he gives me the bangs. "This and this, therefore that and that. None of the old 'You'll be moving to Manitoba with a tall dark stranger with one leg and Land Rover'. I leave that sort of nonsense to the quacks."

We'd been ambling towards the farmhouse, but then he stopped and grabbed my arm.

"Hey, we'd better stop talking."

"But we're allowed to now, aren't we?"

"Well, yes, but people tend not to. They sort of work back up to it gradually. I mean, if you really get into this silence stuff it can be very affecting, and you don't want to use words too much at first, they kind of break the spell. Words actually feel very coarse when you start talking after a long silence, as though speaking is an inferior means of communication."

I'd always thought words were just about the most superior form of communication. But I suppose they sometimes come too easily, and often without any thought behind them. I know they've got me into a lot of hot water over the years, more than any silent gesture ever has, no matter how coarse.

"And after that snoring business, I don't want to come across like a chatterbox. Most of them here are pretty laid back about how you behave, but some of them are, well, snotty if you don't appear to be getting into it like they do, even if they're really less serious about it than I am."

Which convinced me I had no place at Ravenswood, and I'd call for a taxi as soon as I'd put some food into my now growling stomach.

§§§

CRYING

The dining room was busy and there seemed to be more animation about the eaters than I'd noticed the night before. Fiona had told me that meditation had given her a tremendous appetite, something to do with the outlandish energy requirements of the greedy brain when being threatened with enlightenment, but more likely, I thought, to be brought about by the enforced absence of other pleasures, tactile, sensual or cynical.

There was a selection of cereals and porridge, loaves of bread which you could slice and toast yourself in an industrial-strength toaster, and seemingly endless jars of jams, honeys, nut butters and other weird and wonderful concoctions that I passed over with barely a suspicious glance. The porridge appeared to be safe, and although the bread looked as though it contained enough roughage to keep an army regular, it was actually okay, even if an injudiciously sized mouthful did take five minutes to chew. There was a big bowl of coarse cut marmalade, probably homemade, that ranked alongside the previous night's roast potatoes for quality. I might still have been having doubts about how long I could survive the regime, but I couldn't blame the food or the accommodation. I sorted through dozens of boxes of tea bags until I found one that contained standard-issue PG Tips, and made myself a mug of tea. I would know I'd gone native when I found myself drinking some sort of herbal infusion smelling of Channel Number 5.

"Have you tried the chamomile?" said a voice in my left ear. It so took me by surprise I thought at first it might be some sort of temptress, a siren voice trying to woo me into becoming a full-blown retreatant, but in fact it belonged to an elderly, pleasant-faced lady with an outstanding head of pure white hair.

"No, I think I tried smoking it once, but it didn't get me onto a higher plain."

She giggled and nearly dropped her plate, as if I'd just set new bounds in subtle comedy. I was unjustly flattered.

"I'm Doris. You're Peter, aren't you, the artist?"

"Peter, yes, artist, sort of."

"Have you met Zara Sheck?"

"Zara, yes, if there's only one Zara here, I've met her. Sheck? She's not ..."

"Yes, she's Maria Sheck's sister. You know Maria Sheck?"

"I know of her." Oh, shit! Maria Sheck is just about my favorite living artist, and the blowsy bitch is her sister. Did this mean Maria was also a twat? Did it mean Zara was a good artist after all, and that her insufferable boasts were true? Did it mean I would have to suck up to Zara so I could get to meet Maria? Did it mean I had to stop liking Maria's work because her sister was so off-putting?

"I'm a complete ignoramus when it comes to art," she said, looking sheepish.

"Well, that's not necessarily a bad thing to be. Next time you're in an art gallery, look at the other people there. The artists will take 10 minutes to look at a piece to see if they can understand its "meaning", but the ignoramus will make up their mind in 10 seconds and move on. Life's too short to interpret some of the pointless drivel you see on show these days."

Bob and I had been the last to arrive for breakfast. I've got this silly attitude about eating times I just can't rid myself of. I nurture the belief that it's somehow superior to eat later than everyone else or, in communal situations like this where everyone eats at pretty much the same time, it's better to be one of the last at the trough. I don't know where I get this from, but it seems more civilised to breeze into a dining room gracefully and late, than to storm in early and frantically stuff one's head into the nosebag. It's as though latecomers have shrugged off that panicky, barbaric voice that tells us to get food whilst it's going, and that they either are so rich they know there will always be grub in the larder, or that they've put themselves on a mental plane from which they can disparage frenzy and greed.

This attitude isn't limited to my convoluted brain and insecure personality - it seems to be ingrained into the English class system. Don't the toffs eat lunch at 1 p.m. whilst the plebs are noshing down at noon? Doesn't the dinner bell ring in aristocratic homes at 7:30 p.m., whereas the TV dinner trays slap onto laps at 6 p.m. in the land of the semi-detached? It's got to the point where I feel inferior to everyone who enters a restaurant after me, and I imagine supercilious scorn on their faces as I stumble out, their looks saying "see that poor little savage, couldn't control himself and his incontinent appetite".

I wonder if eating times haven't somehow got into the genes, and whereas the highborn are happy to meander off to a leisurely lunch when the more important parts of their lives have been dealt with, the droning, slaving lower classes are overcome by some atavistically inspired craving for food that pulls them as strongly as the sex urge in the last seconds before an orgasm.

My own genes are at the low end of the spectrum, so in my case the struggle against noon lunch and 6 p.m. dinner is always hard fought, although I've managed to put off my animal cravings in the evening by shuffling a few time-winning aperitifs into the equation. I hate Spain, where they lunch at 3 p.m. and dine at midnight, so I feel inferior to everyone – even babies are still sucking down their dinner after I've swallowed my last mouthful of paella in Alicante.

Anyway, as a consequence of this inane and baseless hang-up, when I sat down to eat breakfast I felt as though I had an advantage over my spiritually-orientated friends, who had rushed back from their transcendental pursuits to gorge themselves on wholemeal this and unrefined that, whilst I wandered back at my ease, discussing the wonders of gravity on the way. No sooner did I think this, than it struck me, for the millionth time in my life, what a pathetic creature I am.

As Bob intimated, breaking our fast was undertaken with a lot less reticence and a lot more gusto than breaking our silence, and nobody was saying much. There wasn't even a lot of smiling, but whether this was because everyone was coming to terms with the outcome of the recently finished meditation, or simply a case of the early morning doom, I couldn't tell.

Then, just as I was trying to decide whether to have another slice of toast and marmalade, I heard somebody sobbing. It was a girl I'd first noticed that morning - she couldn't have been around the night before, because she was pretty enough to have caught my eye if she had been. She had long, curly black hair, and wide innocent eyes that were now filled with tears. For a while nobody did anything, then Dennis, in the act of leaving the room, stood behind her and rested his hands on her shoulders. He bent down and whispered in her ear before leaving. She nodded as he spoke, and then got on with her crying. A few other people patted or touched or whispered to her on their way out, but otherwise she was just left to get on with it. Zara's were the only words addressed to her that I heard. "We're all here if you need us," she said, making it sound as much an instruction to the rest of us as a comfort to the girl.

I was so busy trying not to notice, that by the time I got up to leave I realized I was the last person in the room apart from the girl. It's an odd situation, being alone with someone who's crying and you don't know why and you don't feel obliged to do anything, despite feeling bad about doing nothing. She'd obviously had offers of help and comfort from those who had spoken to her as they left, and as she hadn't taken any of them up, she couldn't have wanted my comfort either.

I was poignantly reminded of a time when I'd been at Heathrow airport, changing terminals. In one of the anonymous underground passages I'd come across a woman leaning against a wall and crying her eyes out. On the spur of the moment I approached her and asked if I could do anything, trying to use a tone of voice that implied I was happy to leave her alone, and I wasn't a predator or a mugger - don't ask me how I presumed I'd got that message into my voice and my body language, but I thought I had. "Fuck off," she said, and I did, angrily biting back an obscene riposte of my own, the role of indignant, rebuffed Samaritan sitting very uncomfortably on my pompous shoulders.

I wondered if I should leave and just let the girl get on with it, and I was about to go when she spoke.

"We must all seem pretty crazy to you. I mean, getting emotional all the time and, well, everything."

Now she came to mention it, I can't say I'd noticed there being a lot of emotion in the air. In fact, I would say just the opposite. Most of the residents seemed to be in control of themselves, somewhat too much in control in the cases of Roger and Zara, and Dennis didn't strike me as the type who dissolved into tears very often.

"Well, I suppose it raises quite a lot of feelings, all this contemplation," I said, as the thought occurred to me that if I ever managed to think hard about my life for a few hours it would cause me to howl with irrepressible anguish.

"Yes, it does. I'm Sandy, by the way."

"I'm Peter."

Her eyes were red, but she was smiling, and it didn't look like a brave, forced smile, she actually seemed quite happy all of a sudden.

"Crying is wonderful, it's such a release."

"Well, yes," I said. I suppose it is a release, but you don't start crying because you're happy, do you? There must be something shitty in your life to start it off. Didn't she mean that stopping crying was good, and the crying part was just a necessary prelude to the stopping part? I find it hard to believe I actually said what I said next, but I did.

"Do you come here often?"

"I live here. Well, not permanently, but I've been here for six months and I don't want to go anywhere else just now. About a third of the people here at any time are long-termers, longer than a week or two, that is. Some stay for years. Monica started as a visitor and then joined the staff, so did Roger. Ken came for a weekend and has been here for eight months. He just never left, I mean really, he came on a Friday but never went home on Sunday night. Gave up his job, left his family, everything, all by telephone. Incredible."

"Incredible," I echoed, but not meaning it as a compliment, as I assume she had.

"What happens next?" I asked, and then added, "On the program I mean," in case she thought I was asking about her life in general. The importance of words was obviously getting to me.

"We have free time until 10 o'clock, then an hour-long session, then a break, then work, then lunch at 1 o'clock."

"What's the session?"

"Not sure, could be anything. Sometimes it's the best part of the day, something completely off the wall that Dennis leads, but it could be just another sit."

"Sit?"

"Sitting meditation. That's really at the heart of what we do here, just sit and meditate in a supportive environment. It's amazing what can come out of just sitting."

"What ..." I said, trying to frame my question sensibly.

"What?"

"I was going to ask you what you get out of it. It sounds like an inane question, but I'm new to all this stuff and it seems, well, I don't know, just, well ..."

"I understand," she said, but I didn't know how she could, because I wasn't aware of what I was asking. "I came here to find out more about myself. I'd just got to the end of a wonderful relationship that had turned painful, and I couldn't see any way forward, so I came to try and find out what's really important to me and how I should put my life back together."

"And did you find what's important?"

"No, well, yes, I did. I found that nothing is important.

Being here is important, but I could be somewhere else. It doesn't matter what you do or where you do it. What matters is how you do it. Relationships are okay, even intense ones, but you have to be yourself, not somebody else, not someone the other person expects you to be. That was where I'd gone wrong. I'd always tried to be the person other people wanted me to be - my family, my friends, my lover - and I wasn't being me, so nothing I did felt right. Dennis told me you can buy the most beautiful pair of shoes in the world, but if they don't fit, they're going to hurt, so you should get comfortable with yourself first, and then everything falls into place."

This all sounded neat and orderly, but what does it mean to "be yourself"? I feel as if I'm myself, but my life is still screwed up, so what do I do now? Get a new self?

"What do you do when you're not here?" I asked.

"Nothing. My father's rich and he gives me a huge allowance, so I don't need to work. I used to have a few shops, boutiques, that sort of thing but I sold them. I owned a restaurant for a while but I sold that too. I used to flit from one silly scheme to the next, most of them were five minute wonders. Now I don't need all that to make my life fulfilling, I just need this," she said, opening her arms to embrace the room and, I assumed, the rest of Ravenswood, and maybe the rest of Wales, and even the rest of the world for all I knew.

"You look puzzled," she said, and I was puzzled, puzzled by what she'd just said, puzzled, for the umpteenth time, by why I'd come to this place, puzzled by the fact I was chatting to an attractive, rich, single woman without thinking about flirting with her. It was all slightly worrying, as if I wasn't being myself, as if I was losing touch with my old standards of behavior, wretched and conniving as they might be. I briefly wondered - ludicrous though it sounds - if Dennis was doctoring the water or the food in order to evoke these subtle personality changes to ensure he retained a healthy number of paying guests who thought they might be on to something profound.

"Well, it may sound naive, but I don't really know why I came here, and now I'm here I don't know what to expect. Dennis started me off by saying I shouldn't expect anything, so if I look clueless, it's because I am clueless, and I don't see any way I'm going to stop being clueless."

A broad smile spread across her face and she applauded. "That's wonderful!" I was afraid she was going to say that, and the laugh I gave in reply was suitably hollow.

"No, really, it is. That's the best place to start. Just go with the flow. Stay clueless, whatever you do! I'm more clueless now than I've ever been, and I love it! I've spent all of my life trying to go somewhere, and not getting anywhere made me angry with myself and everyone else. Now I take it as it comes, so there's nothing to get upset about."

Precisely. What these people found so wonderful about being up the creek without a paddle was beyond me, and given the particular creek I was floating up was called Shit Creek, their admonitions to stay there were leaving a very nasty smell in my nose.

"You can't explain the colour blue to someone who's been blind all their life," she said.

I didn't say anything. I had the impression that another piece of Dennis' sagacity was about to be divulged.

"I can't explain something to you you've never experienced. You have to experience it yourself and then you'll see. It takes an act of faith."

Oh, well that's going to be very hard for me. Faith is the one word I didn't want anyone to mention. If I went to a doctor and he told me to have faith, I wouldn't be impressed, in fact, I would be very depressed and immediately start looking for another doctor, one who dealt in more tangible commodities.

"I bet you're always thinking about how you'd like your life to be, aren't you?"

Well, yes, she's right on the money there. In fact, when life gets me down I think very hard about how I would like life to be, and it's perfectly simple. I would like to be a successful cartoonist, with a regular spot in one of the national dailies and occasional appearances in the overseas press, like Le Monde, Washington Post, New York Times, El Pais and so on. I would, as a consequence of this success, be modestly rich and slightly famous - famous enough to have Channel 4 or BBC 2 documentaries made about me, and to be able to get tables at fashionable restaurants when I want to be fed, rather than when they want to take my money.

My richness would bring me a beautiful home in London, with civilized neighbors - who have hair (neither shorn nor lousy, bleached nor dyed) and noses and tongues without rings and studs in them - and a few other properties in pleasant places. It would also bring me a new, prestige automobile, or two, and an absence of worry over money matters. Lastly, I would like to have a beautiful, loving, voluptuous partner who shares my sexual appetite, both in terms of hunger or abstinence, depending on how I'm feeling, although she should expect a preponderance of the former for a few years to come.

I suppose I should also add good health, but I don't need to add happiness, because if the above criteria were satisfied and I wasn't happy, then God would be eminently justified in ending my life painfully and miserably without a moment's hesitation. Is this too much to ask? Yes, of course it is, but none of it is out of reach. Some cartoonists make money and are marginally famous. I'm not so ugly that, even if I was rich, beautiful women wouldn't look at me. So all I lack is the right breaks and, I suppose, that last bit of talent or luck that would launch my career into orbit, and get it out of the dangerous hedgehopping flight path it's in now.

So yes, Sandy, I do know how I'd like my life to be, very clearly, as it happens.

"Yes," I said, and as I did so, I thought of Amanda, and realized at that precise moment I would have liked to be snuggled up with her. In fact, I don't think my problem is not knowing what I want, but rather I know precisely what I want, right down to the last and frequently sordid detail, but can't do it, either through lack of complicity in others, or lack of talent, guts, attractiveness, confidence or persuasiveness in myself.

We talked for a while longer, and although she was perfectly pleasant, the general tenor of our conversation was that she was enlightened and right, whereas I was unenlightened and wrong. She made me feel inferior and stupid, and despite absorbing her pearls of wisdom, I knew they couldn't untangle my singularly maladjusted view of that part of the universe with which I am in daily contact. I wanted to ask her why she'd been crying, and how it was her grief had come to such a sudden and complete end. But she didn't really give me the opening, and in the belief she was steering the focus away from herself by giving me advice, I didn't pursue it.

§§§

MEDITATING

I sat in the yard simmering under some weak sunshine for a few minutes before Monica sallied from the farmhouse, tolling her large school bell to summon us to the next session.

Once we were all assembled, nothing happened for a full five minutes. We just sat there in complete silence. This, I was realizing, was the way things were done at Ravenswood. Everything was preceded by a period of reflection, and despite my general antipathy to what I considered to be a somewhat self-important mood, I came to enjoy these quiet interludes when nothing was expected of me. At last Dennis spoke, and he spoke very slowly, with long pauses. To begin with, I found this style of delivery irritating, arrogant and not a little spooky, but I gradually let my irritation go and started to pay attention.

"I'm sure you've heard the phrase 'more is less'. It's a very powerful statement. Most of what we do in this world is aimed at getting more into our lives. More money, more sex, more pleasure, more power, more possessions, more knowledge, even more time itself. You could say not many of us seek more pain, more hunger, more misery, more disease, more heartache. But whereas we know when we've shaken off something negative, we seldom recognize we've got enough of something positive. We're happy when we've recovered from an illness, but we're not always content with a certain degree of wealth when we know there's more to be had. This wanting more is never-ending. When we're happy with most of our lives, there's usually something we want more of, and even if our lives are perfect, there's one last thing we want more of, more of life itself. Now I want to give you another phrase to consider, which is really just an extension of the first one. I want you to think about 'everything is nothing'.

"When you meditate, I'm sure it often feels as though everything is struggling to get into your mind, fighting to get its own bit of brain to play with. Our minds seem to have a mortal dread of having nothing to bite on, nothing to consider, nothing to gloat on, nothing to mull over, nothing to worry about. Our minds fear tranquility as if it threatens their very existence, as if stopping the mental processes will stop the brain itself, which will then shrivel up and die and leave us gibbering idiots, or even worse, empty creatures that can't even gibber. Our mind acts like a cart on a flat road that has been set rolling at birth; if it ever stops, it will never start again, and will rest in the same place, doing nothing, going nowhere, for the remainder of eternity."

He paused for a long time. It sounded like a sermon, but he'd accurately described my brief and flimsy meditative experience in a nutshell. My mind acted like a magnet for any stray thought the moment I shut my eyes. I felt as though I was even picking up other peoples discarded thoughts if I couldn't find any of my own to distract me, a sort of radio interference on the extra-sensory-perception channel.

"Our brains want more. They want everything. They're greedy for experience and dismissive of emptiness. They say nature hates a vacuum, well, so do our minds. They're afraid of emptiness, because from that day in the womb when they start working, they are bombarded, nonstop, with information. Even when we sleep they're active, constructing their own imagery through dreams. And then, one day, we sit on a cushion and try to turn our brains off. Just like that!" He clicked his fingers, and the click resonated around the room like a thunderclap, underlining the complete silence we were maintaining.

"After years of having total dependence on our minds for everything, in one moment we want to quieten them and see what's happening when the light of conscious thought is turned off, and when even the surreal world of the unconscious is stilled. Is it surprising then, that our brains can't take the hint? It's like the light that goes on when we open the refrigerator door. If, one day, we decided we didn't want the light to come on when the door opened, but that we wanted to achieve this by simply telling the refrigerator of our wish, would it work? Of course not. We could apply surgery to the refrigerator by fiddling with the mechanism, but that would be heavy-handed and, if we didn't know what we were doing, potentially dangerous and irrevocable. So it is with the mind. Telling it to stop working just doesn't have any effect, no matter how insistent we are, and altering the brain, through drugs or surgery, is even less desirable than it would be to unleash an incompetent electrician on our fridge."

He was an accomplished preacher. He spoke slowly and clearly, no "ums" and "ers" breaking his flow and betraying muddled thought. If he was hunting for a word he simply paused, and resumed the smooth flow of words when he was ready. He might have been talking claptrap - I hadn't made my mind up about that yet - but his manner of expression was so coherent and authoritative that a nonsense rhyme would have sounded profound coming from Dennis' lips. I found myself staring fixedly, not at his placid eyes, but at his mouth as it shaped the individual words, each one deliberately enunciated. I half expected speech bubbles to gurgle up from his throat and plaster words of wisdom across the still air. Even the Buddha seemed to be absorbed by the accumulating pile of wisdom.

"More is less. The more of everything we have, the closer to nothing we become - a situation which converges on my statement that everything is nothing. And here's one last phrase for you. 'Nothing is everything'. This really comes out of what I've just said, but if you need an analogy, consider this - scientists tell us that in the black holes that exist in the universe, immense gravitational forces converge to an infinitesimally small point they call a 'singularity'. Anything dragged into a black hole is irrevocably pulled towards that point, and is compressed to a zero dimensional state, a state in which dimensions actually cease to exist - no length, no width, no breadth and no time. In others word, everything is compressed into nothing, and nothing, therefore, contains everything.

"The state of meditation has been compared to a state of living death in which we can commune with a plane of existence that the humdrum nature of life renders invisible. This isn't a negative state, but, in fact, the most positive state to which the human mind can aspire, because in this state we see what binds all matter, animate and inanimate, human and animal, dead and living. It is the state of transcendental enlightenment, in which the nothing of the stilled mind becomes the everything of the universe and all that lies beyond the universe. It is the moment of truth in which we see the common denominator and in which we are the common denominator. The moment when nothing is everything."

He stopped. People were exchanging glances, and there was a general sense of astonishment in their expressions. But although I liked the performance, and was impressed by it, I wasn't sure it hadn't just been a play on words. What I was sure of, however, was that the man had strong powers to influence people, and I reckoned most of those in the room were in the palm of his hand, then and perhaps always.

In any normal environment someone would now pipe up and say "Come on, Dennis. You just mixed a bunch of metaphors together, stuffed a black hole into a refrigerator and came up with the meaning of life. I bet you don't understand any more about infinite gravity than I do about gynecology, it's just a nicely obfuscating smoke screen for half-baked physics and red-raw philosophy". But nobody did, and although mischievously tempted, I wasn't about to.

The group began to break up. By an adroit bit of timing I managed to find myself putting my shoes on and leaving the meditation room at the same time as Amanda. The bad news was Zara was also there.

"Incredible insight," said Zara, as the three of us walked across the yard. I didn't know if she was referring to Dennis' soliloquy or her own incredible mind. Nor did I know whether she was speaking to me, Amanda, herself or the universe in general.

"Yes," said Amanda. "What did you think Peter?"

"Interesting."

"Interesting?" said Zara, as though she'd just trodden in the word and was trying to scrape it off her shoe.

"Interesting?" she said again.

"Yes."

"Is that all you can think to say about a piece of knowledge as profound as any you'll hear in your lifetime?"

"If it was so peerless, it doesn't really matter what I say about it, does it?"

She snorted, as if the offending word was now removed from her shoe and back in the gutter where it belonged, but her expression illustrated the smell was still bothering her.

"It must be demeaning for Dennis to see his pearls of wisdom cast before swine."

"Well, you'd know all about swine Zara, you bloody, self-important old sow."

For a fleeting moment I thought I'd said this; that the words had come out of my mouth in a reactive, involuntary spasm. Then I thought I'd imagined them, and they would go down in the sizeable annals of the "retorts I wish I'd made but never did". Then I saw someone was walking on the other side of Zara, glaring at her and being glared back at.

"I suppose you also found it 'interesting', being too small brained to understand it?" she said to him, but managing to hit me with the breadth of her insult as well. The newcomer just snorted a derisory laugh and carried on walking past the now stationary Zara.

"I'm Ken," he said to me, slapping me on the back. "I'd like to tell you you'll get used to her, but you won't. She'll seem as poisonous and flatulent on the day you leave as she did on the day you arrived."

So, this was Ken, the family deserter, and now my savior. "Incredible Ken", as Sandy had almost described him. I don't know if I was more shocked by being supported by someone who sounded like he could be a bit of a shit, or by the words he'd used. Of all the emotions and attitudes and reactions I'd witnessed since my arrival, insults and hostility had been completely absent, even Roger's pronouncements were devoid of emotion. Ken's breaking of what was, I assumed, an unwritten rule at Ravenswood, was like seeing a big rock dropped unexpectedly into a completely still pool.

I wanted to ask "Can you say things like that here? Can you be angry and vitriolic and not get expelled or excommunicated or whatever it is that pacifist liberals do to people who shatter their peace? If insults are allowed, can we get drunk, and can I proposition Amanda?" Why should Zara have the monopoly on being unpleasant to people? Even if she didn't use unfortunate language, her insults were a sight more hurtful than many a common or garden Anglo-Saxon blast of expletives I've received from under-tipped taxi drivers or paranoid winos.

Ken was a tall, lean and fit looking man, probably in his mid-thirties. He had a neat black beard and short hair. By both his appearance and what little I'd experienced of his demeanor, he was a direct, no-nonsense kind of bloke. I felt uncomfortable being in his debt. I don't know what I would have said to Zara if left to my own devices. I would have tried to find a sharp, witty response - as much to impress Amanda as repress Zara - but, based on what I know of myself, I wouldn't have got anything stunning together until several hours of seething hindsight and righteous indignation had passed. His blunt intervention left me feeling impotent, as if I needed someone to help me out with overbearing sods like Zara, and although this may be true, I don't like to be reminded of it.

Maybe I should draw a cartoon of Zara. After all, that's how I started when I was a schoolboy, drawing ridiculous sketches of teachers or pupils who intimidated me, reducing them to hideous images, sapping them of other power. My own form of voodoo.

"We have a break now, Peter", Ken told me "to recover from that onslaught and then we work to get up an appetite for lunch. We're starting to dig a new area of vegetable garden today, so an extra pair of hands is needed."

He had no more to say. He just waved a large hand in what might have been a "see you later" gesture and set off towards one of the other buildings that surrounded the yard. Amanda was still close by as we entered the farmhouse, and we exchanged glances. She smiled.

"There are some personalities here," she said, breaking into a gentle laugh. I was immediately reminded of how attractive I found her even, as she was that day, wrapped in some shapeless and strange-smelling piece of clothing, the likes of which I'd never seen before, that could possibly be described as a high-fiber sari. "You'll find they often express themselves very openly, but they don't usually mean anything malicious by it."

"But sometimes they do," I said, and that little laugh bubbled deliciously out of her again.

"You may find them abrupt, but it's not a personal thing. It's just that normal speech is wrapped up in so much waffle, and when you take that wrapping off it can seem a bit blunt, but really it's just honest."

Calling someone an "old sow" might be perfectly descriptive, but it's not factually correct, and I hardly think it wasn't expected to sting. I said nothing, being happy just to soak up Amanda's presence, even if her words didn't ring true.

"Supposing," she said, as we took our drinks to a table, intent on explaining bluntness-that-isn't to me in greater detail, "Supposing, you say to me 'let's have lunch', but for no particular reason, I want to have lunch alone today. Normally, I'd either lie by saying I've got something arranged already, or make an excuse, like I need to spend time on my own, or something of the sort. But the last thing I'd say is just 'no' and leave you to work the reasons out for yourself. A lot of what we say is to lubricate social intercourse," I wondered if she'd chosen those words on purpose, to hint at something, but she just carried on, oblivious to the effect her *double entendre* had on me, "and it's a sort of second-guessing based on how we expect other people to react, and we always base those guesses on our own views of how other people are, which is a recipe for miscommunication. If I just say 'no' to the lunch invitation, I haven't lied, I haven't felt the need to justify myself, so I haven't assumed I know how your mind works, and I haven't made any assumptions about how sensitive you are, or aren't."

"But if we've spent thousands of years constructing a subtle ritual around how we communicate," I said, "isn't it just better to go along with it, even if it is a bit sloppy, rather than make a stand and upset people unnecessarily?"

"Well, maybe, for some people, for most people, I suppose. But if you want to achieve complete honesty, you have to go to the root of the problem and begin there, which means stripping away all the confusion society makes us exercise to spare feelings of people we're not accountable to."

I presumed Roger was an expert practitioner of this approach. There was no overdose of verbal wallpaper in his vocabulary. But I didn't for one minute think Zara and Ken had been exploring honesty - I think they'd been exploring red-blooded, mutual dislike, proving you can't easily live your life in a cocoon, as much as you'd like to, and if you do, you end up like Roger, which is not my goal in this world, and it's hard to believe it's Roger's either.

§

After our break I went in search of Ken, as I supposed I'd been formally invited into the garden digging battalion via the brief altercation with Zara, and partly in repayment for his peremptory settlement of it. The vegetable plot at the back of the farmhouse was already well-cultivated, but beyond it there was a mammoth tract that was probably on its way to becoming overgrown when the Doomsday Book was written - assuming that deepest Wales got a mention in the Doomsday Book. It looked, to my unpracticed and cowardly eye, to be more in need of two weeks with a giant earth-moving machine than the occasional ministrations of a bunch of un-skilled and unpaid navvies.

"The target area," said Ken, who was to prove to com-mand quite a sizeable arsenal of military jargon, much of it offensive, "is from that wall to that fence and from that build-ing to that fence," confirming my suspicions that this was indeed where my cartoonist's hands were needed. Bob was one of the digging team, and he was plainly addressing the problem from the same uneasy and shiftless angle as me.

"Ken," said Bob, "I don't want to appear negative, but wouldn't it be better to get some machine involved in this to begin with, at least to just turn it over, then we could dig it more thoroughly by hand? A tractor, or even just a rotavator, maybe?"

Hands that leaf through star charts are about as well equipped for strenuous labor as those that draw silly pic-tures, so I felt I could keep quiet while he represented my views, not that I would know what to do with a tractor or rota-vator if confronted with one.

"Certainly, we could use a machine, but for two reasons. Firstly, machines are expensive to rent, noisy to run and pol-lute the atmosphere. Secondly, this isn't just for the benefit of the community, the ecosystem and, therefore, the planet, it is also for the benefit of us. Labor is not only physically rewarding and spiritually uplifting in itself, but it also gives us the possibility of extending our meditative practice through activity. In fact, the rhythmic aspect of digging is particularly suitable to meditative goals."

He said all this with a trace of a grin on his lips but a

discernible tone of impatience and irritation in his voice. There was also something in the precise and measured way in which he spoke that seemed to imply a pent-up anger that was likely to be directed at us if we didn't behave ourselves and do as we were told, without further questioning.

But Bob wasn't impressed, nor did I have any reason to believe that he, unlike me, was in Ken's debt for dealing with Zara, so he kept up his criticism.

"Do you have any idea how long it's going to take to dig this over?" he said. Ken moved towards him, bent forward slightly, and put his face about six inches from Bob's.

"No," he said, "do you?" and then added after a significant pause, and making a noise like a cork exploding out of a bottle "Bob!"

Bob jumped back with this last word, and although his mouth started working, he couldn't get anything to come out. I don't think that over-wrapping of words was a problem for Ken, so maybe Amanda was right about the powerful use of honesty, but you could also explain his modus operandi in terms of his being a nasty sod.

"Are there any more questions?" he asked. "Is there an overwhelming need to discuss the matter fermenting in anyone else's brain? Should we adjourn to the meditation room and discuss this issue over a nice hot cup of tea? Explore it from every conceivable angle? Leave no stone unturned? Run through all the whys and wherefores? Or should we just," he said, raising his voice to a shout, "dig the fucking garden!"

Everyone in the group looked either sheepish or shocked.

Bob looked crestfallen. I, if I could have seen my face, would probably have looked something between terrified and delighted, because I could barely stop myself from bursting into laughter. It's not that I like this sort of behavior, I absolutely do not, and I quite liked what I'd seen of Bob, as well as sharing what I assumed to be his indolent tendencies. But there was something about Ken, something about Bob, something about the setting that made it all look perfectly - and I use the description advisedly - perfectly absurd, and absurdity is, after all, my speciality.

Needless to say, we dug, and with considerably more vigor and alacrity than if Monica, for example, had been our smiling and cajoling task mistress. Most of the work proceeded in silence, which I took to be a requirement if we were to get full meditational value for money out of it, and avoid antagonizing Ken in the process. But at one point I found myself only a spade's length away from Bob.

"I still think this is crazy," he said.

"Yes, but I think Ken felt pretty strongly about it."

"Oh, he's always like that. I think he does it on purpose."

"I don't doubt it."

"No, I mean I don't think that's necessarily his nature, but by being confrontational he evokes strong reactions in us that we can meditate on."

"Oh," I said, sounding even less convinced than I felt. To use a suitable metaphor, why not call a spade a spade? If someone's a bit of a bastard, why try to explain their behavior in any other way?

"No, really," he said. "Life here can be very cozy. Too cozy. Going back to the real world can be something of a shock, so I think Ken is here to keep us on our toes, to force us to handle aggression so that when we go back into the real world, we're not intimidated by it."

The "real world". Ah, so at least I wasn't the only one who saw this place as something that definitely wasn't really worldly. But did he really think Ken's mission was to put us through a mental and physical assault course so we would be better equipped to deal with psychopaths when we came across them on the London Underground or wherever they might pop up?

"So, you think he's a plant?" I said, pun intended.

"Well, yes, I suppose, in a way. Well, I don't know if Dennis would actually tell him to do it, but the fact he does do it may work to our advantage."

"But I thought this place was all about inner explorations in a supportive and warm environment. That's what Dennis told me. I don't get a lot of warmth from Ken, or Zara, or Roger, do you?"

"Er, well … no, but, well, whether he did it to help me or not, he's certainly given me something to meditate on." Yeah, right, like you could meditate on a broken leg or a runny nose or diarrhea. But do you really want to? Do you really need to? I didn't say any of this, because it was obviously better for Bob to imagine that Ken's hostility was serving a purpose, rather than just being Ken's chance to be unpleasant to someone when Zara wasn't around.

"Perhaps," he went on, seemingly unwilling to accept that

Ken was just a stroppy git, "perhaps he behaves in that way so the rest of us can see what brutishness and anger are like, without having to be like that ourselves. He can live out the harsh side of our personalities for us, so we can detach from all that stuff."

"What, like the Picture of Dorian Grey? Our sins show up in his image?"

"Yes," he said, excitedly, "exactly! We can live out our negative emotions through Ken. Isn't that amazing?" He'd completely convinced himself he'd got the explanation, so now, I supposed, he could feel alright about the humiliation Ken had subjected him to. I didn't think he was within a million miles of being right, and if he had been, that would have potentially made Ken some sort of surrogate devil, the embodiment of evil, which was pretty ludicrous. But it was an interesting concept. Maybe I should pay Ken to go down the pub and get sloshed for me, then come back and subject Zara to some extreme humiliation, like pissing down her neck whilst she was locked into the lotus position.

Then he could go and force himself on Amanda, and if he got into trouble, I could just watch without getting a telling-off myself. I suppose we do have people like that in society; bad boy tennis players, randy footballers, foul mouthed rock musicians, raunchy film stars - people we can sneer at and tut-tut at, but whom we secretly envy for having the balls to do what they do and what we don't dare do. The only problem is the outward guilt transference is fine, but the inward pleasure transference leaves a lot to be desired. I mean, what would I get out of Ken coming on to Amanda? Not much. In fact, I'd get even less than not much.

After half-an-hour of digging, my hands felt like lumps

of raw meat, and looked much as they felt, so I had a rest, mooched about a bit, went to have a pee, and as nobody showed any signs of stopping work, eventually went to ask Ken, who was digging an immaculate trench like a manic robot, if there were any gloves I could use. He didn't stop at first, and I thought he was either in a trance or ignoring me, or possibly both. But then, in a rapid sequence of movements, he stopped digging, rammed his spade into the ground, wiped sweat off his brow - first with one hand, then with the other, in sweeping swipes - took one enormous stride to stand in front of me, grabbed both my hands in his two, much bigger, hands, turned my palms face up and studied them. Whilst all this was going on I was getting the firm impression Ken was, in fact, some sort of psychopath, and then fear crept over me as I started to suspect that, based on past performances, he was about to subject me to some mental, or even physical, ridicule, abuse or abasement.

"Oh, nasty, nasty. We can't have these precious artist's hands getting a few unsightly sores and cankers on them can we?" He said this in a tone I found hard to decipher. It could have been cynical, patronizing, angry or just histrionic. I hadn't got a baseline on Ken yet, so I didn't really know what he sounded like when he was being normal, assuming he ever was normal. None of this would have mattered, but for the fact he was now peering into my face, his eyebrows raised, from which I gathered his comment, which had been spoken like a question that didn't need an answer, did, in fact, need an answer, in Ken's mind at any rate.

"Blisters won't affect my drawing, but they'll definitely affect my digging."

"Intend to make a profession of it then, do you?"

"Do I have any choice?" I hadn't noticed the place was in desperate need of a few pictures, but I assumed it needed the garden to be dug to sustain the eco-integrity. "If there's a doodling work detail, I'll happily join that instead."

"I think you're in the fucking doodling detail, given the progress you lot are making." With that he marched off to a nearby shed and returned with a pair of gloves that, by an uncanny coincidence, had a hole to coincide with every place I had a blister, but I said nothing, and considered I'd got off reasonably lightly.

§

Lunch time, and I was starting to see what Fiona meant about the effect of retreat centre living on appetite. I sat at a table with Ruben. He smiled, then chuckled, but didn't seem disposed to say anything. He was actually quite an agreeable person to be around, even though he never said much, and even when he did speak it was only to bounce a person's words back at them, albeit cryptically. You could say - not that I'd be caught dead saying it in public - that he put out good vibes. We were joined by Doris, the elderly lady I'd met at breakfast, and a boyish looking girl or a girlish looking boy who unhelpfully introduced itself in a mid-scale voice as Micky, which left me none the wiser as to its sex. I hadn't seen Micky approach, so I couldn't make any judgment based on locomotion of hips, and as it was wearing a capacious denim shirt, I couldn't divine anything from the upper torso either.

Conversation was dominated by Doris, so Micky's occasional alto grunts didn't provide any useful evidence. Then, once it had finished eating, Micky stretched up its arms so that the material of the shirt tightened, and the form of two sizeable tits appeared as if from nowhere and pushed the denim breast pockets towards me by a good few inches. I then paid more attention to Micky, who had an attractive and, needless to say, boyish face. She had short-cropped blonde hair and wore no make-up. When she stood to go, I inspected two well-rounded swaggering buttocks, clenched in a pair of tight Levis. Micky was definitely worth a second look.

When I was a teenager, I went through a year or so of anguished, secret torment as to whether I had homosexual tendencies. I was born at a time and in a society in which being "queer" was definitely not something to be taken lightly. I had nothing against homosexuals, and if I truly were one, I hope I would have the guts to come out and come to terms with it. But, for me, the idea was an unwelcome one, and it became an obsessive priority for me to prove, once and for all, that I didn't find men in any way attractive. I eventually just gave up trying to prove anything, and simply asked myself the question "Am I a homo?" in the same way I would have asked myself "Do I like ballroom dancing", to which the answer in each case was, simply "No", and that was the end of it.

Perhaps I was and am a repressed homosexual, but if true, that part of me is so deeply buried in my psyche that it's never given me any problems since my confused adolescent episode, although situations like the Micky one do cause me to focus on my genital area more than I normally would, and ask myself exactly what is causing things to stir down there. I suppose I would also start asking questions about my aversion to ballroom dancing if I one day found my feet tapping to the distant strains of a *pasa doble*.

After lunch, Monica took me aside and made sure I was aware of where the washing-up roster could be viewed and, as a not very startling coincidence, I discovered my name was alongside the date and time of the meal I had just eaten, together with the names of Roger and Sandy. Roger turned out be as taciturn when washing up as he was when collecting people from the station, or doing anything else I had seen him engage in. I intended thanking him - awkwardly, no doubt - for the flowers he'd put in my room the day before, but I somehow didn't feel in the right frame of mind to give my thanks, and I suspected Roger would never be in the right frame of mind to receive them.

Roger was washing, Sandy and I were drying up and putting things away. I didn't bother to ask why they hadn't invested in a dishwasher, as I assumed Roger was quite capable of giving me an answer similar to the one Ken had given Bob about using technology on the garden. Roger went at it like a demon, and as soon as he'd finished he stormed out of the kitchen without a word. Sandy had said very little while he'd been there, but now she started chatting away like she had after breakfast.

"What did you think of Dennis' talk this morning?"

I struggled to think of something to say other than "interesting", but as I didn't expect her to react in the same way as Zara, I just said it again.

"Interesting. Does he give talks like that every day?"

"No. He usually has a few choice words for us at some point, but it may just be a phrase to think about last thing at night. It's always something worth hearing."

"Is Dennis, well, is he some kind of, well ... just tell me how you view Dennis."

She looked at me as if I'd asked her something surprising, shocking, preposterous even.

"I suppose we shouldn't think of him as anything, and he wouldn't want us to, I mean, he doesn't set himself up as anything."

"He doesn't?" I was in danger of sounding skeptical, as though I was accusing Dennis of putting himself on a pedestal, which I rather suspected him of doing, but couldn't be sure of yet. "I don't mean he considers himself to be, well, superior, but he seems to be regarded as ... Oh, I don't know. I don't want to put words into your mouth."

"He's just really wise. Wisdom is such an incredible gift. The world values people who are rich, or beautiful, or street-smart, or funny, but it doesn't value those who are just wise, even though it's so rare, and you don't appreciate how rare it is until you meet someone who is. Dennis says things that are usually completely obvious once he's said them, but until he's said them, you haven't even remotely thought of them. Do you know what a guru is, I mean what it really is, not what people think of?"

An image sprung to my mind of some sort of eastern, religious figure with a distant expression, long hair and dirty feet.

"No, not really."

"A guru is someone who points the way. They don't tell you to do this and do that and wait for this and that to happen as a consequence. Any revelations that come from outside of you are unlikely to be valid. A guru points inside you, shows you how to set off somewhere and then leaves you to get on with it, until you need more directions."

"And Dennis does that?"

"Yes, but he does it like he's building a wall, one tiny brick at a time. You don't listen to him and think 'Crikey! That's it. The answer to everything!' You just soak up his little drops of wisdom and kind of work on them, meditate on them and see how things start falling into place."

"Where does he get it from?"

"How do you mean?"

"Well, is it a natural gift, or did he have a guru to learn it from, or did he do an Open University course on it, or find it scribbled on a lavatory wall somewhere?"

She smiled, but diffidently, almost condescendingly, and her tone told me she didn't appreciate jokes being made anywhere near the sacred subject of Dennis and his divine pronouncements.

"He studied with a man called Dharavajra, but not every-one who studied with Dharavajra came out like Dennis. Dennis must have a special gift, because he puts everything in a western setting, whereas Dharavajra hasn't left his ashram in India for donkey's years."

I nodded. If Dennis had a spell to cast, it had worked on Sandy. She was his acolyte alright, hook, line and sinker. It wasn't her words that told me this, as much as the Monica-like beatific expression, which had grown stronger on her face as we'd been speaking.

"So everyone looks up to him?"

"Oh yes."

"Even Ken?"

"Yes, why not?"

"Well, from what I've seen of Ken, I should say he's pretty down to earth."

"Yes?"

She wasn't going to make this easy for me. How did I go about saying that surely someone at Ravenswood must be a bit of a rebel, a cynic, must question Dennis now and again, and not give him a free run in the unimpeachable truth department.

"Well, you don't seem to discuss things here. It's as though you just absorb. I'm not used to that, and I got the impression Ken was the sort of person to rock boats."

She was looking at me with wide eyes and a frown.

"I don't understand," she said, and I started to get annoyed at the presumption in her voice that I was talking gibberish or asking inappropriate questions, whereas all I was really trying to discover was whether this place was primarily Dennis' fan club.

"I can see that," I said, and with that our conversation ended on a mildly sour note.

§§§

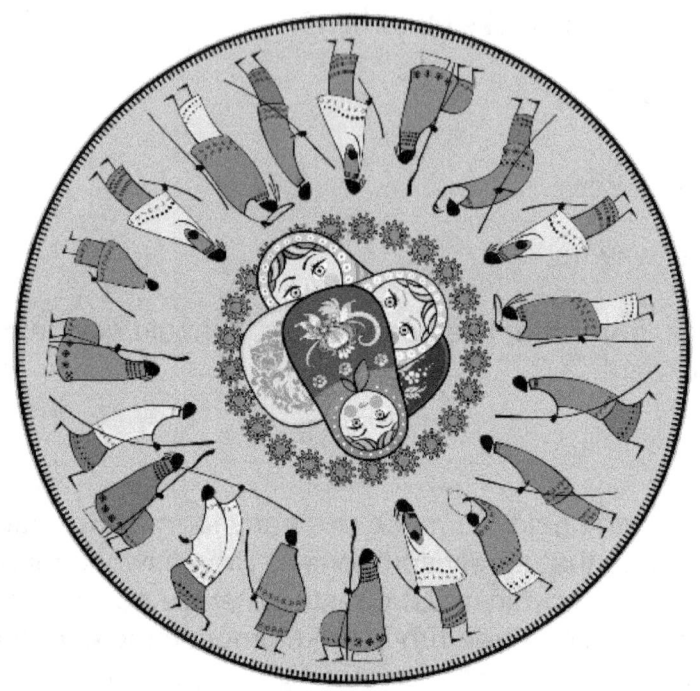

TURNING AROUND

I wandered around outside feeling moody, feeling more than ever like the outsider I was, here more than anywhere. Back in London, I may surround myself with a group of misfits, but they're my misfits, handpicked by me to suit the misfitting bits of my own personality, which is why they give me comfort.

In my mind I started to list the people I'd met at Ravenswood, to try and get some sort of idea how the place ranked on the normality scale, on the cross-section of society index. I was presuming it would come out way off centre. Roger - taciturn even when being kind, not normal. Monica - smiley and laid back, not normal. Bob - pretty ordinary, for an astrologer, whatever that means. Zara - self-opinionated, but not uncommon in the world at large, in fact, quite common. Doris

- a bit hippyish, but if you met her on the street she'd seem like a nice enough old gal. Amanda - abnormally attractive, but otherwise normal. Ruben - likeable, but definitely not normal. Ken - unlikeable, but there are plenty of Kens about. Micky - couldn't say. Sandy - probably a depressive, but not that unusual. Dennis - notable, but in the outside world he'd be running "How to be successful" seminars in California, so no more unusual than other people like that.

This left the rather surprising result that the standard character deviation here wasn't too far out of the ordinary, which put me in a quandary as to why I felt different to them all. Did it mean I was the weird one, and the years I'd spent keeping the company of my usual cohorts had turned me into an outcast? This fact, in itself, didn't bother me, but it was a concern that the people here were probably looking upon me as the newly arrived nutter from Planet Peculiar, whereas that was the handy pigeonhole I'd been inclined to put all of them in.

There were a couple of people I hadn't spoken to yet; a girl who dressed head to toe in black and walked with her head down, her eyes concealed behind a mass of black hair - I think she was called something like Clemmy - and a young man who looked forgettable and kept himself very much to himself - I think his name was Justin. There was reference to a few others who were temporarily in India or Hounslow or some Scottish island I'd never heard of. So the reckoning came up with a largely unremarkable mix, but I still felt like the normal one in a sea of whackery.

Perhaps it was Ravenswood itself, I thought, and I toyed with the idea that it was the setting, or the daily ritual, or the food; but then I stopped myself as I realized it wasn't the place or the people that were odd, it was the purpose. It was what they did and why they did it; it was the sense of direction they had that I wasn't a part of. They were all steaming along the track to Nirvana Junction, whilst I was sat on the platform, waiting for God knows what train, going God knows where, when or why, and if I ever did end up getting on a train, it would take me up Pointless Sidings to Desolation Halt. It's not just innate traits that define people, it's where they're going that characterizes them as well. But realizing this didn't help. I still didn't want to embark on a journey if I didn't know where it was going, which brought me very firmly back to square one, like a metaphysical train hitting a very physical buffer of doubt.

I was wasting my time. Why the hell had I come here? I'd acted like a sick man who had wandered up to the first doctor he'd come across, asking him to fix a problem I couldn't accurately define, and without knowing whether he was an MD, dentist or psychiatrist. Do you know that distant, slightly impatient look which comes across a doctor's face when you tell him or her you can't quite describe what's wrong with you, and the pain comes and goes, and it's not bad today? Most of my illnesses seem to be like that. For me, pains don't fit into the stabbing or aching or throbbing descriptions doctors think in terms of – and anyway how do I know my stab is not their ache? - so they end up writing a prescription for painkillers and kicking me out with barely disguised derision. This might be how the people at Ravenswood see me. A man adrift, but not aware of what he's drifting away from or towards, and with no clue as to where he should be going or what he should be doing. I walked back into the farmhouse to look for the Yellow Pages, and I felt a thrill of anticipation as I thought of my seat on the very unmetaphysical London-bound express.

As luck would have it, or perhaps you could call it fate in

light of later events, the first person I bumped into was Dennis. If it had been Roger or Zara or Sandy, my flight would have been unstoppable.

"Hello Peter, would you like to go for a walk?"

"Oh, well, actually I was thinking of ... well, yes, okay."

"Were you planning something else?"

"Not really. A walk would be good."

Why did I say this? It seems that the *volte face* is a fundamental part of my personality. My inconsistency is the one thing I know I can rely on, personification of an oxymoron that I am. We walked across the yard and along a track up a hill. Just as other people might be happy to sense space opening up around them, I was discomforted to feel countryside girdling me - greenness and brownness were threatening me from all sides.

"Ravenswood was a derelict farm 10 years ago. We bought it for next to nothing and have been spending a fortune on it ever since. Well, not a fortune by normal standards, but it seems like a lot of money to me."

"Where were you before this?"

"I had a house in Exeter I used for meetings, and I had access to various other places where we could hold retreats for weekends and longer. This is my first retreat centre."

"I'm told you were in India for a time."

"Yes, I studied at an ashram there with a very great man,

Dharavajra. I was there for five years, on and off. It was very hard to pull myself away, but Dharavajra insisted in the end. He told me I could do good work in Britain. I'm sure I've done nothing like as much as he would have hoped, but we've made a start."

I watched my feet as I walked. In London I walk with my eyes cast down to avoid stepping in something unpleasant or making eye contact with skinheads or ex-girlfriends, here I was doing it to avoid seeing too much of rural Wales.

"Look Dennis, let me be honest with you. When you asked me to go for a walk just now, I was just on my way to pack my bags and get out of here. I think I'm wasting your time and my time. I've no idea why I came here, and I can't achieve anything with this attitude."

I got the impression this was no surprise to him, and he'd sensed my unease - perhaps that was the reason for the walk. He said nothing. He was waiting for me to dig a hole for myself, I assumed, and then he could talk me out of it, or let me talk myself out of going. I kept quiet too.

"Okay," he said, but instead of feeling a wave of relief rush over me as I saw my planned flight wasn't going to be challenged, I felt just slightly disappointed. God knows what I'd expected. I suppose I was dog-in-the-manger enough to expect him to try and persuade me to stay, as if the place just wouldn't be the same without me, but he called that bluff sweetly enough. Neither of us said anything for a while, and I was just about to say I'd like to be getting back to the farm-house to call a cab and get away, when he broke the silence.

"You'll probably come back. Not to here maybe, but once you've started looking for something in your life, the need doesn't go away, it just nags you until you get an inkling of what you're looking for, and then you spend the rest of your life searching for it." He turned to smile at me. "I'm not trying to be smart. I'm just telling you what happened to me and what's happened to most people who get that feeling of unsatisfactoriness that leads us to look deeper into ourselves. Most people never even ask these questions. Well, maybe once in a while over a pint of beer or when they see a spectacular sunset, but they never take it any further. The ones who do are the lucky ones, and you're now numbered amongst them. Congratulations," he said, smiling and patting me on the shoulder.

He was softening me up for the sell. "You, Mr. Wickham of Kensington, London, have been selected by our computer to qualify for our wonderful star prize, all you have to do is pop your soul and trust into the envelope provided and mail it without delay ... etc. ... etc."

"I don't know that feeling pissed off about life has got anything to do with filling a spiritual vacuum," I said. "You can go on holiday to Greece without thinking you might want to live there for the rest of your life. Some people might decide to buy a timeshare and develop a liking for Retsina, but most of us just go home and go somewhere else next year. I've known people who take one holiday and decide never to go away again - it's just not for them. Maybe that's how it's been for me coming here."

"Perhaps," he said, and again we walked in silence for a while, and I really thought we'd said all we had to say, but we hadn't.

"Peter, I suppose I was very much like you. I never had any time for anything I couldn't relate to through direct physical experience. I was comfortable with that. For me it seemed like the only way to live, the only model of the world that couldn't be criticized because everything was visible, tangible. I don't know if I would ever have got off that track without an almighty shove. I was happy, really happy, but the impetus to change came in a big way, and although I wouldn't ever want to go through it again, or see anyone else go through it, the long term effect on my life has been transformational."

I really didn't want to know what this dramatic shove that had sent Dennis on his new course was, but it seemed impolite just to leave the subject hanging there.

"What happened?"

He didn't answer at first, not that there was anything unusual about that, not for Dennis, nor anyone else at Ravenswood. But I didn't get the impression the silence was the normal, laid back silence that seemed to characterize the place and everyone in it, mainly because an expression had come across his face that I hadn't seen before. His face and neck muscles tightened, his eyes seemed to double in size and his lips puckered, making him look a bit like he would if I drew him. He took a deep breath, as if preparing to do something intimidating or unpleasant.

"I was living a normal family life - wife, two children, suburban home, office job. Everything was completely ordinary about me and my life and my family, and I suppose it would have continued to be ordinary."

It was strange to think of Dennis as having lived an ordinary life. I'd assumed he'd always been somehow distanced from the rest of us plebs, in attitude as well as lifestyle.

"Peter, this is an unusual story I'm going to tell you, but it's one I recount every now and again to remind myself of what I was and where I was. I can't really explain why I need this catharsis, but it's important to me that I do this from time to time. It may or may not help you, but it will certainly help me. Do you mind?"

"No, not a bit," I said, expecting to hear something fascinating, or bizarre, or even salacious. He paused as we climbed over a stile and headed along a path that led across a field full of sheep. I wondered if we should be doing this, but I assumed he was as conversant with the Countryside Code as I was ignorant of it.

"My daughter Gillian was eight and my son Jack was six. We were living in a very uninspiring part of Southampton - the sort of quiet area where people bring up children and don't expect anything out of the ordinary to happen. It was an evening in August. I'd not long got home from work and my wife was making dinner, lasagna. I was sitting at the kitchen table drinking a glass of wine and the children were outside playing. It was a completely regular scene of domesticity, nearly 20 years ago, but I can see it as clearly in my mind's eye as if it were happening now, right down to the way the wine was glistening in the sunshine coming through the kitchen windows, and the smell of the baking meat and pasta filling the kitchen. Jack came in and my wife asked him where Gillian was. He said she was outside. My wife asked him to go and get her because dinner would be ready soon. He came back a few minutes later and said he couldn't find her. I felt a frisson of anxiety, for no reason, it was likely she was with one of her friends somewhere, but I couldn't help feeling more unsettled than I should have done - this isn't hindsight talking, I really had some sort of premonition.

"I went outside. Gillian was nowhere to be seen. I ran back into the house and asked Jack who she'd been with when he'd left her. He told me it was one of her friends, Linda, who lived across the road. I rushed over to Linda's house, but Gillian wasn't there. I asked Linda if she knew where she was." Dennis paused and breathed deeply two or three times. I could see his jaw was tightly clenched.

"She told me that her 'Uncle David' had asked her to help him look for his dog. I asked Linda who this man was, if she'd seen him before and what had happened next. Linda didn't have any idea that something terrible had happened. She was a petulant child and was bored by my questions, so I had to drag answers out of her. At one point I grabbed her shoulders to try and make her concentrate. Her mother intervened and I started shouting that Gillian had been abducted. Linda started crying, so her mother comforted her and tried to cajole the facts out of her.

"I ran out into the street. It was empty. I suppose it was often empty, but I'd never seen it looking as empty and desolate as it looked that evening. I went back to our house and told my wife to call the police, which had the unfortunate result of infecting her with the same panic I was experiencing. Then I ran back to Linda's house. Her mother translated Linda's blubbing and told me a man had pulled up in a car, a complete stranger to Linda, who had introduced himself as Gillian's Uncle David. He said he'd lost his dog in the park and could Gillian help him look for it, and that her Mummy said it was alright to go with him for a few minutes, and they would drive there and straight back. Gillian said she'd have to go and ask her Daddy, but the man said he already had and that I'd said it was alright and they would be back in no time at all.

"By this time I was in a hell of a state. The police arrived and I more or less screamed the story at them. They kept telling me to calm down, but I could no more do that than I could reach out and collect my daughter in my arms. I spent the next five or six hours touring the streets in my car, returning home every now and again to see if there had been any news. The police called our doctor, and he came round and gave my wife and I sedatives. They told me there was nothing I could do for the time being, that they were doing everything possible to find Gillian, and that the best thing was for me to take the pills and get some sleep. I didn't. I threw the pills away and I just cruised around the streets all night.

"There was no news by the morning, and that day was as close to a living hell as I ever hope to experience. It was worse than the night before, because by this time I'd run through just about every horrific scenario of what could have happened to her in my mind, and had convinced myself that one of them was being acted out at that very moment by the bastard ..." He stopped momentarily, as if surprised by his use of the word, but then continued, presumably happy with his choice of description, "... by the bastard who'd taken her. I wanted to be out on the streets again, doing something, but the police told me it was pointless and my wife asked me to stay with her. One of the officers was a specialist in child abductions, and he wanted to get as much information from us as possible. I didn't know it then, but what he was really trying to determine was whether we were involved in her disappearance. But rather than answer his questions, I took him aside and asked him what the chances were that my daughter was unharmed and what were the chances she was dead. Of course, he didn't want to answer, but I convinced him I was mentally stable, that the information wouldn't unhinge me, and that I had to know so I could prepare myself for the inevitable. Eventually he told me there was only something like a one in 20 chance she was unharmed, and a one in 10 chance she was still alive."

Dennis paused. His face was expressionless and his eyes seemed to be gazing blankly into the distance, but I'm sure he could see something very clearly in his mind's eye. He started to talk again, but his voice choked. He cleared his throat and lowered his head. I was going to tell him not to go on, but telling the story was for his benefit, so it was up to him whether he should stop or not.

"Nothing happened for three more days. I succumbed to our doctor's advice and used sedatives to get to sleep at night and more tranquilizers during the day. Taking pills seemed to be the only way I could function. Then, on the fifth day, the police came to the house and I could tell at once they had something unpleasant to tell us.

"It was strange. I was so mentally fatigued and full of pills that my whole life had become flimsy and dreamlike. Reality didn't seem to be affecting me the way it should, but if it had been, I really don't think I would have been able to handle it. The police told us the body of a young girl had been discovered that matched Gillian's description. I didn't feel grief as much as the sort of sadness I would have experienced if what I was going through had happened to a friend, not to me. My wife was sobbing, and I felt sorry for her, not for myself and not even for Gillian. I suppose I was going through some drug-induced mental disassociation, exacerbated by exhaustion. I know now that disassociation is dangerous, and I've seen from my work here and elsewhere that it has to be countered if it comes about through meditation, as it can. But back then it was a tremendous relief not to be feeling what I should have been feeling. I went to identify the body. It was Gillian, but they only let me see her face. She ..." He

stopped for a long time before going on. "She'd been molested and killed, strangled. They never caught the man who
did it. There were several cases the police had linked to the
same perpetrator, but the crimes stopped and they believed
he was either imprisoned on some other charge or dead
- these people often commit suicide.

"So, there we were, the three survivors. My son was
okay, thank God. He was sad to have lost his sister, but too
young to understand the true gravity of it all, and I don't think
it scarred him permanently. He's in his twenties and has his
own life now, of course, and he seems like a well-adjusted
sort of person. But my wife, well, somehow it seemed to
push us apart. You would expect an incident like that to bring
people together rather than separate them, but I think the
fact we didn't naturally look for solace in each other proved
we weren't that close, so 18 months after Gillian was killed
we split up, and it seemed like the most natural thing in the
world. I suppose events like that are a quality control test of
a marriage - if the relationship doesn't break under the strain,
it will probably survive anything, but if there are any weaknesses in it at all, it'll break apart and never work again."

All the time he was talking I hadn't had any idea where
we were going, but at this point we emerged from a long
pathway, enclosed on both sides by thick, dank-smelling
woods, to a view of the valley and, in the middle-distance,
Ravenswood, snuggled in its womb. For some reason I was
actually very glad to see it, but I suppose I would have been
glad to see a rusty tin shed after all the greenery I'd just
been exposed to.

"The whole sorry business revealed a vacuum in my life.
I suppose I could have interpreted it as a bottomless well
of despair, and to begin with that was exactly what it was

- I hadn't just lost a child in the most unspeakable circumstances, I'd also lost a wife and, because she took custody of my son, I lost a part of him too. We'd also seen a graphic manifestation of evil. It probably sounds strange to you, but I saw this vacuum as an opportunity to build my life up again, starting right from the foundations. I was on the floor, devastated, but I had nothing to lose by reconstructing myself, on my own, in a new place at my own pace.

"We normally put our lives together from a standpoint of relative ignorance, starting as children and learning about ourselves and other people as we go along. Now I could start over, with the brain of a man. You can't really understand it unless you've been there, but when everything you've striven for - your job, your family, everything that you and society at large have considered to be valuable - is either laid waste or made valueless, it's actually easier to start afresh than it is to re-erect what you had before, at least, that's how it was for me. I couldn't even think of going back to my job, it seemed almost laughably absurd after what I'd been through."

Another long pause. We stood looking at the view. The sun was trying to battle its way through an ominous, galloping grey sky, and I don't know if it was Dennis' story or the sweeping panorama, but I felt terribly melancholy. It's one feeling I have more than any other, and views often seem to trigger it, usually in paintings. Dejection also weighs me down at about 4 o'clock most afternoons, which is a phenomenon I find as impossible to explain as I do to avoid. A girlfriend once told me it was probably induced by blood-sugar deficiency, so she persuaded me to eat bananas as a mid-afternoon snack, which had no effect on my state of mind, apart from making me consider the banana to be the most dismal of fruits.

"I really had no idea what to do, so I decided, like you, to go somewhere and try to sort myself out, to get rid of some of the confusion I was feeling. Life is a very perplexing business, or can be, as you've found. I could have ended up anywhere - a monastery, Club-Med, a hut in the middle of nowhere, a slow boat to China. I wasn't even sure it mattered very much, as long as it was a change of scenery and a chance to be alone with myself. I picked a retreat centre in Devon a friend had heard of. It was a place a bit like Ravenswood. There wasn't much of a program, and it was more a self-sufficient smallholding than anything, but it gave me the mental and emotional space I needed, and it was someone there who suggested I go to India and listen to Dharavajra.

"So I did, and like you I had practically no idea what to expect. I remember sitting on the plane at Heathrow, seconds before takeoff, thinking "What the hell am I doing?" I needed to get off that plane so damn desperately I wanted it to crash more than I wanted it to lift me up and deposit me in Delhi."

I thought back to my own emotions on the station platform while I was waiting for the connection that would deliver me to Roger's loving arms, and I empathized, but I also felt uneasy, almost as though he was reading my mind and manipulating me.

"I know the feeling," I said, wanting to establish some sort of connection with what he was saying, despite my suspicions. He turned and looked at me earnestly, more earnestly than I deserved.

"I'm sure you do. People predominantly have one of two reactions when they're coming to a place like this - ridiculously high expectations or terrifying reservations, and I can assure you that those in the second category are much easier to deal with than those in the first. When I say 'people' I mean Westerners. Taking time out for contemplation and meditation is so alien to most of us it's scary, but people brought up in a spiritual environment, like Indians, treat it like going to a health farm."

I could understand that, but as I would be the last person on earth to go to a health farm, his analogy hadn't helped me at all.

"I'd been at the ashram at Rajapundi for over two weeks before I even knew who Dharavajra was, let alone heard him speak. Whenever I asked about him, they just told me he'd introduce himself eventually, when he was ready. But that was no bad thing, because I spent the best part of a month getting over the culture shock of living in a poor Indian village, and it was more like three months before I could spend over an hour at a time away from a lavatory. Then one day I was brushing my teeth, and this pleasant looking old boy I'd seen doddering around the place a few times, and I thought was one of the janitors or something, stood by my side, and when I looked up he smiled and said in perfect BBC English "Hello Dennis. I'm very pleased to meet you. I'm Dharavajra." I couldn't believe it, because by then I'd heard so much about him and read two of his books, that I thought he would be some remote and intimidating figurehead. But here he was, and with the warmest smile you could hope to see.

"He was a rare mix of characteristics, profound but light-hearted, intense but self-deprecating, very Indian in his looks but very English in his speech - he'd got his cut-glass accent from listening to the BBC World Service for hours on end when he was growing up. I was entranced by him for many reasons, but none more so than because he was one of the few truly happy people I've met. Not happy because he was simple - he was obviously an intelligent man who'd seen enough of the world to know it's not a very nice place and there's a lot for a thinking person to get depressed about - but happy because he seemed to know something the rest of us didn't, and that's really what made me stay at first, because despite mild dysentery and severe alienation, I was desperate to find out what the hell he was so damn happy about!" Dennis laughed as he said this, picturing in his mind, I assume, the image of the jolly, enigmatic Indian.

"It sounds trivial, I suppose, making it your goal in life to discover some sort of spiritual punch line to a joke you've never heard and probably wouldn't understand if you did, but it was goal enough for someone who was putting his life back together, someone who hadn't seen much fun for a while and certainly hadn't expected to find it at the feet of a famous mystic in a Hindu ashram. We underestimate joy. We attach value to so many material things, like money and sex and power and comfort and family, but if you say your aim in life is to be happy, everyone thinks you're an idiot, and if you want to be happy for no reason, you're practically certifiable."

I knew what he meant, I'd never had much time for those perpetually grinning individuals - like Monica - who tell you they're happy because it's Tuesday, and are permanently disposed to make the best of a thing, life, that has never struck me as being designed to cause happiness in any but the most irrevocably demented. But it illustrates the extent to which Dennis was winning me over, when I admitted to myself I saw some attraction in what he was promulgating, and found myself questioning my lifelong adherence to the undemanding faith espoused by the Church of Doubting Thomas. He lapsed into silence. As we got closer to Ravenswood, I prompted him to go on.

"Well?" I asked.

"Well what?"

"What was it that made him so happy?"

He laughed. "Oh, so you want the answer before you ask yourself the question?"

"Of course, doesn't everyone?"

"Yes, I suppose they do, until they realize, unfortunately, it doesn't work like that. What I learnt from Dharavajra ... well, I learnt so many things from him, but *a propos* happiness, I learnt that you don't achieve it by making it your goal. If you do, you can become a happy-clappy convert in seconds, but that's just treating the symptoms and it doesn't achieve anything that will stick. Like any good cure, you have to treat the disease, which means opening your eyes wide and looking at what's made you unhappy, rather than squeezing your eyes tight shut and telling yourself you're happy."

"Sounds intimidating."

"No, not at all, because it's a continuous process of revelation, and every fresh revelation takes another load of misery off your shoulders. I'm not going to tell you what you should do, Peter, nor will anyone else here. Nobody can design your salvation because only one person knows what it is, and that person is you. We'll show you methods for looking within yourself, and we'll advise you as to what you can try when you hit problems, but you'll be doing all the work yourself, and there are no magic short cuts. All I can tell you is that there is only one way to solve unsatisfactoriness in a life, and that's by looking inside, not by applying remedies to the outside. No pleasure or drug or mantra can heal a wounded soul, but it can heal itself."

"You realize," I said "that none of this makes a blind bit of sense to me?"

"Yes," he said, laughing and putting his arm round my shoulder "but it will."

§§§

THOUGHT STRIKES

Dennis' pep talk, if that's what it was, had the effect of delaying my immediate plans. Even if it wasn't too late to get a London train, I was sufficiently mollified by our conversation to postpone my departure for another day. He'd told me, as we walked back into the welcoming arms of Ravenswood, that he'd leave me to my own devices for a day or two, just so that I could "pick up the spirit of the place and see if anything emerges naturally", but after that he would like to give me a bit more help with meditation.

"We do a number of things here to help people to gain insight, but the fundamental practice is simply the mindfulness of breathing. If you do nothing here but sit on a cushion and observe your breath, you'll probably achieve a great deal."

I wanted to say "Like what?", but I knew by now you weren't supposed to ask questions like that, and, if you did, you got infuriating answers that made you wish you'd kept your mouth shut, which is what I decided to do.

The next item on the program wasn't a meditation session, but was what Dennis termed "an exercise in communication". As he announced this to the assembled group, I noticed a few winces and heard a couple of barely audible groans emanate from the collected truth-seekers. Five minutes later I understood why.

We were told to select someone to pair off with, then to sit facing them, with noses no more than three feet apart. We were to take it in turns to make faces registering whatever range of emotions we felt up to displaying, whilst the other person watched. The watcher was then at liberty to remark on what he or she had been feeling whilst observing these facial contortions, and the contorter could add their own comments on what they had been feeling or what they had noticed in the watcher's reaction. Roles were then to be reversed.

"The purpose," Dennis started to say, and then stopped himself. "No, let's forget about the purpose for now, and see what emerges." Bloody typical, I thought, do something completely inane, and probably embarrassing, depending on who you partner with, without any idea of why you're doing it. I immediately regretted my decision to stay. Private, individual meditation might be all right, just, but this touchy-feely stuff was completely alien to me, and when I thought I could be in a taxi going somewhere else at that very moment, I felt as though I'd been tricked. I would have felt doubly tricked and trebly scared if I'd known that a couple of minutes later I'd be sitting three feet from the threatening face of Zara.

I don't even know how I ended up with Zara, but, looking back, it doesn't surprise me. If you filled Wembley sta-
dium with 100,000 people and told them to pair off, I would
be the last person to make a match and would end up with
the loony with the personal hygiene problem, so to get Zara
from a group of a dozen or so was practically inevitable. I'm
sure she wanted me no more than I wanted her, it was just
that as the person on my left looked to their left, and the
person on my right looked to their right, I noticed Zara being similarly ostracized on the other side of the room. We
both then quickly scanned the group to see if there were
any other floaters, and there was one, Dennis, who promptly
announced we had an odd number so he would drop out,
leaving Zara and I to glare at each other before we circled
and approached like two wary animals preparing for a fight,
and eventually sat down opposite one another.

"I'll go first," she announced, imperiously, and she then
plastered a phony smile across her chops. I laughed, which
caused her to change, involuntarily I think, to an angry glare
which, being more in keeping with what I'd seen of her
personality so far, was not at all unexpected. From this she
went to a petulant pout, and from that to a sad expression
that was so convincing I was about to start feeling sorry for
her, until she turned it quickly, almost imperceptibly, to a look
of cunning and evil that almost took my breath away. From
this she went to a kind of smoldering look that I think was
meant to be sexy, but was so inept it had the curious effect
of making me feel depressed, and made me realize fleetingly
that Zara had her own problems to deal with. Then she went
on to just plain bored, and climaxed with her most natural
look and the one that seemed to suit her resting features
best, supercilious hostility. It was actually quite a bravura
performance, but then I had to decide whether to be honest,
because nothing I had to say about her expressions could be

taken as a compliment, and some of it would be potentially insulting. Dennis must have expected this potential dilemma for those of us who were not Roger.

"When you make your comments," he said, "just tell your partner what feelings went through your mind. Don't embellish or explain. If they don't like what they hear, that's for them to resolve."

"Your happy look made me laugh, as you heard, your sad look made me sad, your evil look made ..."

"What evil look?" she said.

"The one after the sad look."

"That was intelligence, cutting through to the truth, sweeping aside all nonsense. You thought that was an evil expression?" she said, sweeping me and my opinions aside as nonsense.

"Yes, well that's how it looked to me."

"So you think intelligence is evil, and vice versa?"

"No. I'm saying what your look put me in mind of."

"And my intelligence looked evil to you?" she said.

"No, your face looked evil, that's all."

She muttered something that could have been "idiot".

"What did you say?" I said, and then I muttered something that was definitely "Shit bag".

"What did you say?" she said.

"I said 'What did you say?'"

"And what did you say after that?"

"I said 'shit bag'," and I said it loudly.

Zara got up and stormed out, thumping her bare feet on the floor. Somebody whimpered, somebody tittered, and somebody sighed. I laid back and shut my eyes, feeling juvenile but happy. Yes, honesty can be a great liberator after a period of uncomfortably holding back on one's constipated personality.

§

At dinner I sat with Amanda, which was starting to become a habit, and one I intended nurturing. As far as I could see, the only good thing likely to come out of my stay at Ravenswood was whatever I could extract from Amanda by way of a young girl's favors to an older man, and the thought of it quite restored me after the several vicissitudes of the day.

"How are you today, Peter?" she asked. "Are you managing to make any sense of things yet?" The sympathy in her expression and tone of voice touched me, and I was surprised to find myself abnormally moved. An alarm bell went off in my head as the word "love" lurched across my field of vision. Oh no, I thought, not that bloody thing again!

"No, not really, but Dennis has told me I should stop trying, although I can't imagine I'll be able to. I mean, I could be here for 20 years before I get the hang of it, and actually I don't have that long."

"Well, you have that long if it's important enough."

"Maybe it isn't. I only really came here on a whim, so I hardly feel ready to promote my reason for being here to one of life-changing importance. I ..." I was going to tell her I'd nearly left that afternoon, but I thought it would make me look like a quitter, and I didn't want her to think that, even though it was more accurate than any other impression I could conspire to give her.

"What?"

"Oh, nothing. I'm just rambling."

She smiled, and a warm feeling of encouragement tingled happily in my chest. But I'm clumsy about picking women up at the best of times, and the thought of suggesting intimacy to a much younger woman, at Ravenswood, stone-cold sober, left me feeling I was attempting something far too difficult and too likely to end in rejection, which was an outcome I could do without, today as much as ever. I also felt intimidated by talking in the dining room, because it was generally so quiet that any conversation taking place was potentially audible to anyone. So, as we'd both finished eating, I suggested we went for a stroll. I wasn't planning anything, I just wanted to talk to one of the few people I considered likely to be seeing the world from something close to my perspective.

We went out into the yard and mooched about. It seemed romantic in the fading light, but the yard hadn't changed, I had.

"I've only been here a day, but it feels like a week or more."

"Yes," she said "but when you've been here a week, it will feel like a day."

I must have looked skeptical at yet another perfect answer, because she laughed and said, "But I suppose you're fed up with enigmatic statements by now, aren't you?"

I was finding it hard to listen to the words she used, as I was getting fixated on the delightful noises she made, when she spoke or particularly when she laughed. Even the swish of her clothes as she moved was starting to entrance me. I forced myself to attend, but rather than feeling encouraged by her understanding of my predicament, I was overcome by the idea that she, and everyone else here, was probably starting to see me as the dunderhead who just couldn't get the message, the twerp who had come to a spiritual centre thinking he's signed up for beer and one night stands at Butlins. I was the boy who always came bottom of the class and last in every race, the uncoordinated army recruit who can't make his arms swing in opposition to his legs, the degenerate, middle-aged lout who goes to Bangkok to buy sex from young girls because he's too inept to get it in any other way. As this feeling engulfed me, I had an urgent need to convince her I wasn't stupid, or desperate, although I knew I was partly flying in the face of reality.

"No, I've got the idea. Now all I need to know is whether it's for me or not. We anal types don't find letting go very easy. I may be an artist by trade, but I'm a Tory-voting bank manager by nature."

"No you're not. You're imaginative, witty, attractive, intelligent." She smiled shyly as she spoke, her head tilted down and her eyes on the ground in front of her. I felt as though I'd just drunk a magnum of champagne and then whacked myself over the head with the empty bottle - lightheaded, ecstatic, and a little sick, but the sickness came from plucking up the courage to say what she'd just given me the invitation to say, or so I thought.

"Er," was all I could come up with, and I gulped when I said that.

"What?"

"Oh, I, well ... It's nice of you to say that."

"It's true. Come on Peter. You've surely learnt enough in your time here to know that people speak the truth, maybe too much truth some of the time.

She stopped and turned to look at me. "You're really surprised aren't you? You're so worldly wise that you can't trust a compliment, even when it's directed at you."

"Compliments directed at me are the ones I'm least likely to believe."

"Well, I don't want to steal Dennis' thunder, but I think I may have pointed something out that you need to work on."

"What?"

"Your incredibly low opinion of yourself. Don't be surprised."

I wasn't, but I didn't say anything.

"Most sensitive people think badly of themselves. They're always disappointed with what they've done or how they've behaved, so they never stop being hard on themselves. It becomes a way of life after a while. If you're going to have a good outlook on the world, the first person you've got to like is yourself. You can't conceivably like someone else, not really like them, until you've developed some affection for yourself. Being creative only makes it worse, because your mind is able to manufacture negative things about you that aren't true. If you just saw yourself as you are, without embellishment, you'd see a lovable person. There, now I'm starting to sound like Dennis. I'd better shut up."

I thought of the ever-critical, irascible little red devil who'd popped into my mind during meditation that morning. It's not the act of liking myself I find difficult per se, it's finding something to like about myself that's so bloody hard. When I look in the mirror, I see a nice enough sort of bloke staring back at me, but when I observe all the petty, cynical, pretentious, embarrassing and selfish things I do or think of doing in the course of the day, I have to conclude it would take either a superhuman effort or a hideously distorted view of reality to garner some genuine respect for myself.

As I thought this, I realized I've never really paid this kind of attention to myself in the past and, if I had, it had been from the perspective that I'm unchangeable anyway, so it's more a matter of changing the world to value my characteristics, rather than changing my characteristics to those I can be proud of and the world can appreciate. I'm the sort of person who feels bad about not contributing more to charity, but rather than sticking my hand in my pocket and pulling out some cash, I try to find reasons why I can't afford it, or why charity is a bad thing, or I tell myself the organizers are probably crooks. It never works, and I end up feeling both mean and indignant, as if to say "How dare you ask me for money and make me feel mean for not giving it to you!"

"What are you thinking?" Amanda asked.

"I'm thinking I do have a bad impression of myself, but I can't see why I shouldn't. Do you think someone should like themselves even if they don't deserve to? What about Stalin, or Hitler, should they have liked themselves?"

"Yes, of course. If they had done they would have liked other people and wouldn't have been able to do what they did. Hating is a vicious circle - you start off hating yourself and you end up hating everybody. But the great thing is that loving is the same, if you love yourself you can love everybody."

I must have given her another suspicious look, because she went on. "Well, alright, loving is too strong a word. Dennis uses the word 'metta', which is a Buddhist term for all-pervasive goodwill. Loving can have heavy connotations. Dennis thinks it smacks too much of free love, of the hippy generation, which he hasn't a lot of time for."

"Me neither, and Charles Manson was a hippy."

"We do quite a lot of metta meditation. It can put you at peace with yourself and the world."

"What do Ken and Zara do when these metta meditations are taking place?"

"Sorry?"

"Well, from what I've seen of those two, they don't radiate a lot of goodwill, not to me at any rate, nor to each other, nor does Roger."

"Oh, well, I suppose they're working through their own problems, but you just have to forget about other people."

"But I thought it was about liking other people."

"Yes, but if someone doesn't react to you like you'd like them to, you can't afford to get hung up on it. You've got to make your own feelings towards others unconditional, not dependent on how they respond to you. It's hard enough sorting your own mind out, let alone anyone else's. When I first came here I was having a big problem about my parents. Not with my parents, I don't mean. I just couldn't get my feelings towards them into perspective. So I spoke to Dennis about it and he said just forget it. I said 'How can I forget my parents?', and he told me not to diminish them as people, but that a child's relationship with its parents is so complex you could spend years focused on it and get nowhere, so you just have to push it to one side and sort yourself out, and it will all fall into place anyway, given time. Some problems are best ignored, like the dust behind the cooker - it would be very hard to clean up, it doesn't go anywhere and it doesn't bother anyone, so just leave it alone."

We wandered around for a while without saying anything. I was feeling pissed off. I'm not altogether sure why, but not having had a drink for 48 hours or a fuck for weeks may have had something to do with it. Amanda broke the silence.

"What are you thinking now?"

I was irritated enough to be tactless and crude. "I was thinking how much I would like to make love to you, and as we're making honesty our top priority, I can't lie, can I?"

"I'm flattered, but I'm afraid I have to disappoint you. I

don't do that here. Sex and meditation just don't go together. Monks aren't celibate without reason. As soon as you let people start thinking about sex, they don't think about much else."

"What if we resolve not to think about it, just do it with our minds blanked off?"

"But it never ends there does it? If only life were that simple."

"If only people were that simple."

Well, at least she hadn't screamed, or hit me, or told me what a dirty old man I was, or gone running off to Dennis and demanded my expulsion for a gross breach of spiritual etiquette. In fact, she gave me one of the most acceptable brush-offs I've ever received, apart from a woman who told me with earnest apologies that she would really love to hop into bed with me "more than anything in the world, darling", but she had a minor but irksome sexually transmittable disease and didn't want to transmit it to me. At least, I thought it was nice until a mutual friend told me it was a complete lie, and in fact she'd told our friend she would sooner be fucked by a demented gorilla, and would certainly enjoy it more, and so would the gorilla.

§

A week passed. The days went by smoothly enough, and although I made no major discoveries about myself, life, the universe or anything else in it, I had a few interesting moments.

Amanda and I remained on good terms, despite my hapless attempt to proposition her. She was undoubtedly my best friend there, and fast on her way to becoming one of my best friends anywhere. I'd no idea why this was. I was close to double her age, and I've invariably found that a failure to pick someone up, no matter how civilized the rebuff, is the kiss of death to any friendship you might try to erect in the place of anything more steamy. I suppose we just seemed to like each other, in that rare unconditional way you encounter just a few times in the average lifetime, and when you have the chemistry going for you, it's almost impossible to destroy the resultant friendship, even by consummate crassness. I got to the point - and I assumed she had too - where I wasn't consciously aware of her age, sex, religion, race, wealth, class or anything else that can be a barrier or a catalyst when getting to know someone.

We did a lot of meditation, some of it breath watching and some of it the goodwill thing that Amanda had told me about, and yes, I confirmed I don't like myself, and no, I wasn't able to do anything about it. I hadn't spoken to Zara and I kept out of Ken's way as much as possible. I confirmed Roger was not at all malicious, just inhumanely blunt, and that Bob, Doris, Ruben and Monica were consistently and unremittingly pleasant. Dennis continued to be sage and a little aloof from the rest of us, and I was more aware than ever of the unquestioning respect the people there had for him. He projected his benevolently authoritative persona very professionally, and he was full of useful and entertaining anecdotes - many drawn from his experiences in India. I suspected he used his Indian mentor, Dharavajra, as a mouthpiece for his own ideas, thereby imbuing them with an additional component of mystical gravitas. But I didn't blame him for that. Many of us need a Dharavajra in our lives who can say the things we don't want to say ourselves, because they're either too pompous or too inane, and in the mouth of Dharavajra

- the Dorothy Parker of the metaphysical world - even the most pedestrian remark could sound pithy and elegant to the true believer.

Sandy didn't have much to do with me since our prickly conversation while washing-up, and Micky, the girl whose sex I couldn't determine but whom – perhaps as a consequence - I went on to find beguilingly attractive, didn't seem to have much to do with anyone, of which the same could be said of the few other people I saw drifting around the place and to whom I still hadn't managed to put names. In the real world, I suppose I might just have gone up to them and introduced myself, but at Ravenswood it was as though they were encased in some sort of transparent, spiritual bubble, with "Keep out - person being meditatively mindful!" stamped across the outside, and I got no indication from them that they cared who the hell I was anyway. Actually, I doubted even after a week they'd registered my presence, and if they had, they certainly didn't seem to have any pressing inclination to recognize it.

In general, my stay at Ravenswood was amounting to a pleasant and inconsequential break, which made it nice for the time being, but unlikely to prove of any lasting benefit, although that didn't bother me – a good break is more than I was expecting during my first day or two. Monica was still doling out warm feelings to complement the nourishing comfort food, of which she was the quintessential mistress.

Ruben had become a benign and abstract presence who, despite his almost complete silence, I started to miss if I didn't see him around. His habit of bouncing the odd word back at you - just lobbing it into the air and letting it hang there, forcing you to reexamine your own utterances as reissued from his mouth - mesmerized me. He probably didn't mean anything by it, but it struck me as being a power-ful technique for getting noticed on the minimum of creative input, and made me think a lot more about what I said in his mirror-like company. When I sat with him at mealtimes, it was as though there was another version of me at the table, but because he looked nothing like me, he was more like an interesting caricature than a tiresome copy.

§§§

DEATH

When I saw them, I realized it was the first time I'd seen a dead body in the flesh, and now I was seeing two at once. I'd seen dozens on the television, but they never seemed to have the same stillness that a real, live dead body has, particularly when it's somebody you've known, somebody you saw functioning yesterday, somebody who had no physical reason to be dead today.

I was shocked, of course, because I discovered them first, locked in each other's arms. It was as though they were making love, so tight and abandoned was their entanglement, but the intensity of their posture went beyond love making, and was a desperate clutching that marked their passage into death. It wasn't control they'd abandoned, it was life itself.

Sandy and Doris, before the Buddha, their stillness as perfect as his. Doris' eyes shut - she could have been smiling. Sandy's eyes open – questioning, slightly surprised. The Buddha's eyes softly focused on the infinite - perhaps he could see them there, newly arrived in the timeless state of which he's a permanent, distant resident.

It was morning, and I was first to arrive for the early meditation. My very first impression was of one body, prostrate before the Buddha, but then I noticed an excess of limbs and thought I'd found two people in some private or profane act. I turned to leave, hoping to go unnoticed, but their inertness reached out to me, forced me to turn around again, and I started towards them, gently, afraid of disturbing their eternal clinch. I stopped moving as I began to take in what I was seeing. There was a large bottle of Evian water - Doris' preferred drink - glasses, three small plastic containers, the sort pills come in, and, most surprisingly, an empty half-bottle of vodka, lying on its back, the Smirnoff label staring drunkenly at the rafters. On either side of the Buddha were two burnt out candles, the wax collapsed into overflowing skirts around their holders. Propped in front of the Buddha was an envelope which, even from several yards away, I could see was addressed, in large and flowery writing, "To Dennis".

The scene printed itself on my mind. The image of their eternity will probably be with me until my own eternity beckons. They've shown me what it looks like for those that are left behind. Now I just have to endure a few more years before I become a similar image for someone else to deal with. I wonder who it'll be that discovers my passing?

I felt no grief. I hadn't known them well enough or long enough to qualify for feelings of bereavement. I felt surprise and an urgent need to broadcast the news, not to gossip, but so that I could tell someone who would feel their loss in the appropriate way, and mark their passing with tears and sadness and the other signals and rituals they were due. They needed to be missed for their deaths to have value, otherwise it was just another event that would be remarked upon and forgotten, like an impersonal newspaper story. It's the sense of loss that makes death important and noteworthy, so I had to get the information to the people who could feel it, and sob the sobs that were part of the process. As I opened the door, Roger was about to enter.

"Don't go in," I said. "Doris and Sandy are dead. Keep the others out while I get Dennis."

"What?"

"I think Doris and Sandy have committed suicide. They're dead. Don't let anyone else go in."

"Are you, are ... what?"

"Just don't let anyone go in. I'll be right back."

I left him there, looking scared and inept. I realized, for the first time, that he was very young. His coolness had made him look older, more mature, but now he looked like a young boy, struggling to make sense of one of the nasty bits life throws up. Unexpectedly I felt myself falling into the role of coper, the person who keeps their head screwed on and stays in control. God knows why. I'm not normally to be found playing that sort of part. I suppose I was reacting to Roger's shock. His helplessness made me feel strong by comparison.

I couldn't see Dennis, but Bob was in a group of people

who were walking slowly towards the meditation room, I was going to tell him, but then I spotted Dennis coming out of the farmhouse.

"Please," I shouted, breaking the silence and making Bob, whom I was now alongside, jump with fright, "don't anyone go into the meditation room."

Dennis stood still, taking in the scene, coolly viewing the retreatants stopped dead in their tracks like a frozen frame of video, and me running towards him with, I'm sure, a bizarre expression on my face. I told him what I'd found. I spoke to him with my face close to his. He recoiled slightly, and I thought it was because my breath was probably bad after sleep and coffee. He stared at me, and I saw shock take him over, and I thought he could be reliving the time he lost his daughter, tragedy recalling tragedy. He did nothing. His mouth moved slightly but no words emerged, it was as though he was softly blowing bubbles. Is he still honoring the pre-breakfast silence? I wondered. Should I shake him to make it sink in? Would anyone here be able to get a grip, or would I have to do it all myself? Call the police, the doctor, the undertaker, the priest?

Ken marched up to us. "What's going on?" he said, not angrily, but calmly, pleasantly, in a gentle tone of voice I'd not heard him use before. I told him. As I spoke, I noticed Roger in the distance, squarely blocking the door to the meditation room, not that anyone was trying to get in. "Jesus!" said Ken.

"Dennis, there's a note addressed to you."

"Where?" said Ken.

"In the room, leaning against the Buddha."

Dennis let out a short, sharp laugh, and this sudden, hysterical reaction, which came and went in an instant, seemed to wake him from whatever nightmare he was going through behind his glazed eyes.

"Okay," he said, and the three of us strode towards the door with a purposefulness that had seemed impossible just a few moments earlier. At first I didn't think Roger was going to let us in, and that I would have to re-program him with a new instruction, but then he moved away, slowly and dreamily, his face downcast.

Dennis stopped before opening the door, his hand on the handle. He tilted his head back deliberately, then forward. I saw his shoulders heave as he took a deep breath, then slowly and silently he opened the door. Ken followed him in and then me. I shut the door behind us. Again I felt the stillness of the room, the two bodies and the Buddha statue. Perpetual stillness. It was as though the Buddha was smiling more than usual, as if to say "Yes, we all come to this. Isn't that what I told you? Didn't you believe me?"

Dennis took off his shoes - automatically honoring the rules of the meditation room, even now - and padded over to the two bodies. He knelt down and laid his hand on Doris' arm, and stayed in that pose for a long time. Then he roused himself, looked around at the bottles, pausing as his glance shifted from object to object. He seemed to look at the vodka bottle for the longest, but eventually he stood up and quickly plucked the envelope from in front of the Buddha as if he needed to take the statue by surprise. He only looked at the note contained in the envelope for a few seconds before he handed it to Ken. I'd assumed he hadn't wanted to read it, but when Ken handed it to me almost immediately, I saw there was very little to read. It said "Happy now, united with the metta of the infinite, and with Zoragaia. Much love, Sandy and Doris". Doris' name was written in a different hand to the rest of the note, a shaky, uncertain hand that may once have been a flowing copperplate. I looked down at the gentle, friendly, harmless and dead woman at my feet, and felt warm tears run down my cheeks and curve around my mouth.

"What the fuck did she do that for?" I said.

§

Sergeant Davies sighed incessantly, but I couldn't determine whether it was out of sadness or from frustration with having to deal with a bunch of weirdo dropouts, or perhaps it was simply something to do with his being Welsh, and Welsh amongst a group of English at that. I knew he viewed us as weirdo dropouts from the way he referred to Ravenswood, never by its name, but as a "com yoon", and he always winced slightly on the second syllable as though the word gave him offence to the extent of it being physically distressing, like an acrid smell. Also, I heard his colleague, Constable Llewellyn, refer to the meditation room as "that mumbo jumbo place", which is what I may have called it a week previously.

"So you were the first person to see it, like?" Davies asked me. I thought he hadn't finished his sentence, and the "like" was going to lead on to something else, "like it was" perhaps, but after a couple of false starts I realized he often left his sentences hanging in this way.

"Yes, about an hour and a half ago, just before seven."

We were sitting in Dennis' office. Just Davies, Llewellyn

and me. I was the first to be interviewed.

"And it was pretty much like it is now, like?"

"Yes, we didn't touch anything. Well, Dennis touched a body, and he picked up the note," which was now on the desk in front of Llewellyn, "and somebody came in and kissed them."

"Kissed who? Where?"

"Zara, in the meditation room."

"I mean where on the body, like?" He grinned, and so did Llewellyn, and so did I, sheepishly, because I'd never been interviewed by a policeman before, and I felt uncomfortable and unqualified to do this sort of thing.

"On the forehead, I think. Zara, well she's ... you'll understand when you meet her."

"Close to them was she, like?"

"Not particularly, she's just histrionic."

"What?" said Llewellyn.

"Alright, I understand," said Davies. "Was this a surprise?"

"Totally. I mean, I didn't know them that well. I've only been here a week and had never met either of them before that, but Doris was a pleasant old girl, and seemed perfectly happy. Sandy was possibly a bit less stable, but, well, not suicidal, I wouldn't have thought."

"What do you mean by 'less stable'."

"Well, she cried every now and again, but that doesn't count for much here. I mean, people, some people, get emotional, and she was one of them, but it's ..." I wanted to say cathartic, but I thought I'd better find another word, "it's an emotional release, and she seemed to enjoy it. It's part of what they do here."

Both of them furrowed their brows slightly.

"What is?" said Davies.

"Sorry?"

"What exactly do you do here?"

"I'm not really the right person to ask. I'm just passing through, and I really haven't got the hang of it yet. You'd better ask Dennis, he runs the place. I'll only confuse you. I'm confused myself."

Davies nodded and sucked his teeth, but Llewellyn adopted a look that mixed surprise and skepticism.

"It's nothing spooky." I felt obliged to tell them. "It's just a meditation centre, and some people get very intense."

"And you think this may have contributed to her death?" asked Llewellyn. I was digging myself into a hole.

"No, well, look, I don't know. This is all new to me, and amateur psychology is right out of my field. Ask Dennis."

"Do you know where she got the pills from?" said Davies.

"No, I'd never seen them before, nor the vodka, I didn't know it was allowed."

"Allowed?"

"Well, not encouraged. I guess you can do what you like, but the belief is you can't meditate usefully when you're sozzled, so I wasn't aware there was any booze in the place." And if I'd thought there was any more of it lurking in some dark cupboard, I would have made a bee-line for it right then.

"Were the two of them close to anyone else, like?"

"Not really. I didn't know they were close to each other. I still don't know that they were close to each other. Maybe they just decided to do this together for some reason."

"What, you mean a coincidence?" said Llewellyn.

"No," I said, sounding more annoyed than I'd intended. I was getting frustrated, and I seemed to be saying things I didn't want to say. If I'd ever harbored any ideas of becoming a criminal to relieve myself of my incessant financial worries, my clumsiness in handling these two would have convinced me I should reconsider. "No, I don't mean that, but, well, maybe they just found they agreed about this and, you know ..."

"Agreed about committing suicide, like?"

"No." Again, my voice was raised too high. I could imagine them marching me off to jail on suspicion of every unsolved crime on the books of the Welsh constabulary if this went on much longer. "No," I said again, but quietly. "Look, I'm completely baffled by this, as you can surely tell. It was a complete surprise to me and everyone else, I should think, but if anyone knows more about them and their states of mind, it's Dennis." The two of them exchanged glances. I don't know why because no message seemed to pass between them, but it must have been obvious I wasn't enjoying my moment in the limelight, and my constant recommendations they should talk to Dennis probably made it look as if I was desperate to get away from them, which, of course, I was. Really, I wanted to spend some time on my own to let things soak in, although I didn't know what useful purpose the soaking in would achieve.

"How did Mr. Foulds react when you told him about the deaths, like?"

"Er, who's Mr. Foulds? Is that Dennis?"

"Yes, Dennis Foulds."

"He was very shocked. Speechless. It was a few moments before he could rouse himself, which surprised me."

"Why?"

"Dennis is a very stable and capable sort of bloke. If I could think of anyone likely to be able to handle a situation like this competently, it would be him."

"So would you say he was unusually perturbed, like?"

"What's usual and unusual in a situation like this? You may come across it all the time, but most of us never come across it. Who knows how they're going to react?" Of course, Dennis had been through much worse in the past, but I had no reason to suppose he was immune to new tragedies.

"How did you react?"

"Well, I was shocked, but I managed to stay in control."

"In control of who?" asked Llewellyn.

"Of me," I said, again showing my irritation. I couldn't understand why I was getting the third degree for what looked like an open and shut case of suicide. I knew I shouldn't say anything more, but I couldn't help myself. "Why are you asking all these questions? Isn't it obvious what happened?"

Davies looked up at the ceiling and Llewellyn at the floor, but both put on almost identical expressions of mild frustration, like any traffic cop would do when asked why he stopped you for speeding, and not the young hoodlum in the red Ford Escort who had just overtaken you doing about 110 mph.

"Mr. Wickham," said Davies "I don't know how it is where you come from, but when we come across two bodies in a sleepy little part of Wales, bodies of two individuals who showed no inclination to kill themselves, and nobody can give us any reason why they should want to kill themselves, like, we have to make sure we get the story absolutely straight. If anything is lurking under the surface that's likely to come back later on, like, something that should have been discovered at the time, I want to know about it now. I'm sure you understand," he said, in a bored tone which indicated he really wasn't awfully concerned whether I understood or not. "Now then," he went on, "do you know anything about the backgrounds of either of the deceased?"

"Not really. Sandy, the young one, had a rich father who kept her afloat, and she spent quite a lot of time here. I think

Doris was just here for a short stay, but I don't know anything beyond that."

"Were either of them ill?"

"Not that I know."

"Had they argued with anyone recently?"

"Not to my knowledge."

"Were they emotionally involved with anyone here or anywhere else?"

"I've no idea."

"Had anyone discussed the matter of death recently?"

Oh.

§

It had happened two days earlier. I was starting to get the hang of the scenery, and was almost beginning to appreciate that fields and foliage and birds and fresh air might have something positive to be said for them after all. The day had been tranquil in terms of what I'd done, what I'd felt, and even in terms of the weather. There had been no wind, not even a trace of a breeze. This stillness seemed to have infected me somehow, and I got the impression I wasn't the only one who felt calm and generally slowed-down. It was the last meeting of the day, and if the daytime had dawdled along quietly, the evening was so laid back that time was in danger of coming to a stop altogether, which made me appreciate Stephen Hawking's line that time exists simply to stop everything happening at once. We were in the meditation room, and the silence that preceded everything had gone on even longer than usual, but I didn't mind, and if I didn't, I'm sure nobody else did either. Dennis began to talk.

"I want to raise a subject none of us like to think too much about, but which is equally the most significant thing that happens in our lives. The subject is death, and I've always found it ironic that there's so much more to say about death than about the other significant event, birth. The idea of death mystifies us, terrifies us, and inspires us to cram activity and achievement into the lives it terminates. Sometimes it relieves us.

"So what is death? Is this a question we can attempt to answer, or can we only add one more useless speculation to the millions that already exist? Perhaps a constructive way to view the subject isn't to address it head on, but rather to ask what there is in the absence of life. A piece of stone exists, but it doesn't live. Our remains, when we die, will exist in some form or another, but they won't live. So what is existence without life? Is it something the existing entity is aware of? Is there consciousness without life? We assume not. We assume that atoms and molecules have no awareness, but is that a valid assumption? Is there, perhaps, some force that suffuses everything, a force that never ceases to exist, whether it's in a rock, a packet of energy, a piece of ash, a bone, a human body, a human brain? Is that force what we experience when we meditate and quell the noise that thought and life impose on us? The same force that exists innately in every atom, whether it's part of a living animal or an inanimate object?

"I can't prove to you that it is. I can't give you a logical explanation that incontrovertibly illustrates that an all-pervasive, loving, timeless, beautiful, single consciousness suffuses us all, and welcomes us back when the frenetic noise of life is extinguished. But I know it does. I know it more certainly than I know anything in life we might conceitedly label a 'fact'. I can tell you we all return to a unitary, harmonious consciousness when our lives end. Call it heaven if you like, Call it Gaia. Call it a singularity, a perfect mathematical entity, a point. Call it nothing. Call it everything. Call it God."

Call it what you may, at the time I wouldn't have called it an inducement to commit suicide, a rallying cry to rush off and experience Dennis' perfect state a bit ahead of time. But when directed at a particular sort of mind, in a particular state, well, yes, it could have pushed Doris and Sandy over an edge of some sort, especially if they had already peeped over that edge at times in the past. I suppressed a shudder.

"No," I said, looking Davies and Llewellyn squarely in the eye, first one, then the other, "not that I remember," I said, and I went on to shake my head and adopt an innocent look, as I warmed to the task of lying to policemen.

§§§

TALKING OF DEATH

The day went on, but without the regular timetable of Ravenswood I had to keep looking at my watch to see what time it was. Despite my surprising tears over Doris, I can't say I felt her passing too keenly. She'd looked so content in death I made the baseless assumption that her passing had been painless, although nobody knows what agony we may go through as we slip out of life - death masks leave no evidence as to what happened next, or what it felt like. As for Sandy, I'm slightly ashamed to say I felt nothing about her decease. I don't know why I should be ashamed. I didn't know much about her and I actually thought she was a bit of a twat. Feeling nothing about her death made me an outsider amongst the controlled and, I think, genuine displays of grief that others felt. Micky was inconsolable, and illustrated the sincerity of her feelings by trying to hide them, but I didn't know which of them she was missing, or why she, of all people, should be suffering so badly.

By mid-afternoon the business part of dealing with death was taken care of. The bodies had been removed, the police had left and I was dawdling in the yard when Dennis approached me.

"Peter, I need to stretch my legs. I'd be grateful if you'd come for a walk with me."

We hadn't really had much of a conversation since the first and only walk I had with him the day after I arrived. But I suspected we weren't likely to have a normal chat given the events of the day and the fact he just may have had an unwitting but powerful role to play in them, a possibility that Davies and Llewellyn had almost certainly raised when they'd interviewed him.

We set off at what I, an inveterate ambler, considered to be a breakneck pace, but I kept up with him, uncomplaining, assuming he needed to exercise or exorcise a few demons. After 10 minutes or so we came to a place that gave us a good view of the valley - perhaps you'd call it a promontory, but I'm not really well enough up on geography to know exactly what a promontory is. We stopped and gazed at the panorama below us. Well, Dennis gazed at the valley and I stared mainly at Dennis, trying to read in his face what he was thinking and going through. Eventually he spoke without looking at me, his eyes looking blankly into the distance but, I suspect, focused on something deep inside of him.

"Quite a shock."

I nodded but didn't say anything.

"Doris was ill, terminally ill. She may have lived for a couple of years but she was bound to die before very long, possibly within six months. Cancer. She'd spoken of taking her life, but only in vague terms, and she seemed to be looking forward to the rest of her days as a way of preparing for death."

"Perhaps she was ready," I said. "Perhaps she got the preparation done sooner than expected and decided to go before the pain started. She looked content, as though it was what she wanted."

"But not Sandy," he said, and looked at his feet, his chin tucked against his chest. "Why Sandy? I've spoken to the people here who were closest to her and Doris, but nobody has a clue. But ..."

"What?"

"My talk, two days ago. You remember?"

"Clearly."

He nodded.

"Yes, so does everyone."

"What do you mean?" I asked.

"One or two people have mentioned it."

"Did the police ask you about it?" I said.

"They asked me if death was often discussed, and I said yes, but I didn't volunteer that I'd made that particular speech so recently."

"They asked me."

"What did you say?"

"I said I couldn't recall anything that would have had that effect on them."

"You lied, like me."

"Yes, but I don't have any problem with that. Anyway," I went on, "if you believe what you said, and I've no reason to doubt you do, you've nothing to regret. You've done them a favor."

"Possibly. No, I mean ... I mean I don't doubt what I said, but life happens for a purpose, and we're not supposed to give it up just because someone tells us they've found solace in the thought of death. I should have made that clear. We have to find our own, innate rationale for doing things, not swallow someone else's and act it out."

"So what's the purpose of life?"

I thought he might grin, or even laugh, and accuse me of trying to find shortcuts again. But he didn't. He turned sad, empty eyes to me and said "I don't know."

He paused and looked ahead again. "Does that surprise you?" he said.

Actually, it did, but I felt unjustified in being surprised. Dennis never told anybody he knew all the answers, he just somehow gave the impression he did. Perhaps I should have told him this, for future reference.

"Well, no, but it wouldn't have surprised me if you had known the answer either, or at least that you had a fair idea." This time he did laugh, albeit without a lot of conviction.

"Peter, you make it sound like a game. A computer game. Search for the buried treasure."

"Well, it is, isn't it?"

"Yes," he said, smiling "yes, it may be, in a way. It's certainly a treasure, and it's most definitely buried."

"Not only is it buried," I said, "but we don't know where it's buried, or even if it's buried on this planet." He looked at me, as if surprised for some reason but said nothing, so I carried on. "If I've only learnt one thing here, it's that problems are for the individual to sort out. By that token you're not responsible for what other people do with your ideas."

After more gazing into the distance, by both of us this time, we started walking again. "Mr. Tinburnell is coming down tomorrow," he said.

"Tinburnell?"

"Sandy's father."

"Is that Tinburnell as in Guy Tinburnell, the financier?"

"Yes. Have you heard of him?"

"Oh yes. I know him."

Guy Tinburnell and I got acquainted through a cartoon I drew of him when he was under the scrutiny of an investment watchdog for some very dodgy share dealings he'd been involved in about 10 years ago. Normally I don't get involved in that sort of arcane business story, but it was big news at the time, as was anything that smacked of the type of greed the Thatcher years were blamed for fomenting. My cartoon showed him feeding at a trough with a few other notables and politicos of the day, surrounded by some other, unnamed fat capitalists. The meal comprised of frail bodies of the very old and the very young, as a coarse, Hogarthian allegory for Widows and Orphans Savings Funds and the like being pillaged by fat-assed bankers. There was nothing subtle about the content, but I made a reasonable job of the drawing and I managed to produce a good caricature of Tinburnell, which was no great achievement as he obligingly had a large one of just about everything I could exaggerate.

Guy avoided prosecution on a technicality and sued the newspaper that was chasing him, and in which my cartoon appeared. They settled out of court, and a few days later he called me and asked if I would sell him the cartoon for a mouthwatering amount of money. We agreed to complete the transaction over a dinner at the Savoy, at which we both drank a load of superb claret and from which sprang an occasional acquaintanceship that caused us to have the odd drink or meal together over a few years.

I can't say I liked him that much to begin with. He was pompous, classist, misogynistic, probably racist, supremely arrogant and just about everything else it's fashionable to disdain. But he was good company and always insisted on paying, which was just as well because we never went anywhere my credit card could withstand the heat. His major redeeming feature was he could always laugh at himself, which explains why he bought the cartoon to hang in his billiards room, rather than destroy it, which is what I'd first assumed was his motive in buying it. I hadn't seen him for several years.

"How well do you know him?"

I told him the story of the cartoon. "I wouldn't say we're close friends exactly, but we got on well enough. He'll be surprised to see me here."

"Why?"

"Anyone who knows me would be surprised to see me here. Unless he's changed a lot, I would guess he didn't think much of Sandy being here either. He's got very black and white views. I didn't know Sandy was his daughter, but now I come to think of it, there are some similarities."

"Like what?"

"Well, there were expressions they had in common, and I got the impression she was single-minded. Guy is absolutely single-minded. He ..." I paused whilst wondering how much I should say.

"What?" said Dennis.

"Did he say why he's coming?"

"No."

"Well, I'd prepare myself for a storm if I were you. I'm sure he'll be upset, but if he's not happy with the explanation of the way things happened, he'll turn the place upside down as he tries to find out. He's a self-made man. His father lost the family fortune to gambling and misjudged business deals when Guy was a baby, and then spent the rest of his life drinking to try and forget what he'd done. Guy rebuilt it a hundred times over by the time he was 30, and he didn't construct his empire by stepping deftly around live bodies, he did it by trampling over dying ones."

To say he would turn the place upside down was an understatement. If Guy got even the remotest whiff of the fact Dennis may have influenced Sandy's demise, I had no doubt he would smack a legal case on him that would bury Dennis, Ravenswood and anyone within a hundred miles of it.

"He deserves my honesty, if nothing else."

"Well, that's up to you, but if Guy thinks you or Ravenswood were in any way connected with Sandy's premature departure, he'll squeeze you until the pip squeaks. Of course, he may have mellowed, but he seemed to be getting even more reactionary with the passing years during the time I knew him."

Dennis sighed.

"Sorry Dennis. I don't like being the harbinger of doom and gloom, but it's best you go into this with your eyes open. He'll roast you alive if you don't, and Guy's not a vegetarian."

"Are you advising me to lie, again?" he said, matter of factly.

"No, you're the last person in the world I would advise to do that, but you ought to be aware what Guy's capable of, and even if there's no connection between your speech and Sandy's death, he'll find a lawyer who can prove one and make it look watertight. Any man who can shake off the Treasury, the Bank of England, the Stock Exchange and the Serious Fraud Squad as though they're a bunch of bothersome schoolchildren, won't see too many problems in taking Ravenswood to the cleaners." I glanced across at Dennis' glum face. "I bet you wish I hadn't said anything."

"Not at all. I'm glad you told me what you have. I can't even begin to imagine what pleasure anyone would get out of ruining the centre, but I don't suppose he's exactly looking for pleasure right now, and retribution may be a good substitute."

It struck me that Dennis was reacting and talking just like a normal man. He wasn't being cool, he wasn't eschewing practicalities, he wasn't being enigmatic or philosophical or aloof in the way I'd come to associate with him, he was just being downright depressed by a sad event, by an equally sad prospect for the next few days and, if things turned out badly, much longer than that.

"Peter, I don't need you to lie for me. Sandy's father is bound to ask for your version of events, and when he does, you mustn't be constrained by considering what effect the truth will have on me."

"I understand, but I'll try and make him see sense."

"And what exactly is sense in a situation like this?"

"We don't know why she did it, do we? Did you have any idea what was going on in her head?" He didn't answer. "She was a mature adult. You had no way of knowing she'd react as she did, and nobody in their right mind would blame you with doing anything immoral. Maybe he'll take the same view."

"But maybe he won't."

Well Dennis, I thought, I can assure you of one thing, unless Guy Tinburnell is a different man to the one I knew, he won't.

§

Just before dinner, Dennis let it be known, via assorted emissaries, that he would like to see us all in the meditation room at eight. Monica passed the news on to me.

"Do you have any problem with going back into the meditation room? she asked.

"No," I said, without thinking.

"Dennis believes it's important we meet there and expunge any bad feelings about the place. Instead, we should take strength from what happened there, and use that strength to show our feelings towards Sandy and Doris. If we're afraid of the meditation room, it means we're afraid of what they did, ashamed of what they did, but we're not, or shouldn't be. We need to tell them that."

"Who?"

"Doris and Sandy. They're still with us, Peter. Not in this existence, but they're still with us."

I couldn't imagine Dennis putting it in these words, so I guessed Monica was *ad libbing*. I suspected Dennis' motive was to get people back in the room straight away before they started to brood on it and imagine evil to reside there. He couldn't afford to let such a large piece of real estate fall into disuse for fear of bad vibes or ghosts, and if anyone was likely to believe in spiritual influences, it was the people at Ravenswood.

Dinner was a desultory affair, conducted in almost total silence, and when we assembled at 8 p.m. I didn't exactly expect a party to break out. Zara wasn't there, but Micky was, although she was clutching Amanda's hand as though her life depended on it. Dennis began speaking. He was calm, but his voice lacked its usual resonance and authority, and I guessed he was still firmly rooted in the troubled world of mortals and mortality, and probably morality as well.

"I don't want to talk about what happened, I just want us to commune with the spirits of Doris and Sandy. I don't mean we should hold a séance or anything like that, I'm simply suggesting you take your memories of them and quietly wish them both well. As you know," he swallowed hard, "I spoke about death the other day." Is he, I wondered, going to fill them in on Tinburnell's visit, and even prime them as to what they're going to be asked?

"I want to reiterate that I think ... that I believe totally in what I said, and that Sandy and Doris are now part of that universal consciousness to which we'll all return one day, where we'll exist as one with the energy that suffuses every-thing, animate and inanimate, human and animal. But life has a purpose, and we shouldn't treat it as a mere obstruc-tion to higher things, something to be got out of the way as quickly as possible. I'll say more about this soon. Doris and Sandy have done nothing wrong, and I really don't know precisely why they decided to take their lives."

Micky let out a loud sob and Amanda stroked her back. "But they found their own way forward, and I'd now like us to recognize that and have them with us in our meditation."

The gong donged three times as an accompaniment to Micky's soft cries. She left after a few minutes and Amanda went with her. I was tempted to go myself, because I thought the possibility of being able to meditate was negligible. But, surprisingly, after I cleared my head with some rhythmic breathing, I spent the rest of the session observing a mind that was just about as blank as a meditator could hope for, and although it didn't get me anywhere in the metaphysical sense, it was very relaxing.

After the meditation I went to my room with a cup of tea. My mind was clear and I could see the events of the next day unfold in front of me, and I had the distinct impression my forebodings were accurate. Tinburnell would turn up and would determine, probably by lunch time, that his daughter was influenced to take her own life by Dennis, Ravenswood, the Principality of Wales and any other thing he considered to be worthy of suing. My vision didn't have sufficient acuity to tell me exactly how he would find this out, but I had no doubt he would. I didn't plan to give him any evidence. Not because I sided with Dennis, but simply because I didn't think it was right that Dennis should take the blame. But then I asked myself exactly why Dennis shouldn't take the blame? Did I really think Sandy would have taken her life if Dennis hadn't convinced her that the land of the dead was a great place to be? No, I realized, I didn't, but I still didn't plan to make matters easy for Guy.

I started to feel confused, and I didn't want to be confused because I was tired and wanted to sleep. So I just told myself to trust my intuition and do what felt right, which wasn't much help because my intuition seemed to be telling me the right thing to be was confused. But soon the draining events of the day took their toll, and when I went to bed I feel into a deep, unbroken sleep, from which the only dream I can remember consisted of a not unpleasant scene in which Guy Tinburnell and I visited a brothel, at which the madam didn't make an appearance, but whom I somehow knew, instinctively, to be a transvestite Dennis.

§§§

LIFE, DEATH AND MONEY

The next day dawned bright, but a watery sun didn't look very convincing to my untrained eye. The early morning meditation didn't go particularly well for me, as I was far too expectant about what the day would bring. To all outward appearances, Dennis looked as cool and unruffled as usual, but his eyes were roving continuously, and his detachment seemed to be contrived, almost zombie-like, whereas it had always appeared so natural for him until the events of the previous day rocked his calm.

Everyone was in the meditation room at 7 a.m., and although I didn't know if they were aware of the thunderclouds in the shape of Guy Tinburnell that were, at that very moment, rolling towards us along the M4, I sensed an expectancy in the air that I found hard to limit only to myself and

Dennis. Eventually, the gong marked the end of my unproductive meditation and we left for breakfast. Nobody stuck around, from which I assumed either nobody had really got into it that morning, or the contents of the room at the same time the previous day were still vivid in everyone's minds.

In the dining room, large helpings of food were ladled into mouths. The day before, most of us ate little, and some probably didn't eat at all, but having survived the initial shock, the renewed quest for enlightenment had spurred stomachs into making their emptiness felt, and bulk-bestowing fiber was being peristatically transported to them. Amanda, free at last from Micky's desperate clutches, joined me at a table by the window, where I was sitting on my own.

"How are you?" I asked. I rubbed her arm as I spoke, which was okay for me to do since she pushed sex off the agenda. I have to agree that sex can be such a dominating theme it removes the ability to do certain things without raising complications and miscommunications. But, having said that, although I was playing the "let's just be friends" game for her benefit and public consumption, there was a barely concealed part of me still holding out desperate hopes that frequently washed over and through me.

"I'm fine. How are you? It must have been a terrible shock to be the first one there. I don't know what I'd have done if it had been me."

"It was very tranquil in there. It was only later the full force of it hit me, and by then I couldn't be shocked anymore."

"Why were the police here so long? A girl killed herself when I was at college, and they hardly seemed to be around for any time at all."

I gave her all the reasons I could think of, like the fact Sandy hadn't shown any signs of suicidal tendencies, and the local police didn't see much of this sort of thing so they were making sure they did everything slowly and deliberately. She nodded as I made each point, but as I articulated them, doubts grew in my mind, and I realized there was no good explanation, and that was going to be Dennis' big problem in convincing Tinburnell that he and Ravenswood didn't provide a major influence to Sandy's chosen course of action.

"I dreamt of you last night," she said, snapping me out of my train of thought just about as suddenly and completely as I could be snapped out of anything.

"Oh yes. What did I do?"

She smiled, but said nothing.

"And did I enjoy it? If I didn't, it wasn't accurate."

She laughed, but then looked around furtively and tried to stop herself. I noticed Zara glance in her direction, and Ruben, but whereas Ruben was smiling, Zara wasn't. I felt excited, but forced myself to feel empty. I've had relationships like this before, many of them, in fact, where I harbor lusts and passions long after the object of my interest has turned me down. Women seem to send out so many confusing messages - confusing to me, that is - that I can persist in the belief they may still be interested in getting something going even after they've implied or openly stated they're not. I told myself we were pals, that she was so much younger than me, that I treasured her friendship, that I was old enough to be her father, and then some, but it did absolutely no good at all, and the image of Amanda, naked and passionate in my arms, jumped into my mind's eye and stayed there, and stayed there.

Feelings that remain the same for me throughout the years, frustration and longing, remind me of their chronic potency. Although no food tastes as good as when I was young, no music as stirring, no painting as inspiring, no plea-sure as intense, no flavor as poignant to my jaded palate, I can always rely on frustration and longing to be as stabbing and agonizing as ever.

But our conversation came to an abrupt end, because at that moment, as I looked through the window, a car whooshed into the yard like a roll of brightly colored silk being thrown across a ballroom floor, and stopped, chal-lengingly and insouciantly, in front of the farmhouse. And not just any damn car, but a full-blown bloody Ferrari, and not just any bloody Ferrari, but a brand new, sparkling, red - of course, do serious Ferraris come in any other color? - F130. I imagined it pawing the ground with its wide front tires like an angry bull. Snorting rage and derision from its radiator grill as it challenged any other wheeled vehicle to come out of hiding and take a look at the king of the species.

These cars boast and brag even from the pages of a scruffy, ancient magazine in a dentist's waiting room. The very name jumps at you and raises passions and envies that no other car can match. Although I'm only a halfhearted car aficionado, having a Porsche has thrown me into the pathetic battle played out by owners of cars with a super-car marque, and I have come alternately to embrace and to reject the Ferrari fixation as surely as if one had molested my favorite sister and given me 10 million pounds to keep quiet about it.

Nor did I need to glance at the emerging driver to know

who it was, and even if I had, and even if it had been Elvis Presley, my attention would have been attracted instead by the stilletoed blonde who was getting out of the passenger side, and even if she hadn't been a stunning blonde getting out of a stunning car, I would have been transfixed by the fabulous legs preceding her exit from the clutches of the automotive Lothario, legs displayed from crotch to ankle, as she coped with extricating herself from the low-slung, snarling Italian beast that had enveloped her and transported her here from heaven, via Reading, Swindon and all points west.

By the time I'd recovered, albeit partially and temporarily, from this spectacular vision, I noticed Dennis walk up to Sandy's father and introduce himself. He shook hands with Guy. He shook hands with the woman. No smiles. Dennis turned and led them into the farmhouse and I heard them go into the office and shut the door. Amanda had noticed my distraction, and when I turned to face her she was looking at me.

"Who was that, I wonder?"

"Sandy's father. I used to know him."

"You knew Sandy's father?"

"Yes. I didn't know he was her father until Dennis told me yesterday. He was famous for a while, infamous really, and I drew a cartoon of him that he ended up buying. We got to know each other."

"It must have been one heck of a shock for him."

"What, the cartoon?"

She snorted, and a very nice snort, it was too. "No, hearing about Sandy."

"Yes it must have been. But he's tough. He'll survive. Guy has spent all his life fighting the world."

A few minutes later I got up and wandered out into the yard, but Monica called after me.

"Peter. Washing up I'm afraid."

Dennis came out of his office at the same time.

"Monica," he said "can you get someone to stand in for Peter. Mr. Tinburnell would like to talk to him."

I went back into the house and Dennis opened the office door for me. I walked in, expecting him to follow, but instead he shut the door behind me, with him still on the other side of it. Guy came towards me, hand outstretched, but I was having trouble tearing my eyes away from the expanse of exquisitely shaped leg his companion was managing to exhibit, even without the lecherous Ferrari's help.

"Hello Peter, long time no see. How are you?"

That voice, deep, resonant, gruff, full of confidence, privilege, challenge. No, Guy hadn't changed a bit if his voice was the measure of the man. His face was a little more lined, his girth somewhat broader, and his eyes, although sparkling as they usually did, were sadder than I remember them being, but I assumed this was due to the passing of his daughter and not to the philosophical darkening of the soul that age brings as one of its more questionable benefits. He was a handsome man in a larger than life sort of way. Not a pretty man, but one whose features seemed to hold a story, and to judge from his famous conquests of the opposite sex, the story was a lascivious one.

"I'm fine, thank you Guy. It's good to see you, but not in these circumstances."

"This is Susan Dangerfield, my lawyer."

Well, God the Creator, what a petulant wastrel you are to put a wonderful body like that around a lawyer's cynical brain. She didn't stand up, just shook my hand with her cool and slender digits and stared at me. Perhaps there was a hint of a smile, but nothing more than that. It was more of a visual sniff she gave me than a look, a quick appraisal from which she gathered I was unlikely to taste of anything, and then I was of no more interest. Despite feeling I had made no impact upon her whatsoever, I was disappointed to discover she wasn't Guy's mistress, but perhaps she was - it would be just like Guy to have his employees and amours double up on their roles.

"Peter, what goes on here. In general, I mean?" said Guy.

"Didn't Dennis tell you?"

"I want to hear it from you, please."

The "please" was a mere afterthought, the interrogation had begun and the style had been set.

"It's a retreat centre. People come here for a number of reasons, but I should think a lot just come for a bit of mental recuperation. It's nothing weird, nothing cultish, just a nice place to take some time out and get your thoughts in order."

"Why are you here?"

"Just for that reason. My career's going nowhere, my social life is stuck in a groove. Someone suggested I come here to mull things over, so I did. Butlins may have been just as good, but they haven't opened for the season yet."

"Has it worked for you?"

"Not really, but it's been a break." I spoke as straightforwardly as I could, just as I would have done when the two of us used to meet for dinner. If he thought it was another Peter Wickham standing before him, a hippie twerp who was spouting mystical hogwash, I wouldn't have been able to do Dennis any favors, should I have wanted to. I noticed I was speaking quicker than I had been for the previous few days. Words were tumbling out carelessly because I knew they didn't carry the same weight in the world of Guy as they did at Ravenswood beyond the closed office door, where every utterance was measured and assumed to be valuable. But I reminded myself that even if I was at liberty in this company to prattle, Guy would be attaching his own probing interpretations to whatever I said, or failed to say. His presence had already filled Dennis' office and taken ownership of it, and I assumed he'd do the same to me if I wasn't guarded.

"Didn't Sandy tell you why she came here?" I asked.

"She told me it was to discover herself. To shrug off conditioning and imposed personalities. To get to the truth, uncover her soul, something like that. Fucking claptrap, and I told her so, of course, but I didn't think it would be the death of her."

I put on a surprised expression. "You think Ravenswood

contributed to her death?"

"Of course I do. She may have been a bit loopy at times, but suicidal? Never. How long have you been here?"

"Just over a week."

"Did you have much to do with Sandy?"

"No, we spoke a couple of times, but that was about all. I didn't know she was your daughter until after ... until yesterday."

"Mr. Wickham," said Susan Dangerfield, "did she seem at all unstable to you?" Her face was expressionless as she talked, her voice icily confident. There was a woman who had spent her whole life tying men's tongues in knots, intimidating them through her aloof beauty and intelligence. She stared levelly at me, knowing what thoughts were going through my head as I struggled to keep my eyes from straying to her long, long legs and the mysterious regions from whence they came and to which they led. Why the hell are female legs so fascinating? I've never been even remotely interested in a man's legs, never even had that aesthetic appreciation of them that I could have for a handsome man's face. Why are female legs so damn alluring? Their elbows do nothing for me, nor feet, nor hands, nor even stomachs - making me immune to belly dancers - but shapely legs set my pulse racing before I even realize I'm gaping at them. I used to be passionate about women's breasts, but now fine legs can forgive a flat chest, dull hair and a plain face, not that in the present specimen, Miss Dangerfield, there were any noticeable deficiencies in those areas either, just the opposite.

"No, she was emotional at times, but not suicidal."

"What do you mean by emotional?" she asked.

"She was always bloody crying," said Guy, sparing me from answering. "Nothing unusual in that. If she had nothing to cry about, she'd cry about having nothing to cry about. Same all of her life, like her mother."

"Had the subject of suicide or death been discussed recently"? asked Ms. Dangerfield, her name suddenly striking me as very appropriate as I entered the minefield I'd been expecting and, I then realized, dreading. I knew they would be talking to more people at Ravenswood, and I knew that if those people were true to everything I'd learnt about them so far, they wouldn't lie, so I supposed I wouldn't need to or be able to lie either.

Yet again, for the umpteenth time in a week, I was reminded of what a bloody nuisance the truth can be. It's not lying that causes problems, it's the inability of the truth, no matter how painful, to lie dormant and keeps its nose out of affairs that are proceeding perfectly well without it. Truth can be the most pious, self-righteous busybody. If I'd been able to maintain the lie to my wife and daughter that I'd loved them, or even liked them, or even found them barely tolerable, I could have blundered on with a reasonably contented existence, suffused with occasional sex, a healthy diet and some genuine moments of shared joy and familial warmth. But for some reason I couldn't or wouldn't do it. And who was the hardest person with whom to maintain the lie and reinforce the fiction of slight domestic bliss? Well, myself, of course. My bloody self. The angry little devil who jumps up and down inside of me, himself capable of every whim, deceit and petulance, wouldn't accept being lied to for one moment longer, which opened the floodgates to lawyers, sharp-tongued in-laws, childish insults - both given and received, from both adults and child, mental and physical - alimony, recriminations, surgically bisected kitchen appliances and irascible, slovenly bachelordom.

"Dennis discussed existence in general terms the other day, and life and death came up in that, of course."

"And what did he say about death, exactly?" and when she said "exactly" she meant, as was obvious from her strident emphasis and her chilly demeanor, that exactitude was precisely what she wanted, and nothing less would do. Despite her intoxicatingly obvious attractions, I thought it improbable I was going to like anything else about her, so I had no reason to play up to Ms. Dangerfield.

"Why have you brought your lawyer with you Guy?" I said to him, but looking at her, and half expecting him to say "Because I'm fucking her, you idiot!"

"Isn't it obvious?"

"No, and even if it were, I'd like you to explain it to me."

"I don't believe my daughter was inclined to kill herself, so I find the fact she did extremely fishy, and I'm of a mind to suspect someone or something here caused her or persuaded her to do it, actively or passively. If it was passive, I'll ruin them. If it was active, I'll see them in prison, for a very long time."

"So," said the lawyer, "please answer my question." She had a supercilious smirk on her face, and her eyes were full of contempt and impatience. I was amazed at how clearly I could see it. A week of meditation had obviously heightened my perception of interpersonal communications, although what good that would do me, I couldn't even begin to imagine, ignorance being the bliss that it so frequently is in our coarse and hurtful world.

"I'm sorry Guy. But you and your legal eagle are barking up the wrong tree. I'm very sorry about Sandy, but I've no reason to believe she was induced to do what she did, and ..."

"We're not asking what you believe, Mr. ..., er, Wickham, we're asking what happened."

"Go screw yourself. Go and find a criminal if you want to play Perry Mason. I'm not one, and nor is anyone else here as far as I can judge." I said this coolly, but I leant towards her and glared as I spoke. Women make me feel inferior at the best of times. My daughter, even when she was an incontinent infant, made me feel inadequate, so it's hardly surprising a beauty like Dangerfield had me in a corner from the beginning, and I was now turning a sharp, adolescent tongue on her as my last, clumsy defense. I made to leave.

"Peter," said Guy "I'm sorry, we're pushing too hard, but you can understand my feelings. Please, sit down, there's something you should know."

I sat, absorbing the daggers Susan Dangerfield's eyes were sending in my direction, daggers so sharp I could almost feel them piercing my flesh and deflating my ephemeral self-confidence. She had stopped being attractive. I could still see her legs, and I'd become aware of sizeable breasts, which protruded arrogantly and provocatively from her otherwise slim frame, but her antagonism towards me was so obvious and so intense, though unspoken, that I'd given up any suspicion of having anything other than a highly acrimonious relationship with her, and my lust had subsided under the reality of knowing that if she had any feelings about me at all, they were contemptuous.

"When Cynthia was born - that's her name by the way, Christ knows where 'Sandy' came from - I put two hundred grand in trust for her. In fact I put it under the control of a chap I'd reckoned to be a wizard on the stock market. In five years the fucker had nearly lost the lot, and it was down to under fifty thou, but damn me if it didn't balloon after that on the back on some high-tech stocks he'd banked everything on, and although it's been in less speculative but safer hands for the past 15 years, it's now worth around nine million. It's all her money. I can't touch a penny of it. Despite her best endeavors to piss some of it away on one hare-brained scheme or another, she's barely made a dent in it, so she's ... she was a very rich young lady."

He stopped and I nodded. I saw clouds gathering on the horizon. I didn't know why, but money and death, particularly sudden and unnatural death, don't sit easy together – I'd read enough pulp fiction to know that.

"Three months ago my daughter made a will using some tin-pot solicitor down here somewhere. She told her mother, Belinda, not me. I haven't spoken to Belinda for ages, but she called me soon after hearing from Sandy and told me about it. Frankly I didn't think much about it. She made a will once before and left the bloody lot to some bunch of soft-headed lesbians in Northampton, but I knew she'd rescinded that one and I assumed she'd do the same with this when she left the place and was getting regular sex again. But she hasn't cancelled the will, and who do you think is named as the beneficiary?"

I said nothing.

"Go on, please try to guess."

"You wouldn't be here, telling me this, in this mood, if the answer wasn't Ravenswood."

"Precisely, and she even added the caveat that should Dennis what's-his-name and Ravenswood be parted at the time of her death, the money was to go to him rather than the place, or any recipient of his choosing."

He'd been calm thus far, but now he raised his voice in frustrated anger.

"Peter, can you fucking well believe it?"

I didn't answer. There was nothing I could usefully say.

"So now, perhaps, you can see why I'm so keen to deter-mine whether the admirable Dennis did anything to influence this particular course of events, because it was certainly in the bastard's interest to do so!"

"I can see what you're thinking, and why, but I've no rea-son to believe he tried to persuade Sandy to kill herself. Do you know that he was aware of the will?"

Guy smiled slightly.

"Interesting question," he said. "Yesterday we called the Welsh solicitor, Roberts, who drew up the will, and asked him who was aware of its contents. He blustered a bit, said he couldn't possibly divulge that sort of information, client-attorney privilege blah-de-blah-de-blah-de-bollocks. But Susan can be very persuasive, and she has some powerful contacts in legal circles." The two of them exchanged a conspiratorial grin, and I saw the chemistry flow across the room between them, leaving me in no doubt as to the extent of their relationship beyond matters legal. "Dennis knew alright. Sandy told Roberts she'd made him aware he was a beneficiary. But, funnily enough," he said, grinning again, but this time with a malicious look in his eyes, "Dennis was very vague on the subject when we asked him about it just now."

"Did he deny he knew?"

"Not precisely. He said Sandy had mentioned something of the sort, but he hadn't dwelt on it and certainly didn't know how much it would amount to."

"You don't believe him?"

"Why the hell should I?"

"Because it could be true."

"Yes, and it could be complete hogwash, and that's where I'm betting my money right now. Don't misunderstand me, Peter. The moolah isn't the issue. It wasn't mine and Sandy could do what the hell she liked with it. She could have given it to the lesbians or any other crackpot cause that took her fancy. But if that bastard talked my daughter into killing herself so he could get his hands on her cash, I'll put every ounce of my being into making sure he pays the price for it, because he as good as murdered her." He dropped his head and looked at the floor.

"So," said Ms. Dangerfield, "would you now like to answer my question?"

"Which was?"

"What did he say about death, exactly?"

"I don't remember. Ask Dennis."

"He has a personal interest in giving a biased answer."

"And you have personal interest in applying a biased interpretation to what I, or anyone else, says."

"Are you saying you won't answer my question."

"I have answered your question, not that I had to. You may not like my answer, you may not believe my answer, but my answer remains the same. I do not remember exactly what he said, and given the importance you seem to attach to my answer by asking me the question repeatedly, I'm damned if I'm going to dredge up something from my memory that could be wholly inaccurate.

"Guy, for all I know your suspicions are absolutely correct. Maybe Dennis found out Sandy was rich, maybe he got her to make a will naming him as beneficiary, maybe he persuaded her she should kill herself, maybe he laid on the pills and vodka, maybe he even fed them to her and hung around to make sure it all went according to plan. I can't say that any of that didn't happen, but if you're asking for my opinion, I would say that two people, for their own reasons, decided that death looked better than life and chose to investigate.

"Doris was terminally ill and probably had an easier

decision to make, but in Sandy's case, I don't know what her thinking was, and I believe, yes believe, because I don't know," I said this looking at the lawyer, "that Dennis was as surprised as the rest of us, and I certainly don't think he's happy about it. He doesn't give me the impression of a man who's seen his plan work out and is now dreaming of what to do with the loot. I think he's devastated, and the one thing I do remember is how he looked when I broke the news to him, and if that wasn't a look of shock, then I don't know what is. Perhaps he does think the soul-searching some of the people here subject themselves to could have affected her deeply. Perhaps he does blame himself, but only in the way we all blame ourselves for not noting some sign of what she was planning, no matter how deeply it was hidden. But ..." I paused. I was talking too much.

"What?"

"No, I've finished. I didn't know her, and to be honest I'm not grieving that much - she was a stranger, and it would be phony for me to start wailing and gnashing my teeth. But some of these people are deeply distraught about it, and if any of them had suspected something fishy, they would have raised it by now."

"Unless they were part of it," said Guy.

"Yeah, okay, well if you're into conspiracy theories I'm probably part of it too, me and Lee Harvey Oswald, so why bother asking my opinion?"

"We're not asking for your opinion. We're asking for facts," said Susan.

"Oh, okay, well you've had them." I got up to leave, again.

"We have some more questions for you," she said, coolly.

"But I don't have any more answers."

"Peter," said Guy, "let me be open with you. Please sit down, this won't take a moment but I'd like you to hear it."

I sat, with a sigh, and he sighed too, then continued.

"I have three children by Belinda and two by the wife who followed her. Sandy was my eldest child, but, to be honest, my least favorite. She was born at a time when having a family was a low priority for me. I was more intent on making money and getting the power and influence that goes with it, and my neglect of my kids, particularly Sandy, has been re-paid by them feeling nothing for me and, in her case, treating me and people like me with a large amount of contempt.

"A few years ago she heard of some fucking nutcase kid in the States who had tried to divorce himself from his par-ents, and although she was well past the age of majority at the time, she told me she wanted to do the same, just as a gesture to show me what a subterranean form of lowlife she thought I was." He shrugged and spread his hands. "What can I do? I'm a greedy capitalist, always have been. You know my life history. I've been dedicated to making money since before I could walk, and I still don't see anything wrong with it. I love making money for Christ's sake! Who the hell was she to deny me that fundamental liberty? Anyway, we'd rubbed along a bit better over the past couple of years, but only because she'd mellowed. I'm not aware I've changed at all, or ever will. I'm not devastated by her death, but I am sad about it, because if her mellowing process had continued, she might, just might, have got to like me a bit by the time she was 30 or so. By middle age she may have understood me, and if she ever got as far as seeing out her days in a comfortable nursing home, rather than in some shabby council shit hole, she might even have thanked me for the wealth I'd built up on her behalf, and which she was patently incapable of building up by herself. But, as it's turned out, she won't do any of these things, and she's thrown the final insult at me by leaving her money to some brain-addled creep who probably feels the same about me as she did at her worst."

I went to interrupt, to tell him that hate and derision weren't Dennis' style, but he silenced me with a raised hand.

"Just let me ask you this," he said. "If Dennis is such a high-minded hero, wouldn't his reaction be to say 'Okay. Money's not important to me. If you want it so badly, take it'? He could rub my nose in it and maintain his lofty, unquestionable, otherworldly superiority. Why wouldn't he do that, rather than risk being ridiculed and dragged through the courts, upsetting his karma for the next few lifetimes?"

"I don't know, Guy," I said, with a strong note of exasperation, "but if he knows he's done nothing wrong, why should he? Philosophers need money as much as anyone, to some degree, and Dennis isn't exactly dripping with cash." Out of the corner of my eye I noticed Dangerfield scribble something on her legal pad, but I pressed on. "If he thinks Sandy made the will in all earnestness, and knows he didn't contrive to make her kill herself, why should he refuse the money and ignore her wishes? And anyway, how do you know he won't refuse the money, once he's had time to think it over? All this has been so sudden. He may decide to deny the bequest when he's considered his options," or lack of them, I thought to myself, once Guy begins to tighten his litigious screws on Dennis' testicles.

"His options being prison and/or ignominy - an outcast from the mystic elite," said Guy.

"His options being blamelessly taking a freely made gift or being bullied out of it by you," said I.

Guy snorted to show disbelief, and then went on to tell me why he believed his snort was the more suitable rejoinder.

"Well, Peter, I can assure you he didn't come across to Susan and I as a man who's going to roll over and let me take the money. I think he can already see that parade of neat black digits in his bank account, and he likes the look of them. What did he say, Susan?"

"He said 'If your daughter meant the money to go to Ravenswood, then that's where it should go'".

"And when he said it, Peter, he looked as though he was ready to fight for it."

"Why shouldn't he? Dennis doesn't know you from Adam. Why should he just let you storm in here and intimidate him into doing something against Sandy's wishes. Put yourself in his position. If he's done nothing wrong, why should he look a gift horse in the mouth?"

"You really are on his side aren't you?"

"No, I'm not on any side. I hadn't seen it as a battle until you got saddled up for action and stormed in with Sancho Panza here. I just think you've got an extreme and slightly screwy view." I didn't think either of them would appreciate the quixotic allusion, although it seemed appropriate from my perspective. Guy ignored it, and Dangerfield just shook her head disparagingly.

"So how do we get to the truth?" he asked.

"What constitutes the truth?"

"How do I find out the circumstances in which Sandy made her will?"

"Well, I'm sure you can talk to anybody here who's willing to talk to you, and you'd better go and see the solicitor you mentioned."

"And can I ask you to do me a personal favor, Peter?"

"You can ask."

"Will you try and find out the truth for me, too?"

I stopped to think. In all honesty, I was interested in finding out what really happened, if anything, and I also reckoned that if Guy thought I was working on his behalf as an insider, I might be able to influence him if he looked like getting carried away.

"Well, okay. I don't mind doing that, but if I come up with anything that doesn't suit your purposes, I assume you'll ignore it."

He guffawed.

"Oh, Peter, ever the cynic."

"It goes with the territory."

"Yes, indeed, and I see you haven't lost your touch. I always look out for your drawings."

"Well, you must be looking bloody hard, because I haven't had a lot published lately in anything you're likely to browse through, unless you've developed a passion for reading Model Railway News, or maybe you saw something I did for Real Estate World recently, page 83 I think it was, an absolute blockbuster."

"You really haven't changed, have you, despite your newly acquired spiritual aspirations."

"I don't have spiritual aspirations, just physical encumbrances."

"We must have dinner again when you're back in London. I used to enjoy our meetings."

"Even if I don't help you prove your point?"

"Especially then. I'll need to have my spirits raised."

§§§

DIGGING

I left the office, made myself a cup of coffee and wandered around for while, thinking. Did I want to prove Dennis blameless, or guilty? Did I want to prove Guy right, or wrong? Was I batting for one team or bowling for the other? I had no clear idea. I'd come to respect Dennis, and like him, but if Guy was right, and if his most cynical scenario was correct, then the Dennis I'd come to like was no more real than one of my grossly distorted cartoons. I would probably also have liked a crafty, conniving, duplicitous version of Dennis, and up until a week beforehand I would have said that this version, full of human frailty and self-interested deception, was more my cup of tea than the paragon of virtue I'd known since coming to Ravenswood. But I supposed I needed to determine which was the real man, so that at least my friendship was being bestowed on the correct image.

Having justified the investigation, how was I to carry it out? I thought that just by hanging around and keeping my eyes and ears open I'd possibly learn something, but that could take forever, and given Dennis knew I was a friend of Guy's, he wasn't going to take me into his confidence or let me hear of anything that supported his guilt, if guilty he was. The more I thought about it, the more Micky's image drifted into my mind. Given her grief at Sandy's death, I believed she might have some answers, but as she and I had barely spoken since I'd been there, it was going to be difficult to get intimate with her all of a sudden.

In an attempt to regain normalcy and "commence the healing process" (Monica's words) we had reverted to the usual timetable, which meant I found myself alongside Bob digging in the patch that we had christened "Ken's folly".

"So," he said, "what's going on?"

"How do you mean?"

"I understand the chap who came this morning is Sandy's father."

"Yes, I used to know him, well, I still do know him. He just wanted to get my version of events."

"Oh," he said, with raised eyebrows.

"What's up?" I asked.

"Well, why should he need more than one version of what happened?"

He was fishing, of course, but so was I. I wanted to know

if there was suspicion in any head apart from Guy's, and if anybody there was realistic enough to look for the less than perfect in his fellow mortals, apart from Zara - who seemed to assume it was there even without looking - it was Bob.

"He's baffled as to why it happened, having had no idea Sandy was suicidal."

"Mmm, and who was the woman?"

"His lawyer."

"Why did he bring his lawyer?"

"I don't know about you, but if I had a lawyer who looked like that, I'd take her everywhere she was willing to go. I'm sure I could find a use for her in almost any setting, though not necessarily a legal use, or even a lawful one."

"Are they still here?"

"Yes, you'll know when they go. Ferraris have a habit of leaving a palpable vacuum behind them, and making a lot of noise in the process."

"What're they doing?"

"I think they're talking to Micky."

"Why?"

"What is this, Twenty Questions? I don't know. Was Micky close to Sandy?"

"Well, yes, well." He found a reason to dig a spot about

six inches from my right foot, and somehow managed to do it with his mouth no more than two inches from my right ear. "They had a bit of a fling, I think. Well, you know, sex is supposed to be kept out of things here, but I think they were both, well, you now, that way inclined, and there were, well, rumors, and, well, you know what I mean."

"I see, I think. But it was over, was it?"

"I thought so. I believe Dennis put his foot down, gently, of course, and asked them to cut it out. Must have been about the time you arrived. Sandy burst into tears one day in the dining room. Were you here then?" I nodded. "Yes, that was about when they agreed to stop, well, stop ..." he giggled, so did I. Two middle-aged men chuckling like schoolboys over a pair of lesbians, each conjuring up a mental image of exactly what they had stopped doing to each other.

We dug in silence for a while.

"You don't have to tell me if you don't want to," he said.

"Tell you what?"

"There's something going on, I know that."

"Well Bob, you are an astrologer. If you don't know what's going on and what will become of it, it's a pretty poor advertisement for your profession."

"Come on, what is it? I heard raised voices when Dennis had them in the office, and why were the police here so long? Is there something that doesn't hang together about it all?"

If I'd just said no, I wouldn't have got any more out of him, so I had to keep his interest alive.

"Well, there's something that has to be resolved, but I really can't say what, you'll have to ask Dennis, it's his concern, not mine."

But instead of taking my bait and telling me what he knew, he just continued probing, from which I assumed he knew nothing of any importance.

As I walked back to the farmhouse at lunchtime, Guy and Susan Dangerfield emerged.

"Peter, we're leaving, but I'll be back." The lawyer prepared to lever herself into the car, and despite the barely suppressed hostility between us, I would have liked to watch her doing it, and maybe even offer my assistance by supporting any part of her body she needed to have supported. But Guy grabbed my elbow and led me in a wide arc that would arrive at the driver's-side door. He spoke in a voice only I could hear.

"Peter, did you know that Sandy and Micky were lovers?"

"I found out about half an hour ago. I'm told it ended last week."

"I don't attach any significance to it. Sandy had more lovers, of both sexes, than I've had hot lawyers." He paused for me to acknowledge his joke and his machismo, so I duly obliged with a lecherous grin, taking the opportunity to cast another glance in the direction of those wonderful limbs.

"The girl, Micky, obviously thinks that ending their affair

might have tipped Sandy over the edge, but I've told her I believe that interpretation to be unlikely in the extreme, and although Sandy wouldn't have admitted it, and Micky didn't like to hear it, Sandy was mainly interested in sex, not love. Oh, sure, she always claimed it was much deeper and likely to be everlasting, but I think she was just bloody randy, like her old man, except I'm on the straight and narrow, not in the candle and cucumber brigade. Despite our differences, I understood Sandy better than anyone, because we were so alike, which probably explains our disagreements. Anyway, I just thought you should know, because if anyone tries explaining Sandy's death away through a failed love affair, it's bollocks, okay?"

He got into the car with surprising agility, given his girth and the fact that Ferraris are designed to accommodate sprightly Italians whose bulges are in altogether different places, and of a temporary nature.

"Nice car." I said, as if he needed me to tell him that; as if "nice" is an adequate adjective when used in the same sentence as "Ferrari".

"Are you still driving a Porsche?"

"Well, as usual, it's more likely to be found up on jacks than being driven, but yes, I still own it."

"Tell you what," he said, lowering his voice "if you help me out with this, to the extent you get us the right result," he nodded with raised eyebrows, forcing me to nod back in admission I understood what constituted the right result, "I'll give you this car, how's that?"

I would like to have asked if I could have Ms. Dangerfield's body as well, preferably without her disdainful demeanor.

"I'll do as we agreed, no more and no less. But if you want to give me the Ferrari, feel free, 'right result' or not."

"I'll be happy to get rid of it," he said, levering himself into the sleek, red monster. "I'm keeping Armani in business with all the trousers I've split getting in and out of the damn thing."

He turned the ignition, and four and a half liters of automotive perfection roared into life, sending a powerful throbbing through the sleek chassis to vibrate sensuously under the glorious, taut thighs of Ms. Susan Dangerfield.

§

The departure of the Ferrari and its no less beguiling passengers left a gaping hole in the day. Or perhaps it was a whiff of the outside world and ordinary people that reminded me Ravenswood was a very different variety of existence and, recent events notwithstanding, a less exciting one than that peopled by red-blooded sports cars and sublimely elegant females.

Everything was still low-key, and we just got on with silent meditations. No reporting-in, no speeches from Dennis, just breathing and the metta thing, which is where I tried to have good feelings about myself and anyone else I could drag into the imaginary, Platonic love-in. I really got into the metta at the last session of the day, by which I mean I actually started to generate some warm feelings, which made me feel nice and cozy, but I couldn't imagine it was taking me anywhere along the spiritual path - it just felt like I was ladling great spoonfuls of undeserved, self-indulgent complacency over myself. It was as though I was lying in a warm bed, stewing in syrupy self-congratulation, rather than getting up, taking a cold shower, confronting my problems and getting on with my life. If nothing else, my reaction to some successful metta proved I felt bad about myself even when I was feeling good about myself, which was illuminating. And when I shone my metta on Ms. Dangerfield, as a way of dampening our mutual hostility, instead of intro-spection I got an embarrassing e-rection.

§

I had developed a quite repetitive ritual throughout the days, and I can't say I disliked it. Routine usually frightens me because it's too easy, time slips by unnoticed and I feel as though I could suddenly find myself being 80-years-old and about to snuff it. I usually keep disorganization as a vital part of my life so that I notice time passing. But at Ravenswood I seemed to be running comfortably on tracks, and although I had no idea where the tracks led, it was pleasant to just peer out of the window and disengage my brain.

My nightly ritual consisted of getting a hot drink after the last session and drinking it in my room as I browsed through one of the many books that populated Ravenswood, some of which were extremely weird and some intimidatingly erudite; books I wouldn't normally have dared open, but somehow I'd started to get a taste for them, even though I didn't always make much headway.

Somebody there must have had a passion for William Blake, because although I don't know how much he produced himself, there seemed to be books in the library on just about every facet of his life and talents. How great an author do you have to be before there are more books writ-

ten about you than books you wrote yourself? How great
an artist before there are more books about you than your
pictures in galleries? How great a person before other people spend more time investigating and recounting your life
than you spent living it? On this reckoning, Mozart must be
in a strong position, given he died in his thirties, and if you
add up all the time he's stolen from other people' lives - from
biographers, to musicians, to kids slaving agonizingly over
piano or scratchy violin practice - his own brief life looks like
a bright spark that lit a raging fire of artistic endeavor and
music teachers' torment.

That night the heavens opened and I spent some time
gazing out the window of my room. I couldn't see anything
because it was pitch black, but it was a muggy night so I had
the window open in order to smell the rain and the vegeta-
tion it was soaking. I was about to go to bed when I heard a
familiar tapping. I say familiar, because having lived in some
very old and crumbly buildings over the years, I know a leaking roof when I hear one. I turned from the window to see
water dripping from a damp patch in the ceiling and making
a similar patch in the middle of the floor. I went out onto the
landing. There was a stairway at the end I'd never been up,
but I climbed it now in the hope of finding where the water
was coming from. I emerged onto the top floor of the building, which was once the attic but had been converted into
extra living space.

I walked along the landing trying to get my bearings and
work out what part of the roof corresponded to the area
above my room. The noise of the rain was loud up there, as
it drummed off the roof and gurgled along the gutters and
into the drainpipes. A door to a room was slightly ajar, and a
faint light was coming from within. I walked past the doorway,
but couldn't stop myself from looking in. The only light in the

room was being cast by a candle, but it was enough to see a bed. On top of the bed I saw a woman on her hands and knees. Behind her was a man. He too was on his knees, but his hands were encircling the woman, cupped around her large breasts as they swung to and fro. If it hadn't been for the rain, I dare say I would have been able to hear the rhythmic squidge of Dennis' penis sliding in and out of Micky's vagina.

§

Well, that was it then. Dennis and Micky had plotted the whole thing. When Sandy's lesbian tendencies were unmasked and they learnt she was filthy rich, Micky conspired to have a relationship with her, while Dennis worked on her from the "glory of death" angle. The combination of Dennis' powerful evangelism and Micky's luscious loins, combined with Sandy's gullibility for things spiritual and sexual, helped them persuade her to bequeath her fortune to Ravenswood. They then hit her with a three-pronged attack - Dennis made her feel guilty about the sex, Micky terminated the relationship, and Dennis stepped up the focus on death being a good thing, enlisting the help of the unwitting Doris for whom death probably was a good thing. The means of skipping gaily off into the afterlife were laid conveniently at Sandy's disposal, any lingering doubts were dispelled by Dennis' tour de force sermon of a few days previously, and the trap was set. Apart from the fine detail, Guy had it absolutely right.

Or ...

... the coupling of Dennis and Micky was a complete coincidence, as was the will, as was the suicide, as was the Sandy/Micky affair, and Guy was barking loudly and aggressively up the wrong tree. Although I shouldn't have read too much into the erotic hanky-panky being played out a few yards above my head, it changed things dramatically, not because it necessarily meant anything in itself, but because it exposed Dennis as a hypocrite - a man who frowned on sex as an obstruction to the spiritual path, but then shafted the lesbian lover of the deceased disciple the day following her demise. And I know it sounds fatuous, but although I might have been able to forgive the missionary position as a bit of sex for comfort, two wounded souls trying to put their feelings back in order with some physical metta, the vigorously pursued doggy position spoke more of animal lust and carnal craving.

I slept badly, not least because the scenes I'd witnessed left me aroused mentally and physically. When I did drift off, I dreamt that as I lay in bed, the leak that had been dripping onto my floor turned into a huge torrent of semen that burst through the ceiling and caused my bed to float away on a wide river of spunk through a vast, desolate landscape.

§§§

OUTLANDISH IMPRESSIONS

I woke up the next day with a thick head, and my eyes immediately scanned the ceiling. Ostensibly I was looking to see if there was water seeping through, but my mind pushed its focus beyond the soggy plaster and constructed an endless variety of images, the common denominators of which were the tightly engaged bodies of last night's protagonists. My first thought was I should confront Dennis, tell him I knew he was a closet fornicator, and infer that one dropped standard could lead to another, and perhaps he was more involved in Sandy's death than he claimed, but at that moment I experienced something unwelcome. Fear.

If Dennis really did usher Sandy to her death, what he did was tantamount to murder, and although the legal system would probably come up with some other description - like manslaughter or assisted suicide - how far was it from what he did to Sandy to keeping me quiet by taking a sledgehammer to my head, as I slept a drugged sleep under the influence of doctored rosehip and hibiscus?

Ravenswood was his territory, surrounded by alien countryside and dozy policemen. I doubted he would have any difficulty engineering my disappearance. But this was stupid, more like an Agatha Christie novel than real life. I tried to push the fear from my mind, but it wouldn't go away. What it did serve to do, however, was convince me I wouldn't confront him, and although I went on to tell myself this was a more prudent form of action for getting at the truth, I couldn't shrug off the firmly rooted suspicion that cowardice was making this decision for me. Funny really, I don't have any problem in admitting openly I'm a coward, but when I'm reminded of it in private and experience the pathetic, clammy feelings it invokes, I feel ashamed.

Scene after scene played itself out in my mind as I scrambled to find the appropriate course of action. Perhaps Dennis would come clean, tell me, or even the whole group, that he screwed Micky last night in a fit of desperation or desecration and was now seeking our forgiveness. Perhaps Micky would die mysteriously, as Dennis disposed of the one person who could expose his lethal fraud to the world. Perhaps someone else would come up with a fact that proved what happened, incontrovertibly, one way or the other. But as I considered these variations, none of them seemed likely, and what was most probably going to happen was nothing, unless I rooted around productively and didn't get discovered in the process. That's another shitty thing about life, about my shitty life anyway. Solutions, like randy women, never fall into your lap, you have to go out and get them, enduring endless trials, tribulations, humiliations and expenses in the process. Nothing has really changed since Hercules' time.

At the first meditation session of the day, Dennis made his appearance with no unusual manifestations. I studied his face and saw nothing out of place, no guilt, no sparkle, no deceit was written there, from which I inferred, by turns, that he was a master of deception, or that he had nothing to feel guilty about, except an opportunistic bit of nooky that had no connection with other events. But in the end I came down on the negative side and gave Dennis the benefit of my disdain.

I really wanted to talk to someone about all this, so that I could get things into perspective and generate a few ideas. All I had at the time were the extreme points of view of Dennis and Guy, and they were so far apart I found myself swinging crazily from one to the other. The only person I felt I could trust, both to offer sound advice and not go blabbing to all and sundry, was Amanda. But would she really thank me for dumping the problem on her? If I disclosed to Amanda all the gory details, which I would be compelled to do if she was to have the whole picture, it would probably subvert her opinion of, and respect for, Dennis.

At breakfast, I went and sat by myself. I didn't feel capable, in my state of confusion, of maintaining the sort of spaced out conversation that took place at Ravenswood. To make it worse, I felt like an enemy agent, as though Guy Tinburnell had "turned" me and I was now in the pay of the enemy. I didn't think I could look anyone in the face without flinching and giving the game away. But, my intention of cloaking my possible betrayal in solitude was ruined when Ken came and sat opposite me, intent on talking.

"You knew Sandy's old man then?"

Again I told the story about the cartoon, in the hope that describing our past relationship would stop him asking about the present one.

"What did he want with you yesterday?"

"To know if I had any particular insights on what happened."

"Such as?"

"Such as nothing. I don't have any. I just told him what happened."

"Didn't he believe Dennis?"

"Yes, I expect so. He just asked me because he knew me - sort of a reality check, I suppose." I regretted using the stupid phrase as soon as it came out of my mouth.

"Reality check? What the fuck would you know about reality that Dennis doesn't?"

"Guy doesn't know Dennis, but he knows me. He wanted an unbiased view of what goes on here."

"And why are you more likely to give him that than Dennis?"

As usual with Ken, his tone was condescending and hostile. I knew I should hold my temper. If I was going to get to the bottom of this business - if, indeed, there was a bottom to be got to - I had to be seen as being calm and disinterested, but Ken had irritated me severely.

"Jesus, Ken. I'm buggered if I know. He asked for my point of view and I gave it to him. He's entitled to a second opinion isn't he? His daughter's just killed herself, surely he can ask a few questions. Anyway, what the fuck has it got to do with you?"

To my surprise, he backed off straight away.

"Yeah, you're right. I'm just being bloody nosy."

We were silent for a while, but I knew he was up to something, so it was only a matter of time before he started talking again.

"Do you think it's a bit fishy?" he asked.

"What do you mean, 'fishy'?"

"You know that Dennis stood to make a packet if Sandy died?"

Surprised by his openness, I looked round to see he wasn't being open at all - everyone else had left the dining room and we were alone.

"Yes, I do now."

"Is that what her old man was digging for? To see if Dennis had a hand in it?"

Ken's whole demeanor had changed. His normal arrogance had disappeared and there was a friendly, conspiratorial, almost humble look about him. That, more than anything, put me on my guard.

"No, he just wanted my version of what goes on here, my impression of how Sandy was behaving, my story of how she was found."

"Why would he want to know that if he wasn't suspicious?"

I sighed, but seeing what was coming, he spoke before I could rebuke him again.

"I'm not trying to put you in an awkward spot. It's just, well, it's just a bit funny, the whole business, I mean, it makes you wonder, don't it?"

"It makes you wonder what?"

"Well, Dennis is a millionaire now, and after what he said the other night about death, well ..."

"Are you suggesting Dennis planned all this?"

"No. No, of course not. No," he quickly replied, almost stammering his words. "But you can understand her father thinking it's a bit, well, you know ..."

"You can't have a very high opinion of Dennis to be thinking along these lines," I said. If that didn't draw him into the open, I didn't know what would.

"I call a spade a spade. I believe what I see, and if I see someone winning the fucking football pools, I wonder if he saw today's papers yesterday."

"Well, I can't help you there, I'm afraid," I said, making to leave.

"Is he coming back?"

"Who?"

"Sandy's old man."

"I don't know," I said, leaving. I hadn't really thought clearly about what was going to happen over the coming days. I supposed the next thing would be the funeral, or maybe an inquest, and I was sure Guy wouldn't wait until either of those unwelcome events before he contacted me again.

I walked outside. The sun was trying to shine, but the sky was predominantly cloudy and there were occasional, half-hearted spots of rain dripping out of the sky – I had noticed the Welsh clouds seemed to be incontinent, unable to restrain themselves from leaking even when they didn't seem to be dark enough to be rain clouds. But I couldn't accuse the weather of not being able to make up its mind, given the difficulties I was having with the same exercise.

On the face of it, Ken was a potential ally who could help me find out the extent of Dennis' involvement in Sandy's death, but my overwhelming impression was he was trying to find out what doubts I and Guy Tinburnell had, and he would convey this assessment back to Dennis. I had no reason for thinking this, as I had no clear idea of his relationship with Dennis, but for the sake of caution it seemed sensible to assume everyone was on Dennis' side, and I should trust no-one. I realized at some point I'd become committed to do as Guy had asked. It surprised me I'd come to this decision, but at least it was a relief to know which side of the fence I was standing on.

§

Monica called from the farmhouse to tell me somebody wanted to speak to me on the telephone. It was Guy.

"Peter, can we meet?"

"Yes, when?"

"This afternoon, but I don't want to meet you there, and it's best if we're not seen to be hobnobbing."

"Well, I'm a bit restricted. If I can't walk there I can't get there."

"Meet me at the end of the lane at two."

"Which lane? Everything round here is a bloody lane once you get off the M4."

"Just keep walking until you get to tarmac, it can't be more than half a mile."

"Guy, half a mile in a Ferrari is a day's march for lazy sods like me. Alright, I'll see you there at two."

I set off at 1:30, believing it was at least two miles to the end of the lane. But I hadn't been that way since my gloomy arrival, and my impression from over a week previously was obviously colored by Roger's oppressive company, because it turned out to be much less than that, and I was there with 10 minutes to spare. I didn't expect Guy's lover/lawyer to be with him, and she wasn't - three is definitely a crowd in a Ferrari, and even the most robust gooseberry would be crushed to a pulp - but I thought it only polite to ask after her.

"Where's La Dangerfield?"

"Running errands."

I laughed.

"What's funny?"

"Women like that don't run errands any more than they do chores. I can't imagine Ms. Dangerfield at a sink somewhere, wringing out her knickers, or yours either, come to that."

"Well, she's not exactly involved in domestic tasks, but she is doing some valuable leg work on my behalf."

The thought of anything to do with Susan Dangerfield's legs was worthy of further discussion, as I'm sure Guy intended it to be.

"The mind boggles," I said. "Snooty bitch, isn't she?"

"Yes, very, but when you penetrate that snootiness," he stressed the word "penetrate", or perhaps I just heard it louder than the rest of the sentence, "you find a heart of gold."

"And a crock of gold too, I suppose, or should that be a crotch of gold."

He gave me a knowing leer.

"Where are you taking me?"

"There's a tea shop near here, I thought we could talk there. The nearest pub is five miles away and the landlord is a poisonous, nosey bastard, so I'd rather steer clear of him and his watery bloody beer."

"Five miles between pubs? I didn't know that was a physical possibility. Doesn't it break some immutable law of nature?"

"You should get out into the world more. Such laws are suspended when you get out in the sticks, Peter. Didn't you know that? All life that's worth living grinds to a halt when you cross the M25 moat."

We pulled onto a main road and eventually came to a hamlet that advertised itself as having some sort of attraction in terms of an "Enchanted Grotto", in Gothic script, of course. At the head of the byroad leading to this spectacle was a car park and "Linda's Tea Rooms". Whether this enchanted location had ever seen elves and fairies before was open to question, but it most certainly had never seen a Ferrari, and Guy's car swaggered into the car park like a hot-blooded Italian sex fiend looking for pubescent virgins.

Once inside Linda's quaint establishment, Guy, who hadn't eaten since breakfast, ordered a cholesterol-saturated cream tea. I made do with the liquid part only.

"So," he asked, "what's happening at the funny farm?"

"Nothing."

"Something surely. People don't just die and leave a place without a trace."

"Oh, everyone is pretty down, but it's business as usual. Well, apart from Dennis buying a brand new Mercedes and dancing naked to Julio Iglesias records."

"Haven't you done any digging for me? You're not going

to win my Ferrari by sitting on your arse."

I thought of the work detail, digging the new vegetable garden under Ken's crusty tutelage, and although Bob wanted to gossip as we dug, I couldn't imagine this was really the sort of excavation that would interest Guy.

"I'm keeping my eyes and ears open, but I can't just turn into Sherlock Holmes overnight. Everyone there associates me with you, so if I start asking pointed questions too soon they're bound to smell a rat."

"Okay, but don't leave it too long. The trail will go cold after a while. You're more likely to discover something while emotions are running high. After a few days Dennis will have had the chance to work on the floaters, but if there are doubts in anyone's mind, you're more unlikely to uncover them while there's still a bit of shock and horror in the air."

"Thanks for the advice, Inspector Maigret."

"Tell me, Peter, ever heard of 'Zoragaia'?"

"Yes, of course, hemorrhoid ointment, very effective, I use it all the time. It's also surprisingly good on buttered toast, tastes a bit like anchovy essence, assuming the anchovies have been fished out of an oil spill or sewage effluent."

"No, really, do you know what it is?"

"It rings a bell, but no, you'll have to tell me, and I assume you're going to."

"Zoragaia is the belief that, amidst all those billions of stars and trillions of planets, there is, by statistical inference, tremendously intelligent life in the universe. Life that has developed along similar lines to our own, but which is millions of years ahead of us. These Zoragaians live on some remote planet with a lifestyle so advanced we can't even imagine it. They discovered us eons ago but, being highly enlightened beings, they realized if they introduced themselves to we pathetic earthlings, it would completely fuck us up, much as we fuck up tribes of savages when we discover them in Borneo or somewhere - you know, give them syphilis and influenza, and pollute them with Coca Cola, pizza, the Rolling Stones and Marlboro.

"So the Zoragaians just watch us, partly to learn how they themselves developed at this extremely primitive stage of their evolution, but also to guide us and make sure we don't destroy ourselves. The theory contends they're watching us all the time, and if some nutter is about to do something that would destroy the earth or cause it irreparable damage, they intercede, but only by influencing people unconsciously. One idea is that they interceded over the Cuban missile crisis for example, that they got inside the Russians' heads at the Politburo and caused them to step down, knowing that a conflict would destroy the world and put an end to their experiment in observation."

"Fascinating," I say. "I wouldn't have taken you for a reader of the tabloid press."

"If you start looking for crackpot theories on the Internet, you'll find 10,000 of them before lunch. Of course, the beauty of all of them is you can't disprove them, so the lunatics who dream them up in the first place can never be proved wrong."

"Do you believe it, Guy? With ideas like that you'd fit in well at Ravenswood. Tell you what, I'll drive you back there then drive myself back to London in your Ferrari. You can have my room, no charge."

"You'll get the Ferrari when you've done your job, not before. Look, humor me on this, OK?"

"As you like, but you don't really expect me to believe, and you surely can't believe, that a new age superspecies of Zoragaians is out there watching us. Have they got antennae that tune into our conversations? What will they do to me when they hear I'm not fooled?"

Guy sighed. "They're not Martians. They have technology which is way beyond anything we pea-brains can imagine. It's a piece of piss for them to look inside our puny heads and see what we're thinking before we think it. If North Korea ever decides to unleash a hydrogen bomb on the decadent capitalists, the Zoragaians will have Kim Jong Whatsit by the balls before he can press the plunger, and he won't even know they're doing it."

"Spooky."

"It would be if it was true, having some megabrained gook watching one in one's most intimate moments," he said.

Talk of intimate moments caused an erotic scene comprising Guy, Miss Dangerfield and the Ferrari to begin to coalesce in my mind, but it quickly evaporated, though whether it was because the tea arrived or because the Zoragaians thought this particular smutty image was extremely dangerous and terminated it, I would never know.

"Okay, it's a load of bollocks," I summarized. "Can we

take the straight road to the point of all this, rather than scenic route?

"There are any number of groups with similar theories, most of them based in the US, all playing mind games with the same 'God was a spaceman' idea, and if you ..."

"Jesus!" I said.

"What?"

"The suicide note. That's where I've seen the word, Zoragaia. I knew it was familiar from somewhere. So ..." I could almost hear my brain ticking as it tried to come to terms with what this meant, but although there must have been some conclusion to be drawn somewhere, I just seemed to wallow in empty space for a while. "So Sandy was, what? Being instructed by Zoragaians to kill herself, or ... Christ, help me here Guy. It sounds like it ought to be important, but what's it got to do with Sandy's death?"

"The people who believe in all this garbage would argue that Zoragaians give us complete free will, both out of respect for us and because it would influence their impartial observations otherwise, so they would never persuade someone to kill themselves, unless that person was intent on fucking up the world in a pretty big way. And although I have the greatest respect for Sandy's skills in screwing up boutiques, bistros and the other poxy little businesses she tried to start, I don't think she posed any sort of major threat to world order, unless I've seriously underestimated her and her hair-brained chums.

"The Zoragaian fan club is divided on the subject of death. One school of thought believes death is just what we think it is, and another group believes the Zoragaians rescue dead souls and zoom them back to their planet, where they let them in on the secret and give them blissful life everlasting."

"Zoragaia must be a damn big planet if it's full of dead earthlings."

"Peter, you're just betraying how feeble your brain is. Zoragaians solved all those trivial real estate problems countless millennia ago."

"Yes, I was letting my terrestrial limitations get the better of me."

He took a huge bite out of a warm and crumbly scone he'd anointed with an inch thick layer of clotted cream and jam, enough calories to feed a peasant village for a week. I saw Guy's arteries clogging up before my eyes as he took one more step on the road to Zoragaia.

"There's also a third group that believes Zoragaians like to have real live examples of earthlings to play around with, but it's hard to remove people without them being missed, so what they do is take healthy bodies and leave fake corpses in their places. Of course, being unutterably stupid, we don't know that they're fakes, and we think the dearly departed have met with some untimely demise, for which the Zoragaians provide ample supporting evidence, like tumors or," he paused, "empty bottles of pills and vodka."

"That's kidnapping. Isn't it against the Geneva Convention?"

"Well, being infinitely compassionate and omniscient,

the Zoragaians know the people they take prematurely are only too willing to go, in their subconscious if not in their conscious minds, and, of course, the life they're going to is infinitely better than the scummy existence we all wallow around in down here, and when you have an endless future ahead of you in paradise, soon to be joined by all the people you've left behind anyway, what possible reason can anyone have for not wanting to zip off there immediately?"

"I've heard the same argument made for heaven, and for time-share apartments in the Seychelles as well, come to that."

"Precisely."

"Oh, I see. So this is an explanation for all religions. Heaven is another planet. The prophets were keeping us on the straight and narrow until we get there. The meaning of life is just that we're an experiment being played out for a vastly superior life form. Death is not a terminal disease after all. Where are the papers? I'll sign up straight away."

"Yes, would be rather nice, wouldn't it?"

"And Sandy thought that was where she was off to?"

"Looks like it, and she wouldn't be the first. In the States there are suicides every week, mass suicide some of them, with people deciding they can hitch their souls to the latest comet and join the immigration line to that perfect little home with the white picket fence 10 million light years away."

"How the hell did you find all this out, and so quickly? I assume you weren't interested in it before you read Sandy's note?"

"Peter, I spend my life poring over financial data, cutting through all the bullshit and making real-time decisions about the strength or weakness of an investment. I've been doing it since I was in my first year at Eton. You give me information and I'll give you a summary and a decision. Looking through intentionally obtuse financial data takes skill, seeing through the addled rambling of would-be salvation-seekers is the work of a moment, given the raw information, and with the Internet you can get the data in a trice. Give me a phone line and a laptop and I might not be able to tell you who'll save the world, but I can tell you what his turnover is."

I thought. Guy ate, watching me think. As he embarked on his second scone - which was even more heavily over-loaded with instant death than the first one had been - I shook my head.

"Well Guy, this is absolutely fascinating, but haven't you just explained why Sandy did what she did and, as a conse-quence, that Dennis is innocent of any involvement?" Look-ing at him, smiling contentedly, I knew this was the complete opposite of being the case, and that he would eventually tell me why.

"Well, just let me lay all the facts in front of you, then I'll let you decide. Who do you think is one of the leading mov-ers and shakers behind the Zoragaia movement in Europe?"

It didn't take the brain of a Zoragaian to guess which name Guy wanted to be on the tip of my tongue, but I didn't feel ready to utter it, yet.

"Come on, Guy. I've been there a week and he's never mentioned any of this stuff, nor has anyone else. If they want recruits, they've got a bloody funny way of going about it."

"Okay, doubt me if you like, but let me add that the same person is in financial difficulties, and you can choose to doubt me on matters metaphysical, but you damn well can't doubt my ability to research facts financial. I can tell you, quite categorically, that Dennis' finances are as flaky as this bloody scone, and unlike this scone, they have no fat or jam attaching to them whatsoever."

He paused. There didn't seem to be a whole lot for me to say, so I said nothing.

"It's also interesting," he went on "that Dennis doesn't use his own name in his dealings with fellow Zoragaian adherents. He goes by the name of Astralector."

"Then how do you know it's him?"

"Because, my dear Peter, despite my boundless faith in your sharply honed investigative talents, I have also retained the services of other professionals who make it their business to look into the arcane and murky backgrounds of arcane and murky individuals."

"You have a private eye looking into Dennis' past?"

"Indeed I do, and not just one."

"So you know about his daughter, the one who was abducted?"

"Yes. I probably know more about Dennis than anyone at Ravenswood and, in time, I expect to know more about him than he knows about himself. He lived a pretty ordinary life until his daughter was murdered. Then, after he separated from his wife, the rot set in and he started pursuing his current line of business."

"Which is?"

"Cults, and how to get rich from them. At least, that's my assumption. I'm not saying he started off like that. The first chap he teamed up with, er, Dharabinda or something ..."

"Dharavajra."

"Yes, thank you. He seemed to be above board, but after him Dennis got involved in some increasingly loopy groups, culminating in his current affiliation."

"But if he's broke now, he's hardly been successful in profiting from these cults, has he?"

"True, but he's travelled all over the place, as have his happy band of followers, he's bought Ravenswood, renovated it, and he maintains a reasonably pleasant lifestyle for himself and his team without working in anything like the conventional, sweat-breaking sense. It's only recently he's got into financial difficulties, which makes Sandy's death an amazingly fortuitous coincidence, doesn't it? He also," Guy paused and smiled slyly, "supports at least two unmarried mothers and their children. Being a guru can have some attractive fringe benefits. It seems at least some of the women who throw themselves at his feet are willing to stay down there after hours and accommodate the master in his other interests."

In my mind's eye I saw the crouched figure of Micky, with Dennis rhythmically pushing her from behind, possibly easing her towards the doors of a Zoragaian spaceship.

"But there's nothing whatsoever at Ravenswood to suggest any of this. Are you completely sure you've got the right man?"

"Not completely, but we're getting there."

"Why haven't they tried to tune me into it?"

"I can't say, but a number of reasons spring to mind. Firstly, you're broke, so they don't see you as a cash cow. Secondly, you're a Doubting Thomas - you don't even believe in something as eminently sensible as the Tory party, so how the fuck are they going to make you believe in this claptrap. Thirdly, the great appeal to the real disciples of Zoragaia is that it's deadly secret. The Zoragaians obviously want to keep it secret, so the people who believe it want to do the same. It would completely screw up the experiment if David Frost did a piece on it tomorrow night on the BBC. Dennis has to walk a tightrope between getting the message out sufficiently to attract wealthy dupes, but not publicizing the fact openly, otherwise his credibility would be shot. When new converts come across it, they're supposed to think they discovered it themselves, or that the Zoragaians decided to let them in on the act through thought transference, then, lo and behold, Dennis emerges to tell the whole story and start pocketing their cash."

"You've obviously given this a lot of thought."

"Of course I have. The bastard murdered my daughter didn't he?"

I realized as he said this I was taking it too lightly, and Guy's aggressive research and barely repressed anger were the only ways he knew of expressing the grief which, I assumed, he must be feeling somewhere.

"So, what do you think?" he asked.

"I think I'm bloody confused."

"Look, Peter. For all I know Dennis is just an opportunist. He finds himself capable of making a comfortable living by spouting the hogwash that comes naturally to him, in a nice country estate, which he owns, and from which he can embark on trips to sunny California and many other pleasant places when he feels like it. He's surrounded by impressionable devotees, many of whom are females, many of whom are more than willing to pander to his ego, and to other parts of him as well. Then one day he finds himself a bit short of cash, and one of these handmaidens, who just so happens to be rich, expresses an interest in hopping on the last bus to planet Zog, and Dennis thinks 'What the hell. If she snuffs it, maybe I can persuade her to leave me with the money she won't be needing on her trip to Zoragaia'. So he works on her a bit, and being gullible, she rolls over and lets him tickle her belly without any fuss whatsoever, and in no time at all she's left her corpse behind and is zipping through space, and Dennis' bank account has taken a cosmic leap out of the red hole and into the black hole. Doesn't sound too bad put like that, does it?"

I said nothing, but I was impressed by his comprehensive reading of the situation, even if it was a singularly one-sided and jaundiced view.

"But, the fucker picked the girl with the wrong father when he decided to help himself to her legacy, and I plan to make him pay for it. Sandy was a silly bitch, and if it was anyone else's daughter I wouldn't give a damn. I'd probably say

"Good luck Dennis, and how can I get a bit of the action?" But people don't mess with me and they don't mess with my family. I don't give a fuck about all the hidden land mines there are in the world, but if I tread on one, I'll care, and I care now."

I poured more tea for both of us. Guy needed soothing, and I needed time to think.

"If, as you suspect," I said, "they don't see me as a potentially useful convert to the mysteries of Zoragaia - and I accept you're reasoning on that - then they're never going to take me into their confidence, are they? I mean, why the hell did they let me come to Ravenswood in the first place?"

"You're a paying guest, aren't you? They've got to meet the bills somehow, and before Sandy's death they were just bumping along the bottom. Also, they have to keep up a veneer of being something legitimate and non-Zoragaian. And anyway, for all they know your career may take a great leap forward at some point, and that could be the time to get in touch with you again."

If the Zoragaians knew something about my fortunes and my earning potential that I didn't, I would rather have liked to be in touch with them myself.

"You're assuming Dennis is just using this Zoragaia stuff to extract money out of women and women out of their underwear, and that he doesn't actually believe it himself?"

"I don't know, maybe he does believe it. That's pretty irrelevant really, from my point of view. It may make the world think better of him if he believes it himself, and he could always say that he's just acting out the destiny that establishes a bridgehead to Zoragaia. My sole interest is in the manner in which my daughter died, just the cold, hard facts - what was going through Dennis' mind at the time doesn't interest me in the slightest."

I didn't believe him. Although Guy was anti-everything that wasn't materialistic, I got the impression he was rather fascinated by the story of Zoragaia, as he recounted it.

"But I still don't see how I can help. I'm only going to be at Ravenswood for a few more days, and they're hardly likely to let me in on the secret now, are they? Especially knowing I'm a friend of yours. I mean, what do you expect me to do?"

"There must be someone there you can approach. Someone you can drop a few hints to and see if they bite."

I thought of Amanda and Bob, possibly Ruben and, as a last resort, Ken.

"But what if they don't bite. What if they tell Dennis I'm getting inquisitive all of a sudden. They'll either clam up altogether, or ..."

"Or what?"

"Well, I don't know. But if Dennis is a murderer, I don't exactly want to get into his bad books, do I?"

He smiled.

"Hey, don't have any doubts about this," I said, "I'm more interested in my personal welfare than anything else in this universe, whether it includes Zoragaia or not, and I don't see any use in having a Ferrari if I can only use it for a hearse."

"So, Peter, at least you're admitting that Dennis has a dark side."

"I'm admitting nothing, but if he has got one, I don't want to see it. For Christ's sake, Guy, I went to Ravenswood for rest and recuperation, not to play some Country House Murder Mystery game where everyone knows the script except me. I'm no Hercule bloody Poirot."

"Peter. I have every confidence the information I've come up with is entirely accurate. But it won't survive in the cold light of day unless I can get firsthand confirmation, and for that I need you to winkle out a definitive connection between Dennis and this Zoragaian bullshit, either from him or one of his confidantes. The next step will be to confirm he's of the school of thought that earthlings should be hurrying off to Zoragaia to fulfill their dreams, rather than waiting for their appointed times. If you can come up with that, then my information resources and a good barrister will tie this business up in no time."

"So if I do find something out, you'll want me to go to court and testify against Dennis?"

"It may come to that, but it may not. He may decide to come clean, or we may unearth other evidence that's more convincing."

"Such as what?"

"Leave that to me and my private investigators. I'm leaving no stone unturned."

"I bet you're not."

"And why not stay another week? I'll meet your expenses. Who knows, you may even get converted yourself."

"I might think about it," I said. "How long are you sticking around? Italian cars don't like damp climates, do they? I don't want you rusting up my Ferrari."

"Not sure. The inquest is on Wednesday, and the funeral will be down here - she stipulated that in her will, and I don't see any good reason to fight it. But the coroner may put the funeral on hold, based on what we propose to tell him, although there's no need - we're not contesting the manner of death, just the events leading up to it."

"Do you expect to have all your evidence in place by Wednesday?"

"I'd like to, but it doesn't matter if we don't. I can easily get the enquiry re-opened later. I don't plan to rush into accusations. I want to have a solid case before I start going after him."

Guy took me back to the end of the lane. I noticed I was starting to pay attention to how he drove, and I felt like telling him to take it easy if he pushed it too hard - I could also feel the car subtly transferring to my ownership, and it was a giddy feeling. We agreed to meet again two days later - same time, same place, same agenda.

§§§

ORBITING

As I walked back to Ravenswood, one thought preoccupied me, and it was not one connected with Dennis or dirty deeds, real or imagined. I was completely taken with the idea of Zoragaia. Not that I believed in it for one minute, at least I don't think I did, but rather the concept fascinated me. As soon as one accepts the existence of vastly superior minds in the universe, minds that would make insightful figures such as Einstein look like incontinent, bubble-blowing, infants, the idea these minds might be viewing us continually, and how they might be influencing and interfering with us, is mind-boggling.

How, for example, did I know any of my thoughts were my own, and not just ones the Zoragaians were permitting me to have? How much were they influencing everything

I did - likewise all other mortals - so as to ensure we look after the earth and continue to provide useful fodder for their experiment? What unthinkable feats can these brains achieve? Every limitation we experience has the potential to have been eradicated by them - intergalactic space travel, time travel, thought transference, everlasting life, everlasting youth, and the (much sought after) endless, perfect orgasm.

I was so transported by all this stuff that I wasn't aware of walking, and I found myself back at Ravenswood as if by magic. I wandered around for a while longer, letting it all soak in. The great beauty of it was that all of the proof was circumstantial, so nobody could disprove it, and if a cosmic numbskull (like me) could make hay with these ideas, just think what a mystical manipulator (like Dennis) would be able to do with them.

Back on the mundane, terrestrial plane, I had no scheme for getting the information Guy needed, but there were now sufficient doubts in my mind about Dennis, and sufficient desires in my mind about Ferraris, that I was willing to try and do Guy's bidding, although the thought of being found in the meditation room in a couple of days time, my corpse surrounded by assorted empty bottles and my spirit on a one way trip to the other side of the universe, was not one I wanted to dwell on.

I decided to do nothing that day. It was unusual enough that I should disappear for a few hours, and I didn't want to compound that minor mystery by suddenly appearing un-naturally inquisitive about unexpected deaths or astral over-sight. I would wait until tomorrow and then sound out Bob as we dug Ken's folly. On the one hand, Bob was a good place to start, because he was low risk and because, being an astrologer, there was a chance he may have a handle on astro-psycho phenomena, or whatever they're called. But, on the other hand, I didn't get the impression he was any more part of the inner sanctum at Ravenswood than I was, so the probability of him knowing anything stamped Top Secret, was extremely remote.

The other thing that concerned me about all this, apart from fears for my safety, was that Guy could have been barking up the wrong tree, in which case I was about to make a complete and utter idiot of myself. I couldn't imagine he was one hundred percent wrong, but it was quite feasible that Dennis was only involved with the Zoragaian business in some peripheral role, and that Sandy's death was no more than it seemed, just common or garden suicide. But then I thought of the Dennis/Micky scene, and my anger at his hypocrisy - which was probably only a self-deceiving front for my thinly disguised envy - made me less inclined to be charitable.

That evening at dinner everyone seemed to be more cheery, and nobody gave any intimation of having noticed my absence during the afternoon; at least nobody remarked on it - long, solitary, ruminative walks being very much the done thing at Ravenswood, to the extent they were a major rite of passage. Back in my room after the meditation, I half suspected I heard the rhythmic squeak of floorboards overhead as Dennis got stuck into Micky once more, but I stopped myself from going up to investigate, realizing I wouldn't be going in search of evidence for Guy, but simply to enjoy a peep show performance and brighten up my celibate night.

The next day dawned inauspiciously with a cloudburst, and it looked as though the digging session would have to be cancelled, and with it my attempt at cornering Bob when nobody else was around. But the rain stopped as suddenly as it started, and I doubt if Ken would have excused us even if it had been pelting down at the hour appointed for spiritually cleansing manual labor. Ken seemed to have developed some sort of obsessive zeal about the new vegetable plot. He reminded me of the officer in the film "The Bridge over the River Kwai", the one played by Alec Guinness who was so determined to finish the bridge that he lost sight of the fact it would aid the enemy. I could imagine Ken out here with Armageddon raging all around him in the final holocaust, a Zoragaian spacecraft waiting to lift him and other selected inhabitants from Ravenswood to safety, but he just keeps on digging, crying "Just bloody let me finish this bloody trench will you!"

As luck would have it, bad luck, that is, Ken took Bob off for some other duty in the small vegetable garden at the beginning of the work period, and I saw my chance slipping away for another day, unless I managed to get him on his own at some other time. But then he suddenly appeared out of nowhere, spade in hand, and started digging just a few feet away from me.

"I'm getting to think he's completely off his rocker."

"Who? Ken?"

"Yes. He asked me to dig up some potatoes, and told me not to make them squeal. He says he can hear potatoes squeal if the fork goes through them, and I'm not sure he was joking."

"Perhaps he's more tuned into the cosmic essence of things than we are," I said, intending this to be a subtle lead in to things Zoragaian, by way of the far reaches of space.

"I think he's just more tuned into the febrile ramblings of his unhinged brain," said Bob, which was the first time he'd been openly critical of Ken, although I didn't think it was the first time he'd wanted to be.

"Speaking of things cosmic, do you know anything about those 'God-is-a-Spaceman sects', you know, the ones who think we're controlled by vastly superior intellects elsewhere in the universe?"

He didn't say anything, and I interpreted his silence as a very bad sign. Normally, silence at Ravenswood was to be expected, but not this time. I took it as an indication that I'd trespassed on a sacred area. Seconds passed, but not a word from Bob.

"Dangerously idiotic," he said at last, and his teeth were clenched as he said it. I actually gulped in response, thinking I'd really set the cat amongst the pigeons.

"Really?"

"Completely."

"Why?" I said, sheepishly.

"Have you ever heard of a potato fucking well squealing?"

I was so relieved I laughed, and I'd never heard Bob swear before, which added to my amusement.

"No, can't say I have, but then I've never listened to one, nor to any other vegetable, so perhaps I'm just not very attentive at their times of suffering."

"Or maybe you're just not a fucking nutcase."

I couldn't really understand why he'd got so worked up about it, and now I had the difficult task of re-raising the Zoragaian subject, which was bound to make it sound more important than I wanted it to sound. I said nothing for a while as I racked my brains to try and think of an off-hand way of getting back to the esoteric subject of Zoragaia, but then Bob helped me out.

"Sorry, what were you saying just now?"

"When?"

"About God as an astronaut or something?"

"Oh, yes, I was just thinking about those theories that superior intelligences on other planets know all about us, and they leave us alone unless we start getting dangerous, but they watch us all the time and covertly influence us to look after the planet and so forth, all without our knowing about it."

"Really?"

"Really what?"

"Do people really think that?" he said, giving me far from the answer I was hoping for. I suppose, in my wildest dreams, I'd imagined he'd respond by saying "Well, yes, strictly between ourselves, I actually know that Dennis is involved in a cult called Zoragaianism, and I wouldn't be surprised if he persuaded Sandy to kill herself, and there just happen to be a few other bodies of dead, rich people, mainly naked women, buried in the woods around here that sniffer dogs wouldn't have any trouble at all in locating," thereby enabling me to rush off and claim my bright red First Prize. But, given his actual reply and his apparent disinterest - I'm sure Ken was much more prominent in his mind than hare-brained theories of space-suited deities - I could barely muster the enthusiasm to continue with the subject, although I felt duty-bound at least to keep up the conversation.

"Yes," I said, "but like all these theories, you can neither prove nor disprove them, so they seem to attract charlatans and cynics in about equal numbers."

"You'd say the same about astrologers, wouldn't you?" he said matter-of-factly.

"I hadn't really thought about it, but I suppose I would, and I'd say the same about cartoonists too, if that's any con-solation."

"In fact, Peter, you'd probably say the same about every profession, wouldn't you?" he said, jolly once more.

"Yes, I guess so, except bus conductors."

§

Unless Bob was a good deal more artful than I'd given him credit for, he knew nothing about Zoragaia, so I decided to move on to my second choice, Amanda. I sat with her at lunch and persuaded her to go for a walk with me after-wards. She seemed moody.

"How are you feeling?" I asked, supposing she was feel-ing depressed about the events of past days.

"Oh, PMT, you know, well, you don't know, being a man, but that's what I've got."

Oh but I did know. I may be a man, and I may be post-menopausal - how do you tell? - but I've had enough vicarious experience of PMT to know it, loathe it and dread its appearance more than just about anything that could happen to me personally. I've been the subject of so much PMT-induced wrath, derision, suspicion, anger and abuse - verbal and, on at least two occasions, physical - that I feel perfectly qualified to set myself up as an expert of the subject of 'PMT as experienced by nearby males', which includes those within striking and tongue-lashing distance, and even those reachable by stony silences at the end of icily frigid telephone lines.

If there was one incident in my brief cohabitation with Fiona that had accelerated its decline more than any other, it was the day before her period started. After a particularly tetchy exchange, I had unadvisedly suggested she needn't be so miserable (I used slightly stronger language at the time, and probably an inappropriate volume and tone of voice). To which she replied by suggesting I should go and do something intimate to myself that I believe to be physically impossible, although if it were to be possible, I would like to know, as I assume that hermaphrodites have more consistently rapid access to consensual sex than the rest of us. She also suggested I should try being a woman and seeing what they have to put up with. To which I replied it was easy to pretend to be a woman, if all you had to do was pour a bottle of tomato ketchup down your pants once a month and be thoroughly nasty to everyone. My so-called cleverness, as I have usually found, didn't get me anywhere.

"I once had a girlfriend who was planning to write a book

on how different the world would be if men had periods," I told Amanda, by way of attempted commiseration from the other side of the sexual divide. "She reckoned there would be unconditional time off work every month, vastly more medical research into how to ameliorate it, counseling, free tampons, automatic discharge for murder during PMT, no household duties allowed, rest in bed with unlimited access to non-fattening chocolates, loads of stuff that, because we live in a male-designed society, doesn't take place. She said that PMT was treated as some sort of a joke subject because men don't get it."

"She doesn't sound like the sort of girlfriend who would interest you."

"She was a nymphomaniac at all other times."

"Oh, I see," she said, giving no indication she saw it as being funny, or even intended to be funny.

We walked and talked, and I wondered if a PMT sufferer was the right sort of person with whom to discuss Zoragaia, and whether I should leave it until another day anyway, just in case Amanda and Bob happened to put their heads together and see that my interest in the subject was unaccountably intense all of a sudden. But I really couldn't be bothered with pussyfooting around. I'd started to get impatient, and I just wanted to get the information Guy needed and bugger off back to London in a Ferrari.

"Have you heard of those cults that believe God is a spaceman; that highly advanced civilizations discovered us years ago and now they're just watching us, making sure we don't screw the place up?"

"Yes, I've heard of them. I had a friend who was really into all that stuff. I can't remember the name of what he called it. Why? Does it interest you?"

"Well, it interests me, but nothing more than that. It's a bizarre theory, but if you believe there's life in the universe, I suppose you can't close your mind to it altogether."

It didn't look as though she was going to say anything else, so I felt that I had to pursue it. If she changed the subject I would be lost.

"I wonder how you find out about them?"

"Try Roger, I think he used to be into a load of funny things," and with that she reverted to talking about how the world would be different if men had periods, which seemed to lift her mood slightly, even though her depression did, ironically, shift immediately to me. Roger was the very last person I would have thought of approaching, apart from Dennis himself. At least I'd proved - I thought - that I wasn't the only one at Ravenswood who was in the dark over the subject. Unless Bob and Amanda were a master and mistress of deception, they didn't seem to have any clue about, or any interest in, Zoragaia.

Despite never having had anything approaching a proper conversation with him, I planned to focus on Ruben next. Given reasonable alternatives, this wasn't something I would have chosen to do, but I really couldn't think of who else I should go to. I'd considered Monica, and although she seemed very open and non-threatening, the fact she was on the staff made it more likely she was part of the Zoragaia faction, if there was such a thing. Because I'd never sought him out before, I would have to pick my moment to sidle up to Ruben and raise the subject. Even then, he was going to be surprised by my sudden wish to talk, but I didn't seem to have any choice in the matter. I'd noticed he often went off for a stroll on his own after breakfast, so I planned to waylay him the following day.

I stuck to the daily program, partly because I didn't want to seem to be behaving unusually, but mainly because there was bugger all else to do in an isolated community with no radio, no television, no newspapers, no romantic interest - at least, not one that was reciprocated by my focus of romantic attention- and no bar. But I'd stopped benefiting from the meditations, a fact I actually found very annoying, because although I couldn't say I was getting anywhere, nor could I say I wasn't getting anywhere either, and who knows what might have popped up if I'd had a mind that wasn't full of recent events and my supposed part in forthcoming events.

I asked myself if, at some point in the future, I would ever go back. It wouldn't be to Ravenswood, of course, because if Guy got his way - and he usually did - Ravenswood would be reduced to a handful of prison sentences and a pile of journalistic rubble once it had fueled the tabloids for a few days with tales of lust, extortion, murder and more lust. But I thought I wouldn't mind doing something similar in the future, and having found there was nothing spooky about meditation, I wouldn't be so intimidated about going second time around.

I wondered if it was me thinking this or some other mind-controlling entity, because it didn't feel like the sort of thought that was wont to spring unbidden to my suspicious mind. But, if it was a thought that was being imposed on me, there was nothing I could do in the face of an intelligence so superior, and I supposed I might just as well go along with it. Believing in Zoragaia was a lot like trusting to Fate, and although I'd never done that in the past, it felt like an oddly comforting thing to do, in that it removed the pressure to agonize over decisions, which would make themselves any-way and with much better judgment than I'm usually capable of unaided.

§

The next day, Ruben ambled out of the dining room after breakfast, and I set off at the same time in a pursuit dis-guised as a coincidence. He dawdled across the yard, and if he followed his usual drill, he would walk up into the sur-rounding hills. I fell in step alongside him.

"Hello Ruben."

He turned and smiled, but said nothing. The walk wasn't going to be the only uphill struggle I was about to encoun-ter. I said nothing for a while, assuming I needed to play the game according to his rules. He didn't seem bothered by the fact I'd unexpectedly materialized by his side on one of his customary solitary morning walks, but as he said noth-ing it was hard to know what he felt about my being there. It crossed my mind he might use this walk at this time of day for a specific purpose, like a particular meditation, or even that he liked to have a shit in the open air, and this was when he did it. Either way, my presence must have been a right bloody nuisance.

"Have you been here long, at Ravenswood I mean?"

"Four weeks."

I left a long gap. I reckoned I might be able to get some

sort of dialogue going if it didn't appear to be one, and that if I left a couple of minutes between each question he wouldn't realize we were having a conversation at all.

"What do you do when you're not here?"

"Southampton University."

Another long gap.

"What work do you do?"

"Mathematician."

Oh well, it wasn't much of an opening, but it was probably all I was going to get, so I plunged into it with about as much subtlety as a fart at a funeral.

"I was reading about how many planets there are estimated to be in the universe, and the statistical probability that life exists on many of them, and the likelihood that some of these life forms are superior to us, vastly superior, even, and that they are already in touch with us but we don't know it."

He nodded at me, and smiled, but didn't say anything, so I continued.

"I mean, as a mathematician, what sort of probability are we talking about? 99%, 1%, one millionth of a percent?"

"Not my field."

And that, I assumed, was that. I felt suddenly defeated and wanted nothing more than to stomp angrily back to Ravenswood - now a clump of buildings in the valley below us

- and shout "Does anyone here know anything about fucking Zoragaia?" But I didn't. I made excuses, separated myself from a bemused Ruben, and trudged disconsolately down the hill. My only hope was that Guy had made progress with the investigation on other fronts, and that he wouldn't expect me to come back after our meeting and start on Monica, Ken and Roger. Of course, my lamentable lack of success put the Ferrari out of reach, unless Guy was feeling particularly charitable, but, to be honest, I can't say I was particularly interested in fast cars at the time, and I was mainly looking forward to putting the whole uncomfortable episode behind me, even if it meant spending the rest of my days driving a clapped-out, rusty, 1975 Ford Escort.

§§§

ENLIGHTENMENT

After lunch, I wandered up the lane to meet Guy. He surprised me by arriving in a rented Audi.

"Don't tell me you pranged my car, you bastard."

"No, don't worry, I'm looking after it for you, well, Susan is."

"You're letting a woman drive my Ferrari? Fuck it Guy, does she know how to handle a piece of equipment like that?"

"Peter, I can assure you that Miss Dangerfield needs no lessons in how to handle any piece of equipment."

I winced, as another reason to envy Guy - apart from Ferrari ownership - stabbed me in the lower stomach.

"Isn't it a bit risky letting a woman who looks like that out in a Ferrari? She'll have every male that sees her undergoing an instantaneous wet daydream. Wales will be awash in a sea of adolescent spunk."

"I can see why you're a bloody cartoonist, with an imagination like that."

"Yes, just what I need to satisfy the surrealists who see my drawings in the East Suffolk Weekly News and Advertiser."

"Well, what have you got for me?"

"Absolutely nothing. I've asked the only three people I hope I can trust not to go bleating to Dennis, and they don't know Zoragaia from a hole in the universe."

"Are you sure?"

"Sure of what?"

"That they don't know anything."

"No, of course not, I mean not in the absolute sense of the word, any more than I can be sure that you're Guy Tinburnell and not some sneaky Zoragaian impostor who's trying to set me up for a nasty end. But I'd be awfully surprised if they do. There wasn't as much as a glimmer when I asked them, and I didn't exactly hedge around the subject - a direct question evinced a consistently, spontaneously, ubiquitously blank expression from each of them. It would have been hard to fake the complete disinterest they all showed in the subject."

This wasn't totally true. My limited dealings with Ruben made it hard for me to categorize his response, but I didn't see any need to cloud the issue and give Guy a reason to believe I should try them again.

"And you don't think they'll tell Dennis you're asking pointed questions?"

"Well, no, I don't see why they should. Why? Are you concerned for my safety?"

"No, not a bit, I just don't want Dennis to get wind of the fact we're after him, if I can avoid it."

The fact that Guy said he wasn't concerned for my safety could either be due to the fact he didn't think I was in any danger, or that he didn't give a shit about what happened to me anyway, but there didn't seem any point in my asking him which it was, especially as I suspected I already knew the answer.

"How about you?" I asked.

"Well, I now know more about Zoragaia and all things relating to it than just about anyone with an earthling brain, but I can't say it's done me much good. Dennis' name crops up quite regularly on the spiritual highway through the Internet, but not in any particularly ominous contexts, and none of my other investigations have come up with anything. Which means ..." he paused and looked at me.

"Which means what?"

"Which means I'm all the more dependent on you, Peter."

"Oh, well, I'm sorry to hear that, because I really don't see there's a lot more I can do. I mean, if I ask any of the others they're bound to tell Dennis, and that'll be that, won't it?"

"As I said, I'd rather Astralector, aka Dennis, didn't know we're onto the Zoragaia angle just yet, but if nothing crops up in the next day or two, I think you'll just have to take the bull by the horns to ask him outright, and see what his reaction is."

"But that'll be the end of it. He's sure to guess I'm working for you after that. I'll just have to pack my bags and leave, and he's not going to hand me a typewritten confession before I go, is he? I think I'd want the Ferrari plus a submissive Ms. Dangerfield if you want me to do that, and I'd want them before I confront Dennis, then at least I could have one last fuck and a fast drive before he blows my head off with a sawn-off shotgun."

"Why don't you try nosing around a bit. Take a look in his office or his room."

"Not bloody likely! That's taking snooping into the realms of burglary, and I'm buggered if I'm going to do that. What if there's nothing in this? I'll just end up looking like a petty thief."

"Isn't it worth it, for a Ferrari?"

I paused, but I knew the answer without giving the matter any thought.

"No, of course it isn't. I might not be a particularly valuable member of society, but I'm not a bloody tea leaf, and I don't want anyone thinking I am. No, sorry Guy, if you want someone to do that sort of work, you better send one of your seedy private dicks down here and let him peep through windows."

"Well, in that case, the next step, if it has to come to that, is that you ask him point blank what all this Zoragaia stuff is, and then just stand back and see what happens. I could ask him myself, but if you do it there's at least a chance he'll see your interest as casual. Just raise the subject with him in some roundabout way and see what he does."

"He's most likely to deny any knowledge of it, and even if he doesn't, he's hardly likely to tell me that suicide is a good thing from the Zoragaian point of view, and that I should consider it, after changing my will, of course."

This was sounding too much like undercover police work to me, and my knowledge of things like that, albeit through the television, is that something nasty happens to someone at some point.

"If he thinks we're onto him he'll try to hide his Zoragaian connections, and if we can catch him doing that, we can prove there's something that needs to be hidden, and that's where incrimination lies."

"So I flush him out and you bang him over the head with a bloody great hammer, is that the idea?"

"Something like that."

"I think you're being very optimistic. If I start asking questions he'll just clam up and make sure everyone else is on their guard until I'm on a train back to London. What will that achieve?"

Guy inhaled deeply, then exhaled deeply, his eyes focused on some point above my head.

"Nothing, but we've got no case at the moment. I know I sound pretty cocky about this Zoragaia business, but we did an audit last night, and when it comes down to it, we've got sweet fuck all, just a load of circumstantial tosh and a good deal of seat of the pants deduction that won't hang together. I just need one common thread to tie it all up, and you, my dear Peter, are currently my only hope."

"I'm flattered."

"And I'm desperate."

He told me to wait 24 hours and do nothing, then he would get in touch and let me know if I was to ask the big question.

"I don't want them to know you're speaking to me, so I'll get Susan to call. Tell them it's your neighbor phoning to tell you about a problem with your flat or something."

"Will she talk dirty to me?"

"If you like. Does your neighbor usually do that for you?"

"My latest neighbor has got so many rings through various parts of her body that I don't see how she can have any blood left. Sex with her would be like sticking another prick into a pin cushion."

When I got back to Ravenswood there was nobody around, so I assumed they had gathered for the afternoon session. Having nothing better to do, I made for the meditation room to see if it wasn't too late for me to join in, but then, to my surprise, Dennis appeared from the farmhouse and called to me.

"Peter, I was hoping we might have a talk, is that okay?"

"Yes, of course."

"Let's walk, shall we?"

I was actually looking forward to sitting down for a while, but I just nodded and we set off into the hills. This, I suspected, was going to be interesting, and it became interesting before we'd gone more than a couple of hundred yards.

"Peter, I understand you're interested in Zoragaia."

I felt my pulse quicken, and I did a quick check to see if there were any bulges about his body that might be hiding a weapon. Despite being flustered, I had the presence of mind to recall I'd never actually mentioned the word "Zoragaia" to anyone, just the concept that described it.

"What's that?"

"The idea we're being observed by superior intelligences from elsewhere in the cosmos."

"Oh, yes, I am sort of. How do you know?"

"Someone said you mentioned it to them."

"Oh, yes," I said, and then I stayed quiet, hoping he was going to tell me who spilt the beans, but he didn't, and if I asked him who it was he would think - assuming he didn't already - my interest in the matter was something I'd been trying to keep under wraps.

"It's an interesting concept," he said.

"Mmm," I said, vaguely, trying to imply it might be interesting, but not very, and it really didn't bother me whether we talked about it or not.

"I suppose you wonder why I'm raising it with you?"

I remained silent.

"I don't want to sound condescending, Peter, have you really thought all this through?"

"Thought what through?"

"The idea that other worlds are in intimate touch with us?"

"Of course not. I don't think things through, Dennis, you know that. I just want the answers without putting in any effort. That's what I told you when I first came here. Just give me the transcendental short cut and I'll leave you in peace."

"Oh yes," he said, smiling, "I remember."

He paused for a while and we walked on. It wasn't a bad day. I couldn't remember seeing the sun, but it was dry and mild, and as I'd overcome my initial trepidation about things rural, I was actually starting to appreciate the countryside, even if I did feel there's just a bit too much of it, and the odd car park or filling station would break up the scenery and make a pleasant change.

"What I'm getting at," he continued, "is that this is pretty powerful stuff." He looked at me to see if any of this was registering, but I remained uncharacteristically inscrutable.

"Imagine, Peter, that we've been discovered by a race that is so far in advance of us that their brain power and state of development is unimaginable. There has been life on earth for millions of years, but humankind has only made significant advances in the past 40,000 years or so. Now imagine a place, let's call it Zoragaia, where, given similar origins to our own, development has proceeded for another million years. We can't even begin to conceive the progress such a race will have achieved. It's completely beyond our comprehension. But we can assume they will have advanced in ways that we associate with civilization, that they will be more caring with a vastly superior sense of ethics, and that they will have developed technologies which enable them to spread their caring tendencies, their metta as it were, beyond their own planet and into the farthest reaches of the universe, even as far as our own primitive earth."

"What if they're not," I interjected. I should really have kept my mouth shut and let him prattle on, but it's not in my nature to let someone state questionable views unchallenged, and Dennis was at his most intimidating when sermonizing, but you can't sermonize easily when you've got a heckler in the audience, even less so when the heckler constitutes 100% of the audience. "What if they're bastards?"

"Every trend in human development has made us better. I say trend, because there have been major setbacks along the way – the Holocaust, Hiroshima - but, generally speaking, we're much better people than we've ever been, and that process will continue. There will be more setbacks in the future we can't predict, but moral progress will beat them, given time, and a million years is a lot of time."

Again we lapsed into silence before he spoke again.

"The practices I've been exposed to, and the ones we teach here at Ravenswood, are exclusively about self-improvement, mindfulness, the development of compassion, self-knowledge, insight. These are all intended to develop the faculties that will take us to a higher plane of experience, to give us a more incisive view of ourselves and our world and, perhaps, what lies beyond it. We know when we move in these directions, that we're advancing. We know, inherently, that we're making progress. The point is, Peter, that we can clearly see when we're becoming better people. We may choose not to improve ourselves, but we still have the ability to register what is progress and what isn't. Do you understand?"

"Yes." I suppose I know when I'm behaving "better". The problem with life is that it doesn't seem to reward us for behaving better, just the opposite, but that wasn't sufficient cause to deny Dennis the point he was making.

"So, if we can understand moral improvement and its overwhelming benefit, we can postulate that a civilization millions of years in advance of ours will have carried this trend to the highest levels. In other words, Peter, if we encountered a person who came from that environment, we wouldn't be struck only by their intellectual and technological superiority, but by their towering moral superiority. To us, Peter," and at this point he stopped walking and grabbed my arm, "to us they would appear like Gods." He stared at me intensely, not like a mad man, but like a complete believer, which I usually think is the same thing, but this time, oddly, wasn't.

"So," I said, "we have the power to become Gods, just by letting our brains develop in the right direction for a few million years?"

"You're not stupid, are you Peter?"

I laughed. He said it as though he really thought I was stupid - spiritually retarded if not completely backward - but he now believed there might be a glimmer of hope.

"I wouldn't go that far, not on account of one sentence."

"But you've just illustrated you know where all this leads."

He was wrong. I was still taking it a step at a time. The final destination was as far beyond me as calculus was when I was at school, hence my artistic choice of career. I stayed silent, simply to avoid saying something inane.

"The great religious figures of the past have all had incredible vision, profound compassion, a view of the human condition that transcends anything possessed by other mortals. In other words," again he stopped and stared at me, "they have all the characteristics that a supremely developed mind would have, a mind that has had countless millennia to perfect itself."

"A mind from another planet?"

"Exactly. This isn't to belittle religion, to undermine it and make it look prosaic. On the contrary, it shows that animal development - from single cells to apes to humans and just as far beyond humans - can lead to a spiritual advancement that is inconceivable. It holds out the prospect that we can reach spiritual enlightenment by walking the path of evolution. It shows that our destiny is to become enlightened beings ourselves, every one of us. It actually takes the mystic out of mysticism and makes it something we can all aspire to."

"But not for a few million years, which rather puts it out of my immediate grasp."

"Ah!" This was an exclamation, and it really was an exclamation. Dennis was in a state of unrestrained excitement I'd not seen him in before, and something in what I'd just said had catalyzed his enthusiasm and cranked him up one more notch of the evangelical ratchet.

"But Peter, we have a vision of the future. Through Zoragaia we have perceived the path ahead. Mankind is obsessed by technological development and what lies ahead of us in the scientific world. But we consider spirituality to be timeless, something that can't change or improve with time. But that isn't right. We can't foresee long-term technical advances. If we could, the advances would take place and become our present. If Einstein had lived in the early nineteenth century and had his brilliant ideas then, he wouldn't have said 'Oh, I can't do that now, I have to wait for the 20th century'. As soon as ideas materialize, they become our common heritage, so to see the future is to jump to the future.

"The same is true of the spiritual world. To see that enlightenment is possible is the most important step on the journey to achieving it. Zoragaia knows it can't unleash its discoveries on us, because to do so would change our lives so fundamentally it could destroy us in the process. We need to develop spiritually so that we can accommodate the culture shock of being dragged forward through a million years of development without self-destructing. Not only do we have to get our minds organized before we can advance in other ways, but this mental development is the goal above all other goals, and the material consequences and advantages of living in a highly developed world are irrelevant by comparison."

"Do the Zoragaians want us to make this leap?" I said. "I thought the idea was to leave us here and make sure we don't blast ourselves to bits. We'll get to where they are eventually, we just have to be patient, very patient, a million years patient, in fact."

"Think of how we view animals. We attribute any number of qualities to them - vicious, mean, stupid, intelligent, kind, hateful, loyal - but whatever we think of them, we believe they have the right to go on being animals, just as nature intended, to live out their time, for better or for worse, in balance with all the other animals on the planet. The Zoragaians see us in very much the same way, but from their own history they know that once animals become intelligent, self-conscious entities - let's call them 'human', for want of a better word - they enter a phase where, alongside tremendous advances, they also develop the propensity to go haywire, to become evil in a way that lower animals can't because they don't have the power and intellect of humans. Animals can go wrong and do evil just as easily as humans, but they can't destroy the planet by doing it, and they can't build and organize that evil into a framework of thought - like the Nazis or the Klu Klux Klan, for example - and propagate it to other animals and other generations like humans do."

It sounded plausible. Foxes commit wanton carnage in chicken houses, but they don't go home and tell their mates that killing chickens is part of their heritage, and go on to form a political party around it, enshrining it with a decency that the elemental, savage act doesn't possess unless it's made part of a self-serving higher purpose.

"And bear in mind, Peter, that Zoragaia is not the only planet out there with life forms on it, and it's not the only one with advanced life forms on it. The Zoragaians have seen the development of life played out in countless settings, so they know what's best for us, and they know that if we're to be improved, then we must be improved morally before we can be improved physically. They could reveal themselves to us tomorrow, give us life everlasting and perpetual bliss, all that's just child's play for them. But they know they have to prepare us mentally first for that quantum leap, and such maturity can only be achieved through a spiritual aware-ness they will give us, each and every one of us, individually, when the time is right."

"But if they can get inside our thoughts, surely they can enlighten us and prepare us without too much trouble." I'd rather have been talking about the perpetual bliss angle, but I saw I had to follow Dennis' argument if I was to get any-where with him.

"Yes, of course they can, but they still believe we should reach out before they hand us the gift without effort, then we're more likely to grasp it, understand it and treasure it."

"Do you mean there are people who wouldn't grasp life eternal and perpetual bliss?"

"No, but the moral dimension that must accompany it is

just as important, actually more important. If we're truly to move onto a new plane of consciousness, we must do it as complete, compassionate entities, not like, like ..."

"Lager louts ordering a pint of bliss and a spiritual take-away on a Saturday night?"

"Precisely."

"How do you know about all this?"

"Does it matter?"

"Of course it matters. Nothing you've said is provable. If you're telling me I've got to meditate for a lifetime before I can see you're right, then you're telling me nothing more than you told me when I arrived, but at least then I didn't have to accept some strange sounding ideas out of a Star Trek movie to make it all fit together."

"There's only so much I can tell you. I don't want to be evasive, but you have to appreciate this is a very powerful concept, the most powerful concept you'll ever encounter, and as well as being threatening to the Zoragaian ideals, it could also be dangerous for you to know too much."

I was tempted ask if this "danger" was the sort of danger that put Sandy where she is now.

"Why dangerous?"

"Because people who can't handle these concepts, but believe them none the less, can be very disturbed by some of the ideas."

"Like what?"

"Like mind control. As a matter of fact, mind control is something Zoragaia practices very rarely, but anyone who thinks that external influences are at work in their mind needs to be well balanced, and anyone who's particularly suggestible can find the whole idea just too much to live with."

"Wait a minute," I said, feigning surprise, "now I know where I've seen that word before."

"Yes," he said, "Sandy's suicide note."

"Are you saying she went off her rocker over this stuff?"

"No, not precisely that, but Zoragaia was definitely a factor in her doing what she did, although it was completely her idea, and as far as I'm aware she was never persuaded - certainly not by anyone here - to end her earthly life."

"To kill herself, you mean?"

"Sandy believes she has only ended her earthly existence, and she's now been ushered to a better place."

"Zoragaia?"

"She thinks that."

"And do you?"

"I'm not going to answer that for you."

"But you're speaking of her in the present tense, so you

can't believe she's dead, not dead-dead."

"But I didn't believe that death is utter annihilation even before I came to learn of Zoragaia. Zoragaia hasn't changed my basic beliefs in the spiritual quest, it's just given it a new and sharper focus, and an explanation for a few more pieces of the puzzle."

I assumed the "puzzle" he was referring to was the puzzle of life, and one with which I was very well acquainted. The image I often had of my own life was a jig-saw puzzle, in the preparation of which the jig-saw used to create it had somehow made adjacent pieces incompatible, leaving me to bend and hammer them into a picture that bore some relation to a life, albeit a cartoon of a life.

"Tell me how you came across it, or did it come across you?" I asked.

"I came across somebody, and that person decided I was worthy of the knowledge. That's how the idea spreads. As I told you, this is perilous territory, so nobody is brought in on the secret unless they've discovered it themselves."

Or, I should have added, unless they have a modem and access to the internet, but I didn't want to burst the bubble of revelation that Dennis thought he was inflating before my eyes.

"And the fact that I've shown interest, that qualifies me for membership? Doesn't seem like a very strong selection process to me, Dennis."

"You've shown interest and you're here. I told you when you first arrived that once you start looking for something deeper in life, you never stop. You may pause, go away, forget about it for a while, go somewhere else, or even come back here eventually. It doesn't matter, once you've embarked on the quest for enlightenment, it seldom deserts you. The fact you've come to Ravenswood right now is particularly relevant, together with the fact you've asked about Zoragaia. The coincidence is too strong for me to ignore it, and it's certainly too strong for you to ignore it."

I hated to bring him crashing down to earth by telling him the coincidence had only been arranged by a vengeful father who wanted to wear Dennis' guts for garters. I couldn't see Guy Tinburnell in the role as cosmic go-between, guiding me towards a fateful inter-galactic tryst. I could only see him as a sharp operator who wanted to floor his opponent and beat him into a bloody pulp. If I told Guy he was just a pawn in the game that was putting my destiny in place - and his as well, given that he also had the sublime knowledge - his laugh would resonate around the valleys, shortly followed by his venomous anger.

"I suppose," he continued," this must look like some sort of weird and wonderful cult to you. Or maybe just weird and not very wonderful from your perspective. But suppose a major news conference was announced, and there on the television you saw the Prime Minister, the US President, the Pope and many other respected and trustworthy figures, and they told you that through secret, painstaking research over many years they'd discovered the meaning of life, where humankind came from, what our purpose is and what happens to us after death. And they went on to assure the world that our destiny is to reach Nirvana, a wonderful place where we live forever, in perfect health and in an idyllic, blissful state of mind. If that happened, you'd be interested, wouldn't you? Isn't that the sort of explanation everyone is seeking."

"Precisely," I said, "it's because everyone is seeking it that discovering it makes it so suspect, like fool's gold. Add Mahatma Gandhi to the press conference as an endorsee – I assume it's a cinch to reincarnate him – and I'm on board."

"Well, Peter, some of us don't need to get our assurances so cut and dried, we can achieve faith ourselves."

"Ravenswood is the center of expertise on Zoragaia at the moment, is it?"

"Not the centre, but a major focus."

"Why?"

"Because we have someone here who has special insight on the matter."

"A direct line to Zoragaia?"

"If you like."

"You?"

"No."

Oh, well that was a surprise. You wouldn't happen to be lying, would you Dennis?

"Who?"

"I'm not prepared to tell you that, and it's really not important at the moment. You need to know more, and I can tell you more, but not right now. I have to go back." And with that he did a rapid about turn and left me standing in the middle of a field looking at his retreating back. He stopped and turned to face me.

"Walk back on your own. Think over what I've told you. These ideas need time to sink in, and you're smart enough to explore them on your own, for now. We'll talk again soon. Very soon."

I stood there for some time, not thinking, just letting the events of the past minutes wash over me. It's at times like this when I most wish I had a logical brain, so that I could sort out the wheat from the chaff. I used to feel the same after heated rows with my wife. She used to throw so many accusations, images, insults and solid objects at me that, for some time afterwards, I was incapable of deciding what had been the essence of our argument and what I should do about it, if anything.

Dennis hadn't told me anything I hadn't already heard from Guy. He may have put a new twist on some of the ideas and, unlike Guy, he put them across as facts and with an enthusiasm that was quite fetching. But Guy's interpretation was factually very accurate, and Dennis had done little more than fill in the details.

Two points stood out in my mind. Firstly, the fact that Dennis said someone else at Ravenswood was the focus of the Zoragaian connection. When he said it, I thought it was a laughable attempt to shift attention away from himself, but what if it was true? What if Guy was right to come up with the trans-universal link between Zoragaia and weedy planet earth as being centered on Ravenswood, but had then gone on to identify the wrong human intermediary? It would be understandable for him to pick Dennis as the inter-stellar junction box, given he ran Ravenswood and was also the man

Guy wanted to bury, but maybe he was only the front for the real genius behind all of this.

Secondly, the fact Dennis chose to give me the Zoragaia story, and managed to weave Sandy into it, could imply he knew I was in touch with Guy and he was trying to influence matters by seeming to be completely open about it all. If his plan in doing this was to confuse me, then he wouldn't find it very hard to succeed, but even if I swallowed his version of events, now enriched by Sandy's additional reason to do herself in - a quick trip through space and perpetual bliss ever after - he wouldn't be able to shake Guy off so easily, and it actually gave Guy another reason for implicating him in actively encouraging Sandy to do what she did.

But at least I felt as though I'd made some progress, and by learning more about Zoragaia, Dennis' connection to it, and the possibility that believing in Zoragaia may encourage suicide, I might have been homing in on some useful information that could incriminate or exonerate Dennis. And behind all this detective work, I was finding the concept of Zoragaia more and more interesting for its own sake.

Although I'm a doubter whose profession encourages doubt and the general debunking of everything, it's also true that most cartoonists live in a fantasy world. I started off, as a child, drawing crazy pictures. Nobody thought I had any artistic talent per se – for the major part they still don't - just a talent to amuse through art, and I found the drawings that amused me and other people the most were those lopsided views that turned reality on its head, making the pompous laughable and the arrogant idiotic. It was but a small step from drawing pictures of my headmaster, beside himself with rage but with his trousers round his ankles and his willy brushing the carpet, to applying the same abasement to politicians and authority figures - the only difference being that now I get paid for it rather than beaten for it, although sometimes I got that as well, verbally. Drawing cartoons is like dragging the real world into a fairground Hall of Mirrors, where everything is distorted but still recognizable for what it is. In fact, if you draw a normal figure in the midst of a bunch of cartoon characters, it looks just as loopy as they do, sometimes more so.

Fruit cake philosophies like Zoragaia are much the same. You heave the real world into a new framework of science, philosophy and religion, and explain everything with a different set of rules. Most of us see the distortion as an invention of similarly distorted minds, a crazy misinterpretation of reality that's clumsily bludgeoned into conforming to a new set of beliefs by some lunatic who thinks his interpretation is a better explanation of life than any that's preceded it. To the dispassionate, skeptical observer it all looks totally suspect and mildly comic, but in the same way that my cartoon characters take themselves seriously whilst the three-dimensional world outside the page laughs at them, so it is with cults and those outside of them.

They say salesmen are the easiest people to sell to, because the suspension of critical faculties that makes it easy for them to sell their products, despite their glaring weaknesses, also makes them gullible when another salesman pulls the same trick on them. So it is with a cartoonist - the skills that enable me to produce fantasy worlds of fat-assed and bounteously bosomed politicians make me a sucker for other people's larger-than-life fantasies.

When I got back to Ravenswood, I saw it differently. It was no longer a place where people come to discover the "truth within" through agonizing hours spent cross-legged on a cushion. It was a place with a mission, and that mission was to launch us all into space so that we should drop swiftly and elegantly into the gorgeous, scintillating, infinitely sophisticated soup that is Zoragaia. Despite being attracted to this idea, I knew I'd never be able to believe it, and that short of being led off to the spaceship and given a clear demonstration of what's coming, I was consigned to stay, like a grumpy and ungrateful Robinson Crusoe, sitting in my earthly cave sucking humbugs and disparaging anyone who didn't agree with me and my negative outlook.

I felt a frisson of envy for Sandy and the literally blissful ignorance that led her to her death, but the feeling passed and left me in a state of mild terror that I should be capable of thinking such a thing, however briefly.

§§§

BUMP IN THE NIGHT

That evening, the meditation seemed to be particularly peaceful. My suspicions about Dennis and, as a consequence, the doubtful pretext on which Ravenswood might have been based, should really have made me feel out of sympathy with things, given that the honesty I thought I could rely on had been compromised by revelations which made the whole setup look questionable. Perhaps I felt relaxed because my brain couldn't make any sense of what was going on, so it had just decided to switch off and switch the rest of my body off with it, or perhaps the Zoragaian influence was working on me and opening a new perspective that would change my life forever.

When things have gone badly in my life, personally or professionally, I get into a state of higher and higher anxiety that seems to have no end and no limit to its frenetic upward spiral. Then, abruptly, it's as though I emerge into the eye of the storm and all is peace and tranquility. I take no credit for this. I know it's just an automatic shutdown mechanism that flips my mental circuit breakers and turns me off before I explode into some new dimension of angst. In fact, as well as taking no credit for it, I believe it probably does me more harm than good. Suddenly becoming an ocean of calm in the midst of a row of hurricane proportions has turned more than one partner or wife completely insane, all the more so because calm is not considered to be a state with which I am normally associated, other than to "be even more fucking annoying" than I usually am. I also suspect my artistic abilities might benefit from a bit of superheated anguish, panic and consternation now and again, but my brain obviously feels I'm not supposed to step foot into that rarefied atmosphere, and it prefers a bucket of cold water to the white hot incandescence of tortured genius that might make me actually achieve something novel, breathtaking and, probably, disturbing.

When I came out of the meditation room, I noticed a figure standing in the yard, looking up at the night sky. As I passed by, it spoke, and as there was nobody else about I had to assume it was directed at me. Dennis had waived the silence after the last meditation since the suicides, for the sake of those who needed the consolation of conversation, so the speaker wasn't breaking any rules.

"Have you ever seen such a beautiful sight?"

I walked over to the figure, which had lowered its head from its starward gaze and, despite the darkness, had revealed itself as Micky, who was now gazing at me. I glanced up at the sky to give the pretence of making an informed contribution to the conversation.

"It makes me feel slightly terrified. All that space, all that distance," I said, being aware I know as little about the heavens as I know about the countryside, and am similarly intimidated by them.

"Doesn't it make you feel so small, insignificant? Like an ant someone could tread on and never notice?"

"I don't need to look at the sky to feel insignificant."

She chuckled, and quickly stroked my arm, gripping it slightly before letting her hand fall limply to her side. Her gesture was strangely meaningful, almost submissive.

"But you're not," she said, "you're valuable."

I recalled the image of Micky and Dennis from a few nights ago, and putting it together with the touch she had just bestowed on me, I felt a sudden arousal she did nothing to dispel.

"Talk to me Peter. We haven't spoken much since you came, and I feel I don't know you." She had a pleasant sing-song voice, deep, but feminine and rather sexy, although I'd find anything sexy given the enforced celibacy of the previous couple of weeks and Amanda's painful unavailability.

"About what?" I said, not wanting to be uncooperative, but suddenly finding myself at a loss for words, particularly words of an astronomical or romantic nature.

"About you."

"Me. Can't you think of anything more interesting to talk about?"

She laughed again. But I'd long since stopped being flattered by the fact that people at Ravenswood found my utterances amusing. I believed they'd got it into their heads that "Peter is a person who says funny things because he's a cartoonist", and without thinking they laughed in some sort of contagious hysteria. I was like an old comic who the public still enjoys, not because he's funny (he's actually embarrassing), but because he used to be funny and they desperately want him to be as they remember him.

"Let's go and have a chat in my room shall we? I feel like talking to someone. Okay?" she said.

Well, of course it was okay. I could have started asking myself questions, like: Why is she interested in me all of a sudden? Has Dennis put her up to this to try and distract me? Is this just a friendly conversation I'm completely misinterpreting? And so forth, but I'd rather just go to her room and see what transpired.

I've never, ever, got lucky in that out-of-the-blue way some men have described to me - including Guy Tinburnell, in a story he once related to me over one of our boozy dinners, about a sex-crazed and insatiable chambermaid in a hotel. All of my conquests - a small number in itself - have been frantically pursued, hard won and grudgingly granted, so the prospect of something being spontaneously and generously awarded to me was still a dream I was chasing with an adolescent ardor in a middle-aged body.

"Make yourself comfortable," she said. "I'll go and get us a drink, shall I? What would you like?"

I would have liked brandy, a lot of it, but I asked for coffee and she left. I looked around the room while she was gone. Overcome with a sudden wish to do something purposeful and not just be overtaken by events, I scoured the shelves to see if there were books on any subject that could loosely relate to Zoragaia, but there weren't. What books there were seemed to be the milder sort of classics, like Jane Austen, the Brontes, Dickens and so forth, although a copy of The Tropic of Cancer sat glaringly and unashamedly amongst them. I found a tatty copy of Ulysses on the floor and a Simenon novel wantonly lying on top of it - a conjunction which put me in mind of the scene Micky and Dennis played out in the attic.

Micky seemed to have the room to herself, which sent another jolt of expectancy through my underutilized (not to say ill-utilized) reproductive system, and I forced myself to calm down, in the almost certain knowledge I was reading things into her friendliness that only existed in my head. She returned.

"How are you liking Ravenswood, Peter?"

"Well, things have got so confused over the past few days, I'm really not sure what I'm thinking anymore." I was reminded of her grief after the deaths of Doris and Sandy, and realized I probably shouldn't be raising this particular subject, but she didn't seem to be affected by it.

"Oh, I know, but I feel as though I've cried all the tears out of me. You have to let go eventually, otherwise mourning just becomes a habit, and the more of a habit it is the less you're mourning the other person. I was really starting to wallow in self-pity."

I'd assumed from my few encounters with Micky that she was taciturn, more of a thinker than a talker, but she was breaking that impression.

"How long have you been here?"

"About two months. I came with Sandy. I worked in her boutique in Kensington before the bailiffs came, and she asked me if I wanted to come along here. I had nothing else to do, so I thought I might as well. It would be better than looking for another bloody job"

"Have you done this sort of thing before?"

"Not really, but I'd always been interested in meditation, and I was keen to give it a try. Sandy offered to pay, so it seemed like fate was leading me here."

Fate or her libido?

"How long will you stay?"

"I don't know. I can't really afford to stay here without Sandy paying for me."

Oh, but I was sure Dennis had a means of extracting payment in kind. She was eyeing me up as we talked. At least, that's how I chose to interpret the open look she was giving me, and which I was doing my best to return in kind.

She told me more about herself. She was in her late twenties, and since dropping out of university she'd just been drifting from one "interesting" job to the next. As the curriculum vitae of someone older and less intelligent, it would have made depressing reading, just a succession of dead-end jobs in some of the less interesting parts of the universe. I suppose "working in a shoe shop in Stevenage" - which was one of her many positions - would just about sum up all of them. But the fact she was young enough to see them as learning experiences, and intelligent enough to know when she was being honest, meant she'd come through it all with her dignity and her sanity intact, although if she was doing the same sort of thing in 10 years time she would have to ask herself whether it was still enriching her view of life and how it's lived.

Then, just when I thought that a friendly conversation was really all she was looking for, she fixed me with a gaze that left no doubt about what she was thinking, and although I experienced a moment of terror, wondering if I was going to be able to grasp the opportunity and live up to expectations (hers and mine), I joined her on the bed where she'd been sprawled and we started a frenetic journey of discovery, the same journey that thousands of new lovers make every day, only to find it much the same as all preceding journeys, not that it stops them wanting to make it again.

I'd never been with a woman whose clothes came off so quickly, almost as though she pulled a cord and they all hit the floor at a speed that would give scientists cause to recompute the force of gravitational acceleration. Perhaps it was something to do with the moistly lubricating Welsh atmosphere, or the fact that clothes are worn loser at Ravenswood, hence encouraging their rate of disposal in times of emergency, such as the arrival of a Zoragaian space craft that demands that space suits be donned in place of Marks & Spencer's accoutrements. Whatever the reason, she was practically naked while the two of us were still struggling to get my Levis over my ankles, and it really couldn't have been more than a few minutes after our first kiss before we were going at it like two people who were trying to beat a world record.

Her body captivated me. There was a lot of it, but it was all so well proportioned you would never have called her anything other than beautifully built. She probably weighed more than me, and her outstanding breasts and formidable buttocks were really those of a much bigger woman. But the other parts of her were smaller, so she looked more like a figure from a Goya painting who had gone to an aerobics class to reduce some of her flesh, but had managed to retain full measure in the parts that men most appreciate and fantasize over. It occurred to me to tell her, when we were finished - which was about to happen very soon, and all too soon as far as my contribution was concerned - that she should consider artistic modeling as one of her future career moves, rather than going back to dispensing burgers in McDonald's in Kettering.

And then, of course, it was suddenly over, and I found it impossible to remember what we were getting so worked up about just a short time before. We gave the necessary compliments to one another, and I told her what a great body she had, and that art classes would "lap her up" - which I realized was not quite the best choice of expressions - if she offered to pose for them. She asked me if I'd like to do a sketch of her and I told her I'm only an average artist - and only an average cartoonist too, come to that - but she refused to believe me, which was nice but very misguided of her. Just because I always belittle myself doesn't mean I'm not telling the truth.

Then before I'd had time to even think about it, she was readying herself for action again, and because things were less manic it actually turned out to be extremely good, but afterwards I started to get concerned she was going to want to keep this frequency up all night, which might find me wanting. But then we both fell asleep, and it was almost dawn before she woke me, towering over me like a statuesque Amazon and bouncing me so hard I thought she was going to break my pelvis, the bed and the floorboards, in that order, and then drive us, still coupled, through the magma and into the molten bowels of the earth. Afterwards, still safely above ground, she advised me to sneak back to my room before anyone else was up.

"Because, you know, what we've been doing isn't really appreciated here." Which was ironic given how much I'd appreciated it, but her statement ignored the fact that at least one other person, the leader, no less, appreciated it very much too, although from an angle we didn't actually get around to exploring.

As we sucked our way through some farewell kissing, I said we should do this again, soon, and she smiled sweetly and agreed, but I got the feeling it wasn't a high priority with her. I may not be very good at understanding when women are interested in me, but I'm razor sharp at detecting when they're not.

Having sex had done me good, and I felt as though something painfully cumbersome had been lifted off me. I breathed the air deeply as I crept back across the yard, even managing to get a slight swagger into my gait and a tentative spring into my step as I tiptoed across the farmhouse's creaky floor. Laying in my own bed, it struck me that Guy was right, and the sort of life Dennis had - a pleasant environment, no sweat-inducing work other than his heroic labors with the occasional acolyte of the opposite sex seeking a bit of divine guidance, physically administered - could be far from unpleasant. But would he have really persuaded and assisted someone to end their life in order to ensure the financial stability by which his life as chief rooster could be effortlessly maintained? I fell asleep as the question formed in my mind.

§

When I woke up to the early morning bell my eyes were heavy, but I actually felt energized. I got a cup of coffee and wandered around in the yard, where a slight mist had formed since I'd crept across it after my night in Micky's arms and other parts of her accommodating body. I looked up at the hills around Ravenswood and felt at peace, much more so than when I was being celibate. I had to accept that my faulty organism needs occasional sex to be holistically healthy, and probably would benefit from a few other things that I was currently denying it - like beer and smoked salmon. I don't see there's anything wrong with admitting my soul has feet; that they are firmly embedded in the real world and probably encrusted with a little earthly mud - it actually makes me feel more stable and less likely to acquire aspirations I'm never going to be able to achieve.

I had real trouble staying awake during the meditation, and every time my mind was alert enough to keep me awake, thoughts of last night rushed into the vacant space and rendered all spiritual efforts futile. Afterwards, at breakfast, Bob joined me, and he seemed to be in good spirits, practically ebullient.

"Fancy a walk, Peter?" he asked, and although I thought the surrounding paths could probably do with a rest from my feet after the exposure they'd been getting to them over the past few days, I agreed.

Unlike Dennis, Bob set a walking pace much more in keeping with my own, so I was surprised when, after about half an hour, I found myself in an isolated area I'd not been to before, and which seemed to be in the back of beyond. I was even more surprised when we come to a hut and Bob strode towards it.

"Have you been here before?" he asked.

"Not in this life," I said, causing him to stop dead and give me a very puzzled look, as though I'd just said something profound or cryptic.

"Oh," he said, now appearing pensive. "Let's go in."

I followed him through the door, which yielded to his push. I didn't have time to ask him why we were doing this or whether he knew what he was up to, before I found myself standing in the semi-darkness of a large room, and as I was about to speak I noticed we weren't alone. No sooner had I detected two other figures, than a match was struck by one of them, its pool of light flaring to reveal a face I saw to be that of Ken. He lit a hurricane lamp with the match, and as the contagion of light spread around the room, I saw the other figure was - no less spookily illuminated - Dennis.

Nobody spoke at first, leaving a random trail of surprisingly coherent thoughts - none of them pleasant - to run through my mind. My first reaction was they had found out about my liaison with Micky, and planned to punish me in some way for my indiscretion. Then I thought it was due to my enquiries about Zoragaia, and they were going to do something that would stop me compromising the wishes of the great force beyond the oceans of space. Then I thought they might just be a bunch of thugs who wanted to do unpleasant things to me because that's what they liked doing to people. But then I looked at the three faces, and although I wouldn't have excluded Ken from any form of nasty business, I couldn't believe Dennis and Bob were capable of anything painful. Dennis interrupted my frantic search for an explanation by speaking.

"Don't worry, Peter, we just want to talk to you."

"Well 'What about?' sounds like the appropriate thing to say." I surprised myself by how controlled I sounded, but I didn't feel it. In fact, breakfast was making its presence felt very uncomfortably in my stomach, and I wondered if it would be making a spontaneous attempt to return to the light of day.

"Have a seat," said Ken.

I looked around the room. It was sparsely furnished but was surprisingly comfortable for what I'd assumed was just a shed. There was a circular, tiki-style rug and some pictures of the interiors of temples or churches. I would have assumed it was another meditation room if I'd stumbled across it by chance, but there were proper chairs to sit on and no sign of a shrine.

I expected Dennis to get the ball rolling, but he didn't and when it was Bob who spoke, I could barely control my surprise.

"Peter, you have shown interest in Zoragaia," he said, but this wasn't friendly lightweight old Bob I dug Ken's Folly with every day and who joked with me about what lesbians do to each other. This voice had authority. It was measured, precise and seemed to be at least half an octave lower than normal. "This is a subject of supreme importance, in fact it is the most significant subject that has confronted the human race since we became self-aware." He paused, staring unblinkingly at me. Dennis nodded and Ken grunted.

"Zoragaia changes everything we know about ourselves and the universe in which we live. It changes everything we think about ourselves and the way we live and should live our lives. Nobody who knows the facts about Zoragaia can ever live their life in the same way again." He paused. Ken said something under his breath like "Aye". Dennis had closed his eyes and was smiling slightly. I felt as though Bob wanted me to say something, but I couldn't, and wouldn't have been able to think of anything sensible to say anyway. There was a strong smell of paraffin in the air from the lamp, and it was casting odd shadows around the room. There were two windows, but they were admitting very little light.

"Zoragaia has revealed itself to you. You are very lucky. You are privileged. You are one of those chosen to be blessed by this special gift of transcendental knowledge."

Well, no, I should have said, in fact Guy Tinburnell came to me in an earth-scorching bolt from heaven called a Ferrari, accompanied by a vision of heavenly loveliness and told me about it as a way of shafting your mate Dennis, but, needless to say, I kept my mouth shut.

"Zoragaia explains everything to us. An intelligence so advanced it has had time to unravel the mysteries that baffle us, the mysteries we haven't even begun to confront, let alone understand. But Zoragaia cannot make itself known to our world, except to those whom it can trust and whom it has prepared for the information by subtly revealing itself to them.

"Mankind has no idea why it has such a large brain. People born with brain disorders, like hydrocephalus, who have a brain that is a fraction of the normal size can live perfectly ordinary lives, can get university degrees and not suffer any privations. Our brain has been given to us so we can use not just a part but all of it to advance the state of mankind to one of mental perfection, and Zoragaia can lead us on that journey. We have ..."

It's as though a switch flicked in my head, and the magic of the moment dissipated to reveal the tableau as it really was - one man spouting portentous nonsense, two men nodding obediently at his side, and one man, me, scared out of his wits. But, seeing this, I could break the spell.

"Wait a minute, Bob," I said.

He blinked. He didn't look startled as much as baffled by my interruption. Dennis opened his eyes and looked at me as though he didn't know I was there. Ken frowned and glared at me.

"Look, I'm not cut out for this sort of thing. You believe what you like, but I'll just stick with the mundane view of the world." I shouldn't have been doing this. I should have sat tight, kept quiet and played along with them if I was going to get to the heart of it, but I found the whole scene too absurd, and unsettling. I got up to leave.

"Stay where you are," said Dennis, firmly. Ken got up and moved towards the door. Yes, I should definitely have kept my mouth shut.

"Peter," said Bob, "I understand how you feel. This can be very unsettling when it first comes to you, very disorientating. That's natural. When you've lived your life accepting one set of beliefs, to find out that something altogether different is true is bound to disturb you. But despite your skeptical nature, you've been selected to receive this wonderful knowledge, and you can no longer turn your back on it than you can stop your heart beating by willpower alone."

I had a sudden, terrifying premonition that I was never going to get out of this room alive, and I didn't expect a Zoragaian spacecraft to bear me peacefully into the distance either. My sole concern was what these three, very human individuals had the power to do to me, in an isolated hut in darkest Wales. I shook my head.

"Peter," said Ken, "you should listen to Astralector."

I looked at Dennis, but he was looking at Bob. So, Dennis hadn't been lying when he told me he wasn't the kingpin. Guy had got things badly muddled. Astralector, star reader, I should have thought of that.

"If Zoragaia is so keen to have me on their side, why haven't they got inside my head and made me enthusiastic about it?"

"It's a misguided belief that Zoragaia controls us," said Bob. "They don't, they have far too much respect for us to do that. They choose people who they feel are worthy of the knowledge and will put it to good use, but they don't exert control on them, they just wait for the knowledge to work on them and gradually make sense to them."

"Well, you're exerting control on me."

"We'd just like to give you time to assimilate what's happened to you. This knowledge is powerful, and because it's powerful it's dangerous. You have to guard it carefully, and we need to help you do that."

"And when I have assimilated it what good use am I supposed to put it to?"

"That will be revealed to you."

"You think a degenerate, weak-willed cartoonist has some role to play is this great scheme? Well, Zoragaia must move in mysterious ways."

"Not mysterious, Peter, just ways that are beyond us. But you will see the reason for what's happening to you in due course, we will all see, soon."

Ken said his muffled "aye" again, and I sensed Dennis' head nodding slowly. "Look, I just find this idea a bit hard to swallow. We've been on this earth a long time, why is it only now that we've found out something so fundamental?"

"Because only now are we ready to receive the idea and understand it. Our knowledge of the universe is proceeding to grow very rapidly. Our knowledge of ourselves and our world likewise. Zoragaia believes we are now in a position to be given the truth, but gradually, individually, and only to enlightened subjects. In several hundred years from now, humans will be reaching further into space and starting to get clues about other inhabitants of the universe. By the time that happens, Zoragaia wants to make sure we can use the information and put it into perspective, so it knows it has to reveal itself to us eventually. Also, our power to do ill to ourselves and our universe increases every day, and Zoragaia knows that at some point it will have to intercede to save us from damaging ourselves and damaging other cultures we might discover and it will not be able to hide that intercession."

He looked smug. An answer for everything in the land of the unprovable and the un-unprovable. I shrugged.

"Why us? Why haven't other 'enlightened' subjects been fed the story? Stephen Hawking, the Archbishop of Canterbury, Eric Clapton? Why enlighten a bunch of misfits like us and not the real movers and shakers?"

"Do you know those people haven't been enlightened?"

"Of course not, but do you know they have?"

"Those who are chosen are directed to use their knowledge in different, subtle ways, not by declaring it to the masses."

How neat it all was, beautifully incontestable, inviolable.

"Well, what happens next?" I asked, not really wanting to know the answer.

"We would like you to stay at Ravenswood for a while longer, so that we can tell you more about Zoragaia and help you put all your knowledge in perspective. Then you'll be able to decide how you can best fulfill your mission in life."

They were all looking at me, and common sense dictated that I shouldn't object to this plan of action.

"But, ludicrous though it may sound, I do have a life back in London, and if I drop out of it for too long, I may not be able to get back into it when I return. The people who buy my cartoons forget about me when I'm not banging on their doors every day, so do my friends."

"We're only talking about a week or two. After that it will be up to you to decide when it's appropriate to leave, where it's appropriate to go, and what it's appropriate to do."

"How many people at Ravenswood are into this stuff?"

"Some, not all," said Bob, his eyes flicking towards Dennis as he spoke.

"Micky?"

"Why do you ask?" said Dennis, probably anticipating this wasn't just an aimless enquiry.

"She seduced me last night. Well, I think that's what she did, but I didn't take a lot of persuading, so it was hard to tell. Did you suggest she did that so that I might feel good about spending extra time here?"

"Yes," said Dennis, with candor so admirable it shocked me, despite my asking for it.

"So Micky knows about it?"

"Yes, also Monica and Roger, nobody else, Sandy of course, but not Doris, although I think Sandy might have told her at the very end," said Bob.

"And how instrumental was Zoragaia in persuading Sandy to do what she did?"

"Not at all."

"Really?"

Bob shook his head. "She had her own way of interpreting things, and obviously felt it was the right thing to do, but it was basically her decision alone."

"Why didn't Zoragaia get inside her head and tell her not to?"

"Because Zoragaia leaves us with our free will, and anyway, she's in a much better place now."

"Zoragaia?"

He didn't say anything, just opened his eyes wider.

"Peter," said Bob "I get the impression you're not quite ready to commit yourself."

"Well, be honest Bob, either Zoragaia has got its wires badly crossed, or its using a very odd strategy if it thinks I can do the cause much good."

"We shall give you more time to consider."

As he said this, I heard a step behind me and then blackness.

§§§

DYING FOR LOVE

I'd never been knocked out before. I was made very groggy once after a heavy rugby tackle when I was at school, to the extent that I fell over again when I tried to get up, but I'd never been laid out cold. When I came to, I was completely disorientated. I thought my eyes were open, but I couldn't see anything, then shapes started to emerge and I realized I was in a darkened room, which was just as well because I was about to assume I'd been rendered blind. As realization started to dawn, it did so to the very unwelcome accompaniment of a pounding headache. I was on a bed, and fearing my eyes would bleed or my head would fall off if I tried moving it, I stayed lying down as I tried to piece together what had happened.

The disorientation was strangely pleasant to begin with

- a relaxing, careless feeling that wouldn't let me hang on to any cogent, troublesome thoughts - but then it became unsettling as I realized this chaos would stop me ever doing anything, even lifting my head off the pillow. I remembered my walk with Bob, and as an image of the strange cabin appeared in my mind, everything else rushed back into my head and I was me again, which was comforting but oddly disappointing, made more so by a renewed throbbing of my skull. I had a moment of panic as I imagined my brain exploding, and I gingerly felt around my head to see if there were any bones extruding or blood oozing from it, not that finding there weren't made me feel any better.

It must have been Ken who whacked me over the head, but Bob and Dennis were facing me so they would have seen what he was about to do, and perhaps one of them signaled to him to do it. I supposed that having seen I wasn't exactly rushing towards the idea of Zoragaia with open arms, they decided I needed to be persuaded a bit more forcibly into lying low for a while. I had no idea where I was, but I assumed the door was locked. Gradually I lifted my head off the pillow and maneuvered myself into a sitting position with my feet on the floor. My head swam, gave a few almighty throbs, and then I heard a rushing sound in my ears, but after that it seemed to settle down into a consistent, but bearable, pain. My knee was sore, which I assume resulted from the fall following the blow to my head.

I got to my feet and explored the surroundings. The walls were of wood and it was small. I paced it out and it seemed to be perfectly square, probably about 10 feet by 10 feet. I drew back curtains to reveal a barred window high up on one wall, through which all I could see was dense foliage. Apart from the bed, which looked as though it had once been an army bed, there was a table with a melamine top, the likes of which I hadn't seen since the '60s, a hard backed chair with a frayed dingy brown cushion, and a circular rug, which looked exactly the same as the one in the building or shed Bob had taken me to. As I walked around, I got the impression there was no solid foundation under the floor - it was like some sort of glorified garden shed. There were books on the table and a torch.

There were two doors and, needless to say, I tried the handles, not expecting to find either of them unlocked. To my surprise, the second door opened, but only onto a small space that housed a portable toilet and a bench on which there was a large plastic container of water with a tap, a mug, various items of toiletry and a recessed sink that drained to the outside. This room also had a barred window high up in the wall, through which I could see a small expanse of undergrowth and dense trees beyond that.

I went back and sat on the bed. Apart from food, I could have survived in the place indefinitely, or, more to the point, I could be kept in the place against my will indefinitely. Monica had told me that people sometimes did solitary retreats at Ravenswood in several huts and caravans in the surrounding countryside, and I assumed this was one of them. But rather than feeling like an eager voyager on the road to enlightenment, I felt like an unwilling hostage in Beirut. The walls were made of thick wood, and although I may have been able to have a go at breaking through them when my headache subsided, I was probably fooling myself to imagine I would be able to get out that easily. I forced myself to think.

There were two main possibilities. The first was that everything I'd been told was true, and Bob *et al* were completely sold on the Zoragaia story and planned to indoctrinate me before letting me go - although if I didn't let myself be indoctrinated, they might choose not to let me go, I supposed. The second possibility was they had colluded in Sandy's death and believed that keeping me out of the way and out of Guy's clutches would serve the purpose of concealing the truth. Taking this second scenario to its logical and unpleasant conclusion - which was that they had actively persuaded Sandy to kill herself and relieved her of her money in the process - I didn't see how doing anything less than killing me, Guy, Dangerfield and the many more characters who Guy had enlisted in his cause would put them in the clear. I couldn't imagine they were naive enough to think I was the only person likely to damage them, and that Guy would just toddle off back to London if I wasn't around to feed him proof of their chicanery. And if they did see me as such a problem, they would inevitably have to kill me, and if they had to kill me, why hadn't they done it already? Surely nothing would have been easier than slitting my throat when I was out for the count?

The criminal explanation didn't hang together. I couldn't accept Dennis was a criminal. Ken was strange enough for anything to be possible, and given that the Bob I'd come to know and like was obviously a fake, I supposed he was capable of greater iniquities than just pretending to be a normal bloke when he was really a cult leader. But I'd developed respect for Dennis, and I didn't see him as a crook, although we were talking about nine million pounds and someone in dire straits might be tempted to do some pretty outrageous things with that sort of reward in the offing.

I couldn't believe this was happening. I couldn't believe I was actually in fear of my life. I pinched myself and shook my head, as gently as I could, to see if I was dreaming, and I then tried to think of something else to explain the events of recent days, but nothing came of it. Then I realized I didn't even know what day it was, how long I'd been unconscious, or even if I was on planet Earth or ensconced in some low-tech, rustic spacecraft at that very moment winging its way to Zoragaia, whilst giving me the impression I was sitting in an isolated hut in the damp, green, Welsh countryside. I felt like crying, but I was sure if I started, I wouldn't find it easy to stop.

I heard a noise outside and then a knock at the door.

"Peter, can you hear me?" It was Ken's voice. I went to the door, expecting him to open it, but he didn't.

"Yes, what the fuck's going on? Do you realize what you're doing, you crazy bastard?"

"I'm not going to talk now. We'll talk later," he said. "You'll see a small hatch by the floor to the left of the door. If you open it you'll find food. Is there anything else you want?"

"Yes, I want you to bloody well let me out of here, you lunatic."

"Can't do that, yet. But if there's anything you need, we'll get it for you. Someone will check with you every couple of hours, and bring you drinks and things. You'll be comfortable in there, and we'll explain everything later."

"When?"

"Later today."

I heard him walk away, and I banged on the door, succeeding only to skin my knuckles. I stooped down and found the hatch he was talking about. Lifting it exposed a small alcove containing a tray of food. I pulled the tray out, slid my arm into the alcove and pushed hard on what must have been the flap Ken opened to put the tray in there from the outside. It was bolted shut, but it might prove possible to break it open and squeeze through, although it would be a dangerously tight fit. I decided not to try it immediately. If I was going to break out, my best bet was to do it at night, so there would be the greatest amount of time before my absence was discovered - assuming they didn't plan to monitor me throughout the night.

I put the tray on the table. There was a vegetable stew, fresh bread and a salad, a flask of coffee and some fruit. There was also a pill bottle with two tablets in it, and a handwritten label on the outside that said "Painkillers, in case you've got a headache. Sorry." which had the unexpected effect of making me laugh, though God knows why.

I ate the food and drank the coffee. I haven't smoked in years but I found myself dying for a cigarette, and a large glass of brandy wouldn't have gone amiss either. I lay down on the bed and tried to think some more about the circumstances surrounding this whole, ludicrous business. I even went as far back as blaming Fiona for advising me to come to Ravenswood in the first place, thinking maybe she knew about the Zoragaia angle all along.

§

Dozing, I felt a sudden draught of air. When I opened my eyes Ken, Bob and Roger were looming over me.

"What's this," I said, glaring at them, "are you going to work me over again or is this the execution squad?"

Nobody laughed and nobody answered for a while, which was worrying. Roger plunked himself down on the floor, huffily, Bob sat on the chair, regally, and Ken stood in front of the door with his arms crossed in the classical "none shall pass" pose.

"Peter," said Bob, "we're really sorry about this, particularly about having to knock you out. Are you alright?"

"No I'm bloody well not, you cretin. What the fuck do you think you're up to?"

"Well, yes, but we really are very sorry. I know you'll find it in your heart to forgive us eventually."

"I don't."

"No, well, we're working towards a higher purpose at the moment, and I'm afraid that means we sometimes have to do things that don't seem understandable or prudent from a normal perspective, but they will, in time."

I shook my head. They could probably excuse filching Sandy's fortune with this line of reasoning, and also doing unpleasant things to me if I stood in their way.

"Peter, when did you become interested in Zoragaia?"

"I wasn't. I was just interested in the idea of humans being unknowingly influenced by inhabitants of other planets. I'd never heard of Zoragaia until Dennis told me about it, and then I remembered seeing it on Sandy's note."

"Are you sure?"

"Of course I'm bloody well sure."

"You see, it's important to know this, because the means by which Zoragaia first contacts an individual often indicates what that person's mission will be," Bob said.

And knowing this would also tell you if I'm Guy's man-be-hind-the-lines, I thought.

"Did the idea just occur to you out of the blue?"

"Yes."

"When?"

"Fucking hell, Bob!" I shouted. "A million people must have had the same thought, and some of them have written best-selling books about it. Why haven't you cracked them over the head and locked them up as well!"

"Because they aren't the same as you, Peter, and they haven't come to Ravenswood. I don't want to be mysterious, but I can assure you that your being given this knowledge and coming here at this time, is much more meaningful than those 'millions' you talk about."

"Well, thank you for the compliment, but I don't see my-self as being particularly fortunate at the moment," I said, feeling my head. "In fact, I see myself as being extremely unfortunate at ever having met you bunch of fucking fruit-cakes."

I wasn't sure being angry was going to get me anywhere, but it certainly felt more natural than anything else. And anyway, if I had to fake a conversion to Zoragaia to get out of the hole I was in, I planned to make it a slow and painful one, so it would appear more credible.

"Can you remember when you first thought of another civilization influencing us?"

I stopped to think, to make something up, which, I hoped, would look as though I was searching my memory rather than inventing a plausible lie.

"I think it was a few months ago," I said, irritably. "I was watching one of those television programs about how big the universe is and how insignificant we are. I usually find that sort of stuff completely pointless. I mean, everything seems to be numbered in billions. They may as well recite telephone numbers for all the good it does. You just can't put all that stuff into perspective. But for some reason it just caught my imagination, I don't know why. I'd probably had too much to drink. But I started to play around with it in my head."

Bob looked up at the ceiling, thinking. The other two were watching him.

"Could it have been March? March 23rd to be precise?"

"Jesus. How do I know? It could have been. But it could have been February the 12th, or April the 6th. I haven't got a clue."

"Mmm," he said.

"Can I go now?"

"We'd like you to stay here for a day or two. We'll make you comfortable. Is there anything you'd like?"

"If you insist on keeping me here, I suppose you could send Micky up."

Ken snorted. Bob smiled faintly. "I'm not sure we can do that," he said, "but in a day or two, maybe she'd like to see you again. She likes you Peter, we all do, that's why we want to help you come to terms with this knowledge and use it in the best possible way, best for yourself and the human race."

"I don't want to be more insulting than necessary, but believing you're under the influence of some other entity, isn't that the textbook definition of schizophrenia? Hasn't it occurred to you you're all suffering from some form of communicable, hysterical delusion?"

They looked at me as though I was the crazy one, which for the briefest possible instant, made me think that perhaps I was.

"Peter, you're an independent spirit, but free will can be like a prison - it takes away the experience of having to do something and knowing you can't choose not to. With free will, nothing is compulsory, unless you want it to be, it takes away the freedom to be constrained and guided by a deft hand and a benign influence."

Very profound, but his allusion to a prison reminded me all the more of my current predicament.

"Look, if you let me go now, I'll just forget about it. I'll pack my bags and piss off and you can set about converting somebody else. I'll write it off to experience and you can write it down to my stupidity. How's that?"

I knew at once they wouldn't buy this, but I thought I may

as well say it. Anyway, it was a complete lie. Even if Guy didn't manage to implicate them in Sandy's death, I planned reporting them for assault, kidnapping, mental cruelty and just about everything else I and a good lawyer could think of and sue for. Maybe I could persuade Susan Dangerfield to take the case.

"Peter," Bob said, "tomorrow I'm going to spend a lot of time with you, telling you as much about Zoragaia as you need to know. Believe me Peter, at the end of tomorrow you will be a changed man. Your life will be transformed to a degree you wouldn't have believed possible. You've got a great experience ahead of you."

"And you've got a great disappointment ahead of you."

"We'll see," he said.

They left, and the silence after they'd gone almost made me wish they were still there. I mooched around the room, tapping on the walls to see if any of them showed any sign of weakness. I leafed through the books on the table. One of them was a book of Shakespeare's sonnets, and I read a few of them, but when you're afraid for your life, anything else, no matter how eloquent, doesn't have a lot of impact.

§

It was starting to get dark when I heard a noise outside, followed by a tap on the door.

"Peter," it was Roger's voice, "dinner," and I heard him sliding a tray into the alcove by my feet.

I sensed he was already walking away, so I shouted to

him.

"Roger, wait!"

"What?" he said, and I heard him walking back to the door. "Do you want something?"

"Roger, do you agree with this?"

"What?"

"Locking me up against my will. You know it's a criminal act. Do you really want to be a party to that?"

"It's for the best. Astralector … Bob, will explain tomorrow, you'll see." I detected a slight quaver in his voice, as though he wasn't sure, and in my mind I didn't see the cold young man who collected me from the station, but the uncertain boy who stood outside the meditation room after I'd discovered the bodies. If there was a weak link in this conspiracy, I thought, it might be him.

"Roger?"

"What?"

"Listen to your doubts."

"What do you mean?"

"If this isn't all as Bob and Dennis have told you, then you might be getting into something dangerous. If this Zoragaia stuff is just a dream you're not serving a higher purpose, you're just breaking the law, and holding someone against their will is breaking the law in a big way, particularly when you use violence on them as well."

"No, it's ... no ... look, I'm going, you'll see ... it'll be al-right. You'll see, tomorrow, really. I'm going."

"You're not sure, are you Roger?" I called, but he'd gone. I thumped the door in frustration, but at least I knew he'd got doubts. I pulled out the tray. I wasn't hungry, but there was nothing else to do. I put the food on the table and was sit-ting looking at it dejectedly when I thought I heard a noise outside again. I sensed someone there, but they were being very quiet. I got up, put my ear to the door and listened. I was sure there was somebody there, but who? Was it Roger with a change of heart? Did my comments get to him? I felt my heart pounding, and then there was a knock that nearly made me jump out of my skin.

"Who is it?" I called.

"Peter, is that you?"

"Yes. Amanda?"

"Yes. What are you doing in there?"

"They've locked me in here."

"Who?"

"Dennis, Bob, Roger, Ken, particularly Ken."

"What? Why?"

"Look, do you think we could have this conversation face to face?" I don't know how you found me but you're my savior."

"But the door's locked."

"Can you see a flap to the right of the door, by the ground?"

"Hang on. Yes, I see it."

"Can you open it?"

"Wait a minute, yes, yes, it's just bolted."

I dropped to the floor and pushed my arms and head into the alcove. I saw bits of Amanda. She shone a torch in my eyes, which blinded me.

"Can you get through there?"

"I'm about to find out."

I stretched my body with my arms out in front of me as though I was diving into a swimming pool.

"What if you get stuck?"

"I'm sure Ken will soon get me back in place quickly enough, but probably not on the side I want to be." I wriggled and Amanda grabbed my arms and pulled, and after a few seconds of panic when I really thought I was stuck, she yanked me to freedom. I jumped up and hugged her, at the same time as thanking God for my wiry frame.

"Oh Christ! Amanda, you've no idea how glad I am to see you."

"What's going on?"

"I'll tell you, but not here. They may come to check on me. We need to get away."

I grabbed her hand and we started walking, but I soon realized I didn't know where I was going, and if I did, I wouldn't know how to get there from where we were.

"I either have to get to a telephone so I can call the police, or I need to hole up somewhere overnight. Where the hell are we?"

"There's a barn over the hill from here. I've been there when I've wanted to be on my own. It's nothing to do with Ravenswood, and the lane that passes it drops down to the main road. You could spend the night up there and go down to the road when it's light."

"Can you find it in the dark?"

"Yes, I think so."

We turned around and went back past the cabin. We were on a path, but it wasn't that clearly defined, and at times I thought we were just stumbling through the undergrowth, but Amanda seemed confident we were going in the right direction. She asked me again what was going on, and although I was nervous about talking in case someone heard us, she told me we were walking in the opposite direction to Ravenswood, and must have been well over a mile away from there by now. When I'd told her what I'd been through, I pulled her to me and held her again.

"Amanda, I was bloody frightened. I was sure they were

going to kill me. I didn't realize at the time, it's only now I know how frightened I was." I was shaking as I spoke to her. "I know this story sounds crazy, but you have to believe me. They're nuts, the lot of them. You have to get out of there."

We kept walking and eventually came to the barn. It seemed warm inside, and when we sat down on some hay bales I felt an intense wave of relief rush over me, but I wouldn't feel safe until I was telling the story to the police and had contacted Guy. In fact, I probably wouldn't feel safe until I was back in London, and maybe not even then.

§

I told Amanda the whole story.

"Peter, this is hard for me to take in. Of course I believe you, but even then, it seems so bizarre."

"It's either bizarre or just plain criminal, depending on whose version of events you follow, Guy or Dennis, and I really don't know which it is, to be honest, I just know they had no right to lock me up, and even less right to make me feel so threatened. I don't know who's telling the truth, but if you asked me to put money on it, I would say they persuaded Sandy to kill herself, and now they're worried the whole thing is going to blow open."

"But Guy Tinburnell knows all about this, about Zoraga-ia?"

"Yes, he knows everything, even though he's got Bob and Dennis mixed up. Christ knows why they think it's such a big secret, it's all over the bloody Internet."

"And Tinburnell is going to tell the police?"

"Yes, when he's got his act together. He's waiting for me to tell him what I've come up with. I may not be able to tell him any more about Sandy's death, but I can tell him for sure that anyone capable of cracking someone over the head and locking them up against their will has got to be capable of other nasty things."

"But what if all this Zoragaia business is true. How does that make things look?"

"Come on, Amanda. It's just mind games. They may be sincere, they may have convinced themselves it's true, but that doesn't mean it is. They're crazy."

She put her arm around my shoulders and ruffled my hair. I leant my head against her.

"This is just one bloody great mess, isn't it? You know, a few days ago I would have said this has been a good experience for me, maybe even a great experience. I've found out things about myself I didn't know were there, and I've made a good friend, you. But now it's all fallen to fucking bits. But I don't know why I'm surprised, that's how it usually is.

"When I started off in cartoons, I really thought I was going to make it. I knew I wouldn't succeed as a serious artist, not as a good one, not even as an average one, and it looked as though I was set for a tedious life of commercial art - sketches for catalogues, illustrating sales brochures, jobbing drawing, all that sort of crap. But cartoons were natural for me, and when I thought I could make a living out of something I was good at and enjoyed, I was happy. Hasn't worked out, though. I wasn't even good enough at cartooning to get to the top, or even near the top, or even much off the bottom, and I was too bloody obstinate and lazy to try my hand at something else. I should have gone to Hollywood to copy for Disney, at least I would have made money in the sun, even though my brain would have dried out along with my skin."

She pulled me towards her and kissed my ear, then my nose, then my forehead, and before I knew what was happening, I was kissing her lips, and her neck, and without hardly being aware of how it happened, I was soon inside her, and warm tears were trickling down my cheeks and dropping onto her face in the dark barn as I let myself go in a painful release of love and hopelessness. Afterwards, she held me like a baby, which is what I was, and it felt wonderful, as if all the need to be a brave human was cast off like a useless skin.

"And now, just to make my misery complete, I've fallen in love with a woman half my age, so you can stick unrequited love on the list of pains I'll be taking away from this place."

She didn't argue. I knew she wouldn't. There was no way in the world she could be feeling for me what I'd felt for her since my first day at Ravenswood. I didn't realize how completely I'd fallen for her until a few minutes before, but I knew now, and the pain of knowing was already starting to gnaw at my stomach. Jesus! Why can't I grow up?

"Peter, I have to go."

"Why, you're better staying with me and keeping clear of Ravenswood. After I've told Guy and the police what's happened, the place will be turned upside down."

"But they'll notice I'm not around, and that may cause them to get suspicious and check on you, and when they find you're not there, they'll start looking for both of us. If they can account for me they probably won't know about your escape until breakfast, and by that time you'll be safe."

"Can you get back all right on your own?"

"Yes."

She got up, we kissed and she left. Almost at once I found it impossible to believe she'd been with me. Had it been a dream? Was the whole sorry business a random mixture of dream and nightmare? I felt desolate without her, and starving hungry. I hadn't touched the dinner Roger had brought, and although the emptiness I was feeling was only partly due to lack of food, at least I could attempt to do something about it if I could eat. I tried to make myself comfortable in the barn, seeing as sleep was about the only thing I could do until dawn. I toyed with the idea of walking down the lane at once and trying to find the main road. But if I got lost I could end up strolling into Ravenswood, given my lousy sense of direction, and that was the last place I wanted to be.

My dejection was made all the more profound by the fact I didn't think Amanda had believed me. I wasn't surprised, the story was still unbelievable to me, but even if I couldn't put any faith in the power of the Zoragaian ideal to make people do crazy things, I could certainly associate with the allure of millions of pounds, and speculate on the lengths some people might embark on in order to lay hands on that sort of money.

§

I don't know how long I'd been in the barn - my thoughts were too confused and my mind too woolly - when I thought I heard a noise outside. I concentrated and I definitely heard something, but as I was about to get up, the door burst open and the barn was flooded with light from industrial strength torches. The beams picked me out and the next thing I knew I was being grabbed from both sides. I didn't even think of breaking free, I just felt deflated and extremely tired, as though life, or at least the will to live, had been sucked out of me with a pump, leaving a mass of spiritless, quivering flesh. Somebody lit a lamp and I made out Ken and Roger holding either side of me. Dennis was there, and Bob. Then I spotted two figures by the doorway, and the first words I heard came from one of them.

"You won't hurt him, will you? We agreed." It was Amanda.

"Amanda?" I said, trying to make sense of what was happening, but already guessing that sense was going to tell me something about betrayal I didn't want to hear.

"Come on Amanda," said the figure next to her, pulling her away. It was Micky.

"Amanda?" I said, stupidly, as though that was the only word I could utter.

"Amanda's told us what's been going on, Peter," said Bob.

"She told you?" I said, sounding like a half-wit, amazed at my own stupidity.

"Amanda is with us, Peter, she sees the beauty of Zoragaia."

"She tricked me?"

"She's working towards the same purpose as the rest of us. The ultimate purpose we will all share and understand, one day."

"Jesus!"

It's then I noticed it. Hanging from Dennis' arm, like the accoutrement of every smart country gentleman. A rifle.

"A gun? You're going to kill me? For Christ's sake, what are you thinking of?"

I felt sick, angry, frightened, but more than anything I felt tired, just bloody tired. I couldn't believe Amanda had done this. I wanted to lie down and sleep, to wake up when the nightmare was over and glorious, boring reality filled my life again.

"Peter, it's the last thing in the world any of us want to do, but we have a higher goal, and you are obstructing it," said Bob.

It was all so weird because he was just speaking normally, as if this - killing me - was simply another chore like washing up.

"And are you going to kill Guy Tinburnell too? Do you know how many people know about this?"

"Without you, he has nothing. Everyone else at Ravenswood will tell the right story, only you can cause problems, so we have to do this, you see?" He grabbed my arm as if desperate to convince me my death was a good idea and I was dense not to understand that. "We just have to, I'm sorry. But death is meaningless. It's a journey you're going on, to Zoragaia, and we'll meet you there in due course, you'll see."

Bob took the gun from Dennis, who just seemed to be staring blankly ahead of him. I started to struggle, and realizing it was the only thing left in my life to do, I struggled as much as I could. Ken and Roger wrestled me to the ground and did a good job of immobilizing me.

"Get him on the tarpaulin, we don't want to leave blood everywhere," said Bob, and they started dragging me onto a sheet destined to be my death bed and shroud. But then I heard a shout, a woman's voice, and by turning my head I saw Amanda had come back and was running towards Bob. Dennis made a halfhearted grab for her but she evaded him.

"You can't do this!" she shouted, and gave Bob an almighty shove as she ran into him. He staggered backwards, and as he fell the gun fired. Nothing seemed to happen at first, then slowly, as though she'd reverted to being an actress, playing her part gracefully in slow motion, Amanda fell to her knees, where she stayed for a second or two, her eyes wide and uncomprehending, an actress who'd forgotten her lines, even forgotten what play she was in. A word, maybe it was "God", gurgled out of her mouth, and a line of blood trickled onto her chin, then she pitched forward.

I realized I wasn't being held any more. Ken was standing over Amanda's body, his shoulders slumped, and Roger was sitting on the floor like a rag doll, almost as lifeless as Amanda. Bob was still lying on his back, his head raised to see what he'd done. Dennis was crouched down beside Ken, staring at the floor.

My mind was filled with one thought, well, more of a blind impulse than a thought. I jumped up and ran like hell. I was through the barn door and away down the lane almost before I knew what I was doing. After an exhausting sprint, with my unathletic lungs about to burst, I chanced a look behind, but nobody was following me that I could see. My eyes were watering. It may have been tears, but I was unaware of feeling grief. I wasn't feeling anything I could relate to any other experience I'd had in my life, before or since.

§§§

REVIVAL

I was on the London-bound train, staring out of the window and trying to put my world in order. It was 10 days after Amanda's death, and during that time I'd been at the centre of a whirlwind that had sometimes left me untouched and at other times made me feel as though I would be torn apart at any moment and scattered to the four corners of the earth, a prospect which didn't particularly bother me, and sometimes positively appealed to me.

I seemed to run down that bloody lane for ever after I got away from the barn, and when I stopped every now and again to get my breath back, I found the silence so worrying I started running again, running from the silences. At one point I thought I heard a noise, so I stood stock still. At first all I could hear was my labored breathing, but when it quieted it was only to be replaced by the manic thumping of my heart. I was just about to start off again when I heard a crashing through the undergrowth by the side of the lane. Terror coursed through me like an electric shock, and it was minutes after the noise had explained itself - in the shape of a deer that shot past me and clattered up the lane - before my heartbeat had returned to anything like a safe level.

Fortunately, it was nearly all downhill to the main road and gave me no opportunities to get lost, as there were no turnoffs as far as I could see. I managed to get to the road quickly, and when I reached it I immediately saw the shape of a house lurking about a hundred yards to my right and ran towards it. I thumped like crazy on the door but nobody answered, and thinking I was probably being pursued I didn't want to stick around banging and yelling and drawing attention to myself if there was nobody in, so I turned to go back to the road. But just then an upstairs window opened and a head appeared. The man who leant out was understandably abusive at first and extremely reluctant to help me, but I told him just to call the police if he didn't believe me, and I'd wait outside until they came. He did, and within 10 minutes - which felt like several lifetimes - a squad car arrived, during which time I crouched by the side of the house watching the road. I don't think I blinked once as I waited, and I wouldn't be surprised if someone told me I didn't breathe either, for fear of being detected.

The next few hours were frantic. I was taken to a police station and I told two sleepy officers the bare bones of the story, enough to persuade them to do something, and I insisted they locate Guy and bring him to the police station, partly because I thought he might be in danger, but mainly because he would be able to corroborate my story and stop me looking like the complete lunatic they seemed to think I was. Llewellyn - one of the detectives who'd come to Ravenswood to investigate Sandy's suicide - turned up after about half an hour and seemed more willing to accept that there might be something in what I was saying, to the extent he told me we would have to go back to the barn, which didn't exactly fill me with glee, but I saw no way of avoiding it.

When I'd first arrived at the police station, a patrol car had been dispatched to Ravenswood to notify them that certain allegations had been made and nobody should do anything precipitate, like boarding a plane for New Zealand in the next few hours. As we were about to leave for the barn, the police radioed from Ravenswood to say we should go there instead. In the car, Llewellyn told me that a man - he didn't know the name, but it sounded like Roger from the description - had admitted to everything, and that the other "suspects" weren't doing anything to contest his story.

The scene at Ravenswood - in the kitchen where the protagonists had assembled - was depressing. Roger looked awful, like a shell-shocked young soldier form the First World War. He was as white as a ghost, shaking uncontrollably, and he seemed much thinner than I remembered him, as though time was running backwards and he was reverting to being a child. Ken sat slumped in a chair with his chin on his chest, looking as though he'd completely lost interest in life, and Bob was wandering around muttering to himself. Dennis was nowhere to be seen and, as it turned out, would remain nowhere to be seen thereafter, likewise Micky.

At one point, while Llewellyn was interviewing Roger in the office, Bob stopped his incoherent rambling and addressed the rest of us.

"You see, the more we've pursued knowledge about our

world, the more competent we've become at understanding our environment, and thus the more confident we've become that we can explain everything in the material universe. But the less confident we've become in understanding our spiritual universe, the less competent we are able to deal with spirituality and the doors that it unlocks. Zoragaia achieved its technical understanding of the universe many thousands of years ago, and since then has focused on developing spiritual maturity and bringing the spiritual and the technical into harmony. Now that Zoragaia understands and masters everything spiritual and technical, they are in a state of grace, and one to which they wish to lead us."

He'd been wandering around the kitchen as he spoke, but he then stood in front of one of the young policeman. "You see? We've progressed intellectually at the expense of our souls. Zoragaia has addressed that fundamental flaw. You see?" he said. But the policeman didn't see, because he told him to "Sit down and shut up, please."

When Llewellyn came back into the kitchen he took two of the uniformed men aside and conferred with them, after which they left. He then took me into the office.

"His story and yours are much the same. My men have gone up to the barn now, expecting to find a body. It was that Bob chap who fired the fatal shot?"

"Yes, they were planning to kill me. It should be my body up there now, or buried in some hole somewhere, and everyone else, including you, should be tucked up cozily in bed. Jesus! Poor Amanda. Fuck those stupid bastards!"

"The only one missing is Dennis Foulds. Any idea where he might be?"

"No, as far away as possible, I assume. He's probably got a woman called Micky with him. She knew what was going on but I don't know if she was in on the plan to kill me - she wasn't in the barn when it happened, but she couldn't have been far away."

"Was Foulds the ringleader?"

"I don't know. It was either him or Bob, but they both seemed to be convinced I was best disposed of."

"And the other two?"

"I don't know. I think Roger was scared stiff, but he and Ken were happy to hold me down while Bob shot me."

It was just starting to get light by the time I was taken to the barn. The whole area was bathed in fierce illumination from lamps the police had set up, driven from a portable generator that was droning away next to a Range Rover. Roger was there too, and Llewellyn led us together into the barn.

"Was this how you remember the scene, Mr. Wickham?" Llewellyn asked me.

I looked down at Amanda's body. She was lying on her back, her eyes staring open. There was blood on her chin and a large red patch on her chest. A dark pool of drying blood surrounded her body like a halo. The rifle was on the floor about two yards away, and the tarpaulin was lying on some nearby hay bales.

"She was on her face when I left. She'd fallen forward."

"Ken turned her over," said Roger, evenly and flatly. "He

checked her pulse at the neck and said she was ... she was ..."

"Yes, okay," said Llewellyn, who then got us to describe the events of earlier. "What happened after she was shot?"

"We just stayed here for a while," said Roger. "Nobody said anything or did anything. I just don't know what happened after that. I just wandered back to Ravenswood. When I got there I saw a car leaving. I suppose that was Dennis. Ken was in the kitchen. Astralector turned up just before you arrived."

"Who?"

"Bob, that's another name for Bob, the crazy bastard," I said. The whole notion of Zoragaia appeared so stupid to me now, I couldn't understand why I had even thought it vaguely interesting before. Zoragaia, or the idea of it, had killed Amanda.

It was mid-morning by the time I saw Guy. We spoke over a cup of tea at the police station. As usual, he seemed to know everything that was going on. Susan Dangerfield was with him, and she smiled at me when she arrived as you would smile at an invalid on a hospital visit, an invalid with not much to hope for in the future.

"Well, Peter, what a fuck up. How are you?"

"I'm devastated. Amanda was, well ... she ..." Tears started running down my cheeks as my mind flicked between images of her smiling face and the lifeless corpse on the floor of the barn, her blood spreading out further and further. I thought of her telling me about her PMT - the PMT she wouldn't be suffering from any more - and I choked. I took a sip of tea to recover my composure, but I could hardly swallow and I felt it in my nose rather than my throat.

"Didn't she lead them to you?"

"Yes." In fact, the whole thing had been a setup. According to Roger, they'd persuaded Amanda to help me escape from the hut so that I would then confide in her exactly what I knew. They told her they may have to hold me there for a while but then they would release me if I still didn't want to convert to their ideas. She was unwilling to be involved, but they told her it was all part of the grand plan, and my salvation would result from it as well as theirs. "But she didn't expect them to kill me, and she didn't deserve to get shot. She saved my life at the cost of her own. I'm not worth it."

We talked a little more, sporadically, none of us really knowing what to say and, in my case, not really caring whether we said anything or not.

"What are you going to do now?" I asked Guy.

"Not sure. Depends on what Dennis' friends have to say. I don't expect to be seeing much of Mr. Foulds himself for a while, unless he's unlucky enough to get himself caught, and if he's not around he can't get his hands on his inheritance. I can't say I'm particularly interested in getting Sandy's money back. In the light of what's happened it's pretty irrelevant. I actually feel partly responsible for this. If I'd let them get away with it, none of this would have happened." He paused and breathed deeply. "But if they did encourage Sandy to take her life, and judging by what they did to you they certainly had something to hide, then they deserve to be caught and punished for the whole wretched business." He sipped his tea. "The Ferrari's all yours, by the way."

"No thanks. I didn't earn it, and Amanda paid for it." I would look at the red car and see Amanda's blood.

"Well, it's there if you want it, see how you feel in a day or two."

Or a month or two, or a year or two. At that time I couldn't imagine feeling any other way than I did then.

§

Looking out the train window, I tried to think about how I was now, as compared to when I was making the journey in the opposite direction about a month previously. I'd made a friend and lost her. The world had lost her. She'd lost everything. I'd found things in myself that were interesting and may have led somewhere, and for a few fleeting, idiotic moments I thought I'd found a fascinating idea about the universe. I was sad now, I'd been anxious then. I was depressed about the future now, I'd been confused about the future then. I thought death was what happened to other people then, but now I knew that its icy finger can rip through space and time and stab any of us in the back without warning, then disappear and leave no sign of its arrival or departure, except the grief of those it pushed aside on its resolute path towards its target. I'd felt full of British Rail tea and sandwiches then, but now I had a void inside of me that I couldn't imagine anything would fill.

The police were bothered by the fact the autopsy showed Amanda had engaged in sexual intercourse shortly before her death, and the obvious question was raised as to whether this had been related to her death and whether she had been a willing participant in the congress. When I first told them what had happened, they didn't seem happy with my explanation.

"Why didn't you tell us this to begin with?"

"Why should I have done. It's got absolutely nothing to do with her death."

"The Superintendent is very unhappy that this has come up now. It makes it look like we believed everything we were told. That we're not protecting the victim's rights. That Christ knows what could have gone on but we've just accepted what we were spoon fed by the perpetrators."

"I'm not a perpetrator. I'm a victim!"

"Then why didn't you tell us?"

"It had nothing to do with her death. It had nothing to do with you. It had nothing to do with anyone apart from Amanda and me." And now it had got nothing to do with anyone at all, not Amanda, and not even me. That beautiful act now seemed more like necrophilia when I thought of it.

Countryside was pouring past the window, but less and less of it as we approached the Home Counties and buildings started to be increasingly evident. I started to feel a little easier and I realized that either my deep-seated fear of green stuff had been held in abeyance whilst I was at Ravenswood, and was now gradually seeping back into me, or perhaps recent events had irrevocably connected the countryside with tangibly unpleasant things, and I'd now got a powerful new phobia to deal with. Either way, I started looking forward to getting back to London, as though I wasn't just removing the malign tumor of thought that Ravenswood now constituted in my mind, but actually applying some metropolitan radiotherapy to my diseased brain as well.

§

I didn't sleep for two days after Amanda's death, but noticing my increasingly fragile state at my daily interviews with the police, Llewellyn contacted a doctor who gave me sleeping pills.

"I'm only going to give you four. That's enough for four nights. Contact me again if you're still having problems after that."

"Four won't kill me then?"

"Pardon?"

"You're worried I'm going to kill myself, that's why you're only giving me four."

"I don't know about that. I just don't want you getting addicted to sleeping pills."

I don't know why I got engaged in that conversation. Despite feeling thoroughly pissed off, I wouldn't have tried to kill myself, but I'm aware that the face I was presenting to the outside world was one of angry desperation. I just couldn't seem to find it in myself to act in any other manner. It was my way of grieving - moody, adolescent, stubborn, pathetic.

For the remainder of my time in Wales, Guy arranged for me to stay in the hotel he'd been using. The police had offered to put me up in a B&B at their expense, while "helping with enquiries", but Guy insisted I stay at the hotel, at his expense. After the first few days of incessant activity, whilst every aspect of the events surrounding Amanda's death was checked and rechecked a thousand times, things quietened down, and although the police asked that I stick around, I didn't have a lot to do, apart from think. But I wasn't desperate to get away. In fact, I felt completely aimless and unable to get interested in anything, and Wales was as good as anywhere given my state of mind. After Guy had gone back to London, I was particularly at a loose end, but I settled into a brooding daily routine that held the first signs of recovery.

I mainly ate in the hotel restaurant. Guy had left the rented Audi with me so that I could take desultory drives around the damp countryside during the day, but in the evenings I preferred to drink, eat, and then slouch in front of the television or immerse myself in one of the steamy novels to be found in the hotel's library of second-rate fiction. One night, about five days after the killing, I drank more than usual, and as I sipped a second brandy after dinner it was as though a long, extinguished light was turned back on, and the cloud of self-pitying depression that had settled around and inside me since Amanda's death lifted briefly, showing me a hint of optimism I thought I'd never see again.

Maybe life was livable after all, perhaps the unpleasantness would fade and I would be able to get some pleasure, however vestigial, out of existing again. I looked into the balloon glass and swirled the brandy round, thinking I might have to rely on this stuff and its alcoholic brethren more than I had done in the past. But so what? At least I would survive, sort of. The next morning, the light of hope wasn't there anymore, but the memory of having glimpsed it was still with me, and I found myself looking forward to dinner that evening and a reprise of the relief that I'd scented the night before, which was the first time I'd looked forward to anything in days.

Trudging round the lanes in the afternoon, I couldn't really put my finger on why I'd let myself get so depressed. A terrible thing had happened, but I wasn't convinced it was just Amanda I was grieving for. It was a bigger disappointment than that. Everyone at Ravenswood had let me down after I'd risked so much of my truculent self in going there, and it was all for money, the complete antithesis of everything I'd thought the place had stood for. I felt my basic skepticism rebuilding itself in my veins, I was getting back in touch with the confused, ordinary mortal who viewed inner explorations as dubious and pointless, and although I felt narrow-minded and defeatist to be putting my spiritual blinkers on again, at least I was getting back onto comfortable home territory.

§

With Reading in our wake, the thought of being back in London preoccupied me. I intended going out and getting drunk that night. Not outrageously so, but enough to tell my mind and body I was back where I belonged, and if I could manage to put the past month into the darkest, dustiest and least-used corner of my brain, I should be able to resurrect the uninspiring version of myself that had never heard of Ravenswood. Normality, boring and predictable and unambitious, started to look attractive in a way it never did before. I browsed through the paper, and even got an idea for a cartoon, not a good one, but something.

When I got back to my flat, I turned on the answering machine while unpacking, and let it beep its way through a succession of strangulated wrong numbers, garbled messages and noisy, clattering hang-ups, before a clearly articulated and shockingly familiar voice began speaking and set me rigid with fright. It was Dennis, speaking as authoritatively and calmly as he did in my early days at Ravenswood.

"Don't forget, Peter, you'll never stop searching, not once you've started. It's there to be found. You can find it. The seed is sewn."

That was all. It was like a voice from the grave. He didn't give a date or time, but the message before his had only been left three days ago. I slumped into a chair feeling sick. Why did he need to do that? Was he trying to intimidate me? Why would he? He would have guessed the police knew everything by then, and there was nothing more I could do to him than I'd already done. Should I take his advice at face value? A hint from a wayward friend who still had my welfare at heart? Perhaps I should, but the way I felt right then was unwelcoming of his eerily offered solicitude.

§

That night, after drinking enough but less than I'd intended, I dreamt I was on a space ship, looking out of the window, when a huge blue orb filled my field of vision. I looked closer and saw oceans start to form, and continents. Then I saw the terrain begin to take on features, all perfect from that altitude, no manmade blemishes distorting the beauty of the planet. I was breathless with excitement, awestruck by the huge, cold, blue beauty of it, which I could feel as much as see.

There was somebody at my side, pointing out features on the planet below us and sharing my sense of childlike wonder. We looked out of the window together, soaking in the experience for a long time before I turned to face him

- it was Dennis. Out of the window I spotted a figure floating about in a space suit - it was Bob, the word "Astralector"
clearly printed across his helmet. He too was pointing out
features on the planet, but he didn't seem to be attached to
our spacecraft and he was gradually drifting away.

We walked through the spacecraft - we didn't float, we
walked as you would on Earth - and came to a room where
there were a number of large chests with pipes and wires
coming out of them. The tops were transparent and I looked
in the first one to see Micky, frozen in a state of suspended
animation. I hurried to the second to find Doris, and in the
third was Amanda. I breathed a huge sigh of relief and had a
sense of overwhelming joy. Dennis patted me on the back.

We went to another window and looked at the planet
again. "Zoragaia?" I asked. "No," said Dennis, laughing, and
all the others in their chests burst into life and laughed too.
"It's Planet Earth, Peter, Planet Earth. We've come to plant
the seed of life, to scatter some microbes, then we'll come
back in a few million years time to see how they're getting
on. They may look like us by then," he said, laughing again.
"Who knows?" and they all laughed.

I woke feeling troubled, but enormously refreshed, as
though I'd been breathing pure oxygen. And then I felt happy,
stupidly and unreasonably happy.

§§§

TURNAROUND

10 years later.

Bob, Ken and Roger were convicted of manslaughter and conspiracy to commit murder (of me). The last I heard, they were all still in prison, but may be out by now. At the trial, Roger looked as though he was headed for a nervous breakdown. Ken said practically nothing and barely reacted to what was going on. Bob seemed to be treating it as some form of earthling idiocy that would soon be put behind him, and when he addressed the court it was with a lucidity that, I'm sure, almost convinced some of those present there might be something in this Zoragaia stuff, so despite the craziness of his basic premise, he wasn't judged to be mentally deficient and he ended up in prison like the other two.

Without being able to interrogate Dennis, it proved impossible to tell whether the whole thing had been mischievously plotted or whether it was just a gradually unfolding shambles.

At some point, Bob and Dennis had come to the belief that I was a real threat to the Zoragaian faction - which found itself in a cash crisis it needed desperately to overcome - and when my death was mooted as a prospective way of removing a potential problem, they assumed they were being guided in this direction by Zoragaia, and that my demise would, in any case, be a means of getting me to that blissful planet even quicker than I could have anticipated.

So, if things had gone according to plan, they would have kept the money and I would have got an express ticket to Zoragaia. I think Bob actually believed this explanation, and that he didn't assume I would suffer by being killed. Ken, surprisingly, seemed to have swallowed everything Bob told him, and so did Roger, although in his case I think there were a few doubts. If anyone had a purely criminal intent, it would have been Dennis, but he wasn't around to defend himself.

No criminal charges were brought in relation to Sandy's demise. The verdict on her death was left open, but her final will was overturned, and when I last spoke to him Guy was still contesting her penultimate will with the lesbians from Northampton - out of the frying pan into the fire.

Monica was never charged, and she took over the running of Ravenswood which, for all I know, is still going, although the mental image I have of the place is that it's now derelict and overrun with weeds and wild animals.

§

Surprisingly, I got back into the swing of things remarkably quickly, and thanks to a documentary on Ravenswood the BBC made, my career took a lucrative leap forward. My drawings are no better but my signature now means something, and I even had a mildly successful "retrospective" exhibition in a cartoon gallery in Holborn a couple of years ago, although how you can have a retrospective when you've never been appreciated is enough to convince me that the art world is as manipulated as ever.

Guy insisted on delivering the Ferrari to me about six months after the killing, and during the two weeks while I was deciding whether to keep it or not, it was stolen from outside a restaurant in Islington and I haven't seen it since.

I've had one substantial affair, a few brief liaisons, a fling with a married woman - which involved a ridiculous, but somewhat stimulating, degree of cunning and subterfuge - and I've made some interesting new acquaintances through the fame Ravenswood temporarily brought me. I also received a lot of mail from people interested in Zoragaia, some of them lambasting me for not being a believer - only a few offensively so - but most of them asking for details of what I learned from the blessed Astralector who, it seems, doesn't answer any enquiries that are sent to him in jail.

I got a letter from some bloke who asked me to consider that if a computer had been built that completely mimicked the construction of my brain, and which was then programmed in exactly the same way as my neurons are programmed, would this computer be a clone of me? He said it wouldn't be, and that Zoragaia holds the solution to what makes a human brain different from a mechanical brain in every other respect but the merely physical one. Zoragaia, he explained, has discovered what constitutes that spark of human spirit that distinguishes the soulless machine from the soulful human, and one day this missing link - which is, of course, God-given - will be revealed to us. He signed off by castigating me for screwing up the Zoragaian quest by running away rather than surrendering myself to a more beneficial fate, for both myself and humanity at large, but he then said it didn't matter that much because the truth would emerge eventually anyway, so I shouldn't worry about the *faux pas* I had committed by skipping out of the barn and saving my unworthy skin.

Nobody - not even my answering machine - heard any more from Dennis or Micky. There was a suspicion they had committed suicide when two charred and unrecognizable bodies were found that summer in a caravan owned by Ravenswood in the Scottish highlands, but it wasn't conclusively proven it was them, and I didn't ever believe it was. Buried deep in both of them was a distinct seam of hedonism.

And then, about six months after the event, it was found that the bodies were in fact those of Zara and her sister who, according to unfounded speculation in the gutter press, had been having an incestuous lesbian relationship for most of their lives and had decided to end it all in an inflammatory suicide pact.

I hadn't thought much about Zara after leaving Ravenswood. In fact, I'd hardly thought about her at all since Sandy's suicide, which struck me as remarkable, given the way the woman had bugged the hell out of me until death stepped in and put petty personality conflicts into a humble perspective. When the press found out about the Ravenswood connection - via the charred caravan - there was speculation that Zara was another person anxious to visit Zoragaia and not prepared to let life takes its normal course, but this was probably nonsense.

Life has gone on, as ramshackle as ever. I've never been back to Wales, to Ravenswood or any place even remotely like it. I've never even thought of doing anything like that again. But sometimes, in the dead of night when trying to make a drawing work, or when walking home from a pub or party with a surfeit of alcohol sloshing around in my veins, I've thought back to the part of me that Ravenswood touched, and I don't feel that I shall ever be able to bury its influence for good and all, or want to.

§

And that would almost certainly have been the end of it, but for the person who started it all for me, Fiona. She phoned one afternoon to ask if I wanted to go to California with her.

"Peter, darling, I've won these two tickets to San Francisco, and a rental car and some hotel vouchers, and I'm not with anyone at the moment, and you and I always have such a good time together, provided we don't actually live together, that is," she said, snorting a laugh, "and I wondered if you'd like to come along. Would you?"

And because all she had said was true, and because the English spring was boorishly trying to convince us it was still winter, and that it would continue pretending to be winter until July at least, and even then all we could hope for was an imitation of autumn, I said "Yes, I bloody well would."

As Sod's Law would have it, we flew out of a warm and sunny Heathrow and arrived in a cold and drizzly San Francisco, but the climate soon got itself sorted out again and we spent our time doodling up and down the Pacific coast under beautiful, clear blue skies. We spent a few days up in the wine country of Napa and Sonoma counties, where we got quite passionate about each other again, but I think our passion was mainly due to the vast amounts of wine we drank there.

We'd made a pact before we set out, that no matter what we did while we were in California, we would revert to our own separate lifestyles when we got back. This rule meant we were free of the obligations that normally go along with a relationship, actual or putative, and it worked out so well that at one point we talked about getting back together on the same basis when we returned to London. But we both knew it wouldn't work, and we agreed to stick to the original plan and just enjoy the holiday. I felt as though I'd secured the immature male's perfect present - free sex with an attractive woman, with no obligations, little expense, and a wonderful environment, and Fiona seemed to like it too, so I thought it was a good deal for both of us.

For the final week, we took the freeway south to Santa Barbara, but hugged the coastline driving back north on the legendary Highway One, through Morro Bay, Pismo Beach, San Simeon, Big Sur, Carmel and Monterey. With just two days left, we checked into a motel in Santa Cruz. Fiona was tired, so I left her dozing in the room and went for a walk on the beach. It was a glorious, mellow day in May and, being a weekday, there weren't many people on the wide, sandy beach. I went up onto the pier and walked along it. A pelican was perched on the railing at one point, and further on people were peering down a hatchway at the fat, smelly sea lions lounging and barking grumpily on the wooden trestle-work just above the water.

I walked to the very end of the pier. There was a man leaning on the railing looking out at the ocean, which was, I supposed, uninterrupted until it washed up against Japan or some similarly exotic shore. I stood about two yards away from him, and when I saw a particularly obese sea lion gracefully swimming in the water below, I said "Amazing how something so fat and cumbersome on land can be so elegant in the water."

It had been a spontaneous utterance, and I hadn't particularly wanted to start a conversation, but when I noticed, out of the corner of my eye, that my neighbor had turned and seemed to be staring at me, I felt uneasy, and I felt a damn sight more uneasy when he said "Hello, Peter" in a voice that was unmistakably that of Dennis Foulds.

He was smiling broadly, probably at my expression, because if I looked half as surprised as I felt, then I must have appeared like a perfect caricature of sudden shock. Dennis was deeply suntanned. His hair had receded but there was still quite a lot of it, and it was fashioned into a pony tail. He was wearing shorts, sandals and a T-shirt with red, blue and green swirls, and a huge yellow sun in the middle. He was every bit the California beach bum in the traditional home of the California beach bum, Santa Cruz.

"God above!" was all I managed say.

"How are you, Peter?"

"I'm suddenly in desperate need of a drink," I said.

"Well, there's a coffee shop over there, would that do?"

We bought coffee and sat on the pier in the sun. I don't

remember the transaction of buying the drinks, but I certainly had a cup in my hand when we started talking and my initial shock began to subside. Incongruously, we talked about the location and the weather for a while, as if we had nothing else to discuss, but Dennis must then have decided he couldn't keep up the pretence of normality any longer.

"Okay, Peter, I owe you an explanation, don't I?"

"You owe a lot more than that, and not just to me, but an explanation would be a start."

He looked into the distance for a while, out over the ocean, in much the same way he'd viewed the Welsh scenery when we'd gone for our walks above Ravenswood. He was still looking out to sea as he spoke.

"It was all just an almighty bloody great cock-up. There was no conspiracy, not to kill Sandy, not to kill you, and certainly not to hurt poor Amanda."

My heart quite literally ached when he mentioned her name, as it still does every time I think of her, though not always as painfully as it did then.

"When Sandy took her life the money was about to fall into our laps, and we desperately needed it. Ravenswood was struggling to stay afloat, and with Zoragaia starting to really get off the ground, we thought that losing the centre would be a disaster." He sucked his teeth and studied a sea gull plodding along the wooden planks of the pier. Dennis was as handsome as ever, and spoke with the same assured deliberation.

"Then it just snowballed. Events overtook us. It wasn't

until the shot rang out in the barn that the bubble burst and I realized what we were doing, and that the whole Zoragaia thing had taken us somewhere completely insane. Does that sound crazy?"

"Coming from you, yes. You always struck me as so damn intelligent and well balanced. I can't believe you fell for that tosh."

"But I did, Peter, I really did. Hook, line and ..." he paused, "sinker," he said, his voice trailing off.

"Where did you go?"

"Latin America to begin with, then Arizona, Jamaica, New Mexico, then here. I'm in the country illegally, but if I never get into trouble with the police I'll be okay. Unless ..." he chuckled and turned away from the ocean and towards me.

"What?"

"Unless you turn me in."

I thought about it. "I don't see any point in doing that. The others may be out of prison by now, but you'll always be on the run. If you don't get caught you'll be locked up in a fugitive's lifestyle until the day you die. I think I'd rather serve my time and get it over with if I were you. The whole world is your prison at the moment."

"You're very observant, and very right. I've often thought that myself."

"Where's Micky?"

"We split up a long time ago. She decided a life on the road and on the run had limited romantic appeal - she hadn't read as much Jack Kerouac as me. The last I heard she had a new identity and was about to marry some rich American twice her age in Las Vegas. She always knew how to use her body to good purpose, as you know."

"Yes, I know." I'd never forget the night I spent with her, the eroticism now tinged with something deeper and darker.

"I was infatuated with her, completely smitten," he said. "It was her fanaticism for Zoragaia that caused me to get even more deeply immersed in it, even though she found out about it long after me. She was young and voluptuous and enthusiastic, whereas I was older and getting bored. It was too easy to fall for her and tag along with her unquestioning belief. Are you surprised I turned out to be so easily seduced, so easily pushed off the straight and narrow? Or perhaps you don't believe me at all."

I thought back to when he told me he and I were alike - the same day he'd told me about his daughter - and I thought of my own infatuation with Amanda and the appeal the idea of Zoragaia had exerted on me too, however briefly.

"No, I understand, being the flawed individual I am. But you seemed to be so much better adjusted than most people I meet. You know, Dennis, once I'd got over the first shock of it all, what really disappointed me was that you'd turned out to be as flaky and weak-willed as the rest of us. I really thought you were a person to look up to. I didn't ever meet people like that, I still don't. You let me down."

"I'm sorry, Peter." He rubbed my arm in the same way he would have done back at Ravenswood. "I don't want to make excuses, but let me just explain something." He paused, collecting his thoughts.

"I was disappointed too, with my life, I mean. I'd developed this model of the world where generation by generation we were adding to the powerful humanizing forces in the universe. Making babies and rearing them as intelligent, compassionate human beings struck me as a kind of recycling process, turning organic matter into people, and encouraging people to look into their souls and see beauty there. It was as though the sum total of love in the world could be slowly increased generation by generation, just as long as we could give people a progressive spiritual framework to live in and give them the ability to look into their own consciousness. I thought we could evolve to be a better species, make the world a better place and, in the fullness of time, millions of years perhaps, we could make heaven on Earth. I thought that was humankind's destiny, to turn ourselves into Gods by processing atoms into life and life into consciousness for endless generations, until every person and every molecule was enlightened."

He paused, looked out to sea and swallowed hard.

"The scriptures bear that out, in various religions. We are the children of God, and we can become one with God, given time, a lot of time, and positive progress." He shook his head, a bitter smile on his lips.

"But then it all just failed me. Quite literally I woke up one morning thinking I didn't have faith in my ideas any more, and I knew at that very moment I wouldn't ever believe in them with the same conviction again. I was devastated, just as devastated as when my daughter died, although in a different way, of course. I'd lost a part of my life, my beliefs, and they were as dead as my daughter, and just as unexpectedly and just as suddenly. This was about two years before I met you. I was in a vacuum, as complete an emotional vacuum as I'd ever been in, and in the same way that I'd gone to India and clutched at Dharavajra when I lost my daughter, I clutched at Zoragaia when Bob turned up one day and started talking about it. You know how Bob was when he talked about his astrology? So matter of fact and unfussy, making you think he didn't want you to believe in it really. That was how he was with Zoragaia to begin with, before he got carried away with it and started calling himself Astralector. I was intrigued by the idea from the beginning, and intrigue led to fascination, and that led to belief and to a dangerous suspension of my critical faculties. Then Micky appeared and I was done for. I would have died for her, but instead we ended up killing for our stupid idea. I was still crazy for her when Amanda was shot, and the main reason I ran away was I couldn't bear the thought of being separated from her."

"You seemed to be so in control when I came to Ravenswood. You didn't come across like a man with doubts."

"Zoragaia gave me some of my old faith back. What Bob told me resonated with what I'd always thought, but now I could believe that Zoragaia would jump-start the spread of enlightenment in the world by speeding us through millennia of spiritual evolution. There's a professor of psychology at the university here in Santa Cruz who gives lectures anyone can attend. He was talking about genius recently, and he said genius can be madness, but in crazy people who can communicate their ideas and have other people buy into them, we interpret madness as creativity and fete the madman rather than lock him up - he uses Van Gogh and Salvador Dali as examples. Bob was the same. He seemed so ordinary and was so lucid that all he said made perfect sense, and I met him when I needed a new explanation for what the hell I was supposed to do with my life, so I was particularly vulnerable. It was only at the very end I saw him for what he really was, and by then it was too late - I was in it up to my neck."

"Why did you get Micky to seduce me? Not that I'm complaining."

"Bob was convinced you would damage us, that you would help Guy Tinburnell make his case and wrest the money away from us. That money would have enabled us to set up a centre for Zoragaia, which was everything Bob wanted, we all wanted. I knew he was going to do something outrageous, so I suggested we let Micky loose on you. I was only too aware of the effect she'd had on me, and I thought she might be able to win you over to our side."

"She didn't even mention Zoragaia."

"She wasn't supposed to. I just wanted to make the whole package of Ravenswood look so attractive you wouldn't want to jeopardize it."

"And you knew I was more likely to be influenced by my penis than my intellect."

"Yes."

I laughed.

"I'm not criticizing you, Peter. We used our intellects and look where it got us. If there were any pricks in this tale, it was us."

"What about Amanda? What role did she have to play in it all?"

"None. She was just a sweet thing who wanted to do the best for everyone, us and you. She was a victim, not a conspirator."

"That's what I thought."

We both looked out at the ocean. Like a log fire, it gave us something to look at when we weren't talking, and it gave me the chance to swallow the lump in my throat that Amanda's memory evinced.

"What do you do now?" I asked. "How do you make a living?"

"Odd jobs. Anything that's going. Mowing grass, cutting trees. I work in a wholefood shop now and again, and I wait on tables in a vegetarian restaurant a few evenings a week. I live in a shack a couple of blocks back from the beach. I can hear the ocean. I run a meditation group and I have the occasional affair, and when nothing else is happening I sit in the sun, like this."

He chuckled and shook his head.

"And do you know what, Peter? I'm happy. Happier than I've ever been. A couple of years ago, not long after Micky left me, I hit rock bottom again, for the third time in my life. I thought it was the end. I didn't know what I planned to do, but the outlook wasn't good. Then I was walking on the beach one day, a sunny day like this, and I felt good. For no reason I just felt bloody good, and I thought 'Well, if I can feel good with my life being in the state it's in at the moment,

I can always feel good'. So that's what I do. I sit in the sun and watch the waves and feel good. My life's become one continuous meditation on nothing. I'm going nowhere and I'm doing nothing. I've given up all quests. I just let life happen to me. I've got the 'beginner's mind' we used to speak about at Ravenswood, and if I feel I'm getting ideas of making something of myself I just let them go and remind myself I have nothing and I want nothing. All my clever philosophies have come true, but only when I let them all go - they're valuable only as long as I consider them valueless."

He stroked his hair and adjusted the way his ponytail sat on his shoulder.

"Being a fugitive from justice helps, because it's a continual reminder that anything I construct can be taken away from me, and my whole life could be turned upside down in a moment, like now if you decide to tell the police about me. All that I have is fundamentally unstable, which makes me appreciate it every second of every day."

Not for the first time, I found myself envying him.

"I must go, I have to work this evening," he said.

I wanted him to stay. I don't know why, there wasn't much more to talk about, but I felt there would be a coldness when he was gone, despite the warm sun. I knew then that I loved him a little. He stood up, and I stood up too and we spontaneously embraced.

"Good-bye, Peter."

"Good-bye ... what do you call yourself now?"

He put his head back and laughed.

"I call myself Peter. Peter Wickham," he said, still laughing, as he walked away down the pier, leaving me to wonder which of us was the real Peter Wickham, and which one the cartoon copy.

§§§

IMAGES by Alison J. Macmillan

OTHER TITLES BY BRIAN STAFF

NO MAN IS AN ISLAND - a novelette and collection of short stories on three dimensions of life

FATHERING SIN - a novel which may turn your usual ideas of life and death on their heads

THE RELUCTANT TRIATHLETE - one of a collection of stories of inspiration, humor and wisdom published in *Chicken Soup for the Soul - Inspiration for the Young at Heart*

THE DOG WHO ESCHEWED TENNIS BALLS - appears in an anthology of stories paying tribute to one of our favorite companions, *My Dog is My Hero*, edited by Susan Reynolds

HEART AND SOLE - a short story which won first prize in a Writers' Forum competition

SCIENTISTS GET IT WRONG, AGAIN - WEATHER TALK. Published in *Weatherwise* trade magazine, it is one of a series of tongue-in-cheek essays exposing the ways in which Scientists turn simple concepts into complex ones so they can keep themselves in a job.

Coming soon:

RICK SHICK - a humorous and unusual detective novel.

Brian Staff is an Englishman living the San Francisco Bay area of California. He has a Ph.D. in Computer Science and has worked for most of his life in selling or marketing information technology. He wrote his first novel at the age of seven for his Uncle Joe, and has now written several more, which are longer than the first one but only a little more sophisticated. He has lived in London, Madrid and Edinburgh, and has traveled widely and wildly. He has published a number of marketing documents, which have benefited greatly from his fiction writing and sense of the absurd.